Grand Portage

by Scott Seeger

ISBN-13: 978-1979311502

CHAPTER ONE

"Ahoy, matey, spare a dollar?"

The homeless man caught Tyler's attention if only for a moment. Tyler turned back to cavernous 53rd Street. There it was, 117 West 53rd. He walked into the lobby through the modern office building and to the elevator bank. He pressed the button and the car pinged and he boarded it, pressing number thirty-five.

On the way up he realized he was violating an old gentlemen's etiquette regarding the wearing of hats indoors. He removed his captain's hat and tucked it under his arm.

He stepped off and opened the double door and the receptionist greeted him. He scanned the lobby with a sense of déjà vu. The marquee over the receptionist's desk spelled out Chambers Foundation in roundish, soft colored font. Accent lights protruding from the ceiling gave the signage a sharp glow.

"I'm here to see…" A vast modern art *masterpiece* to the right of reception grabbed his attention. Some artist from Eastern Europe who had surely used a paintball gun as his brush. Tyler recalled the sticker shock that jetted up his spine when the invoice arrived.

He focused his attention back to the receptionist. "I'm here to see Mrs. Chambers. Is she in?"

She folded her hands together and leaned forward with a warm smile. “I can check with her assistant, may I have your name please?”

“Tyler Chambers.”

She opened her mouth, momentarily losing her words. “I’m sorry, Mr. Chambers, of course, we haven’t seen you in a long time. Let’s see if we can find her.”

She picked up the phone. “Hi Denise, Mr. Chambers is here, is she in? I see. Oh. Oh, I see, I’ll send him back.”

Above the plush chairs off to the left of reception several framed magazine covers featured his wife posing with African children and businessmen in front of hospitals. African? When on earth did she go to Africa? Surely she had them shipped in. Yes, that could be Le Cirque in the background.

“Mrs. Chambers is at the Women’s Lupus Foundation in Bayside. Denise would like to see you though. You’ve met Denise?”

“Um no, I might have. What does she want to see to me about?”

“Mr. Chambers, it’s so good of you to stop by. How long has it been since you’ve been here?”

“Two years, I think. I got the tour when you opened this office.”

“Two years, it’s already two years. It’s been an amazing two years.”

“Can you get my wife on the phone? She’ll answer if *you* call, right?”

“Actually the reason I wanted to see you is that she wanted me to convey some information. She’s involved with the Lupus Foundation’s strategic planning for 2019 so she’s really busy over there getting her hands dirty.”

“I need to talk to her, it’ll only take a second.”

“You’re looking well by the way.”

“Thank you. Can you get her on the phone?”

Her eyes glanced down to the captain’s hat tucked under his arm. If she didn’t notice it then surely she saw the crest on his breast pocket with the ship’s wheel etched in gold thread.

“The thing is she mentioned how busy she is and wanted me to mention a wire transfer you initiated this morning.”

“The wire, yes, how do you know about that?”

“Understand she’s very busy today and wanted to meet you in person but she conveyed how—”

"Tell me why it didn't go through. Did she tell you that?"

Denise's face scrunched into a diminutive submissive shape. Her eyes squinted, her shoulders pulled together. Her head leaned forward. Her voice switched to a whisper. "She said the wire required her approval from a Henry Nicholson over at Madison Trust and that she needed to talk to you more about it before approving."

Tyler leaned back in his chair and glanced over Denise's shoulder at the pictures on the credenza. They shared a commonality, Rachel was the subject and Denise lurked in the background. Her behind Bloomberg and Rachel, behind Oprah and Rachel, her non-assumingly photobombing Rachel, Brad Pitt, and Angelina Jolie. In one it looked as though her face and body were cut off by the edge of the photo since Rachel and Hillary's formal handshake were obviously the subject of the picture.

He retuned his attention to her. She had a toothy, uncomfortable 'don't' kill the messenger' smile. "Where is the Lupus Foundation?"

"Bayside. She mentioned she was very busy."

"Rogers, where are you?" Tyler barked into his phone.

"I'm in East Harlem, sir."

"How long?"

"Oh I don't think it's looking well at all, sir. You may want to sit a spell."

"I'll hop the Lex to 125th and meet you. Is that good?"

"I think that's a good option, sir. Would you be so kind as to phone me when you disembark the subway?"

"Sure."

Tyler tucked his phone into his pocket and glanced up and down the street as the brightness against the five o'clock shadows of Lexington Ave blinded his pupils. He pulled his captain's hat from under his arm and was about to put it on.

"Eh, Village People, you spare a quarter?"

"Sorry," Tyler said with much sourness. He tucked the hat back under his arm and walked up Lex toward the 53rd Street station entrance. People zipped in and out like electrons jumping from their orbitals. He slammed his captain's hat into a metal mesh garbage can. As he descended the stairs he felt around for his MetroCard. He swiped it through the reader. As he stepped through his hips slammed into the turnstile. The little light was still red.

He stood in line at the MetroCard kiosk. He just bought the damn thing a week ago, it should be fine but he would just buy another.

A man walked down the stairs wearing the captain's hat. Dammit if a homeless man hadn't already recycled his hat. He stepped out of line and walked to the help booth.

"Yeah, can I help you," the woman said through the groggily speaker.

"My card isn't working," Tyler said, slipping it under the glass partition.

The woman scanned it and stared at her monitor with a blank look.

"The thing is toast," she said in a thick Brooklyn accent. "Can't read it. You'll have to file a claim with MTA and get a new one mailed."

Tyler tried his hardest not to kill this messenger.

"Go ahead." She motioned to the handicapped gate. She reached down and activated the cage door.

"Thank you ma'am." Tyler shined with sincerity.

He pulled the cage door open for an elderly woman with a walker. When she cleared the entryway he stepped through.

"Eh, Gilligan."

Tyler looked over. A chubby transit cop approached him.

"Whaddya think you're doing?"

"My card didn't work so she buzzed me through."

"Yeah, sure it didn't. Let's us talk to the lady."

Tyler was not wearing a red shirt and a boonie like Gilligan. He wore a white dress shirt, navy blue pants, and a $3,200 blazer etched with the East Hampton's Yacht Club logo on the breast. A navy blue handkerchief peeked from the pocket and he wore a corn blue ascot around his neck in lieu of a tie. This cop wouldn't know an expensive jacket if—no, he wasn't going to be an elitist.

"Eh Mary, Gilligan here says you two are lovers."

"Listen Elmer, how'd you like me to come out of this booth?"

"I'd enjoy that. What's the verdict on the Skipper here?"

"Yeah lost his card or something. He's all right, send him through." She motioned with her hand.

"All right, hope you get off that island, pal."

Elitism existed for people like this. "Thank you, officer. Thank you, ma'am." He offered a polite bow.

He glanced once more at his hat sitting upon the homeless man's head as he disappeared among the uptown commuters.

Tyler peered up Lexington in the middle of Spanish Harlem. A set of headlights blinked up the block. He raised his arm letting Rogers know he spotted him. He walked across the street and Rogers negotiated the car into the far right lane. He opened the door himself and climbed in back.

Rogers lowered the partition.

"Rogers, it's good to see you."

"Thank you sir. Where to? I must admit I'm not familiar with Bayside but I have GPS now."

"Home."

"We aren't meeting with Mrs. Chambers?"

"No, home please."

Rogers raised the partition back up.

Tyler climbed the grand staircase and greeted several of the servants. He tried his hardest to hide everything he felt and instead displayed a graceful demure. He just wanted to get out of these clothes which now felt like a clown suit.

In the master bed he ripped his boat shoes from his feet and threw them to the ground. He stripped down to his boxers and laid his blazer, mock neck, and trousers across the sequined truck at the foot of the bed.

He put on a plain blue shirt and khakis. He threw his sailing clothes into an empty hamper and pulled the canvas liner by the strings and heaved the bag over his shoulder.

He scurried down the south stair and through the garden room to the backyard. He emptied the bag of clothing into the wok-style fire pit. He grabbed the tin of lighter fluid from the grill and squeezed a fountain of fluid on his Gilligan's Island attire. The canister gurgled as air flowed back in and Tyler gave it another herculean squeeze with his thumbs together as hard as he could. Another fountain drenching the clothes. He tossed the empty canister aside and lit a long fireplace match.

The fire pit engulfed the clothing. Through the heated haze of the flames the solarium undulated as he watched the servants dress tables.

The frenzy stopped and the servants set their linens down and rushed out of the solarium.

Tyler knew why they were darting toward the main hall.

When he came in through the servants' kitchenette, a commotion reverberated through the old Victorian mansion. He had become accustomed to this ritual. The servants stowed their tools, dust pans were slammed into closets, orders were hurled in Spanish, and cleaning supplies disappeared. For 23 hours a day, productivity flourished in the Chambers manor but for one hour, half hour in the morning, and half in the evening, productivity gave way to pomp and circumstance.

The commotion became silence. Mrs. Chambers was in the building.

His wife punched through the entryway barking orders at servants about dinner and then turning to Denise and barking a few more in her direction. She noticed her husband. "Tyler, I thought you were in the city."

Denise surely noticed that he'd changed outfits as if he were hiding his shame, although maybe she thought he changed outfits for every occasion as if it were a common elitist practice.

"I want to talk to you," Rachel said.

Rachel held Tyler's two fingers in her hand. "Tyler, Henry at Madison Trust called me and I was shocked to hear what he said. You were in Long Island this morning buying a yacht?"

"You remember. We talked about it."

"I know, but I didn't think it was of this magnitude. I thought you wanted a little boat to get away every now and then and fish."

"I did…and it is."

"No Tyler, this wasn't that. He wanted twelve million. Is that what you were spending?"

"Twelve million, that's the price."

"That's a yacht, not a boat."

"We can afford it."

"Honey, it's not the money. It's what comes with it. Lana Farnsworth recommended against this sort of thing."

"Lana? You talked to her about this?" He pulled his hands back.

"Tyler, she understands us and what we're trying to do. She has a proven track record in philanthropy."

"We have to call her every time we make a big purchase?"

"She's advising us on where to invest our charitable capital."

"We pay a publicist five hundred an hour to tell us not to buy a boat?"

"It's not the purchase price. It's the crowd and stigma that comes with it."

He shook his head. "Why did I drive all the way to Long Island to be made a fool of? I showed up ready to take the keys and the broker told me I hadn't paid."

"We are transitioning over to the philanthropy circuit. We no longer work for Corporate America, we work for Non-Profit America. And the image we project—"

"We could spend more time as a family, it's big enough to hold a fundraising event."

"No, we can't fundraise on a yacht off from some fancy yacht club. Those Hampton yacht club people are a whole different world. According to Lana—"

"It's no different than your events at the Met and Le Cirque."

"I'm not judging anyone. We're no better or worse than the Hampton crowd."

"Then what's wrong with it?"

"It's a branding issue. Our philanthropy investments are geared toward the West Chester circuit. You know how cliquey people are out here. Moving to the Hampton crowd would be like trying to launch a new product in a country you've never been to. Lana says we must focus our efforts in the West Chester circuit and not spread ourselves to areas where we don't yet have a foothold. We risk losing our West Chester crowd if people start seeing us as that Hamptons crowd. A yacht would send that message with the subtlety of a ticker tape parade."

"I looked like a supreme fool in front of those people—"

"What people? You aren't a part of their world, nobody knows who you are out there so there's no harm, no foul."

He hated it when she was right. Technically only two people in the Hamptons knew him. The broker and the broker's assistant.

Rachel wrapped her arm around his waist and leaned her head on his shoulder. "I'm sorry if I made you feel embarrassed. I've worked hard to build the foundation. I promise I'll make it up to you."

CHAPTER TWO

Tyler read pop-lit on his ride into the city. For some reason he couldn't read what he considered fine literature on his commute. The Aubrey Maturin series was a special event read, not a commute read. Lite reads were the reality TV of literature so he pressed on with his Tom Clancy and Danielle Steele novels. Clancy still turned out great reads despite being dead.

The unremarkable West Side Highway traced Manhattan's edge like a trench. Manhattan lost its urban splendor among the low-level co-ops. Rogers turned on 45th Street and the vertical wonder of Midtown came into view.

The Grand Canyon known as Sixth Avenue breathed the spirit of the city—not touristy, but all about business, wide, vast, and tall.

Rogers pulled up to the 860 building, opened the door for him and popped the trunk. Tyler stepped around to the trunk and pulled a five-foot-long fluorescent pink foam tube out. He then retrieved a fluorescent green one and a fluorescent blue. He tucked the three foam tubes under his arm as Rogers handed him his briefcase. He nodded to Rogers and headed for the lobby.

As he stepped off the elevator, the receptionist greeted him with a big smile. The buxom brunette wore a fine pinstripe skirt suit. He touched his wallet to the sensor on the side door and it clicked. He pushed it open with his free shoulder and walked in.

He rarely went through the main entryway, a grand Parthenon of corporate iciness where he had to endure no less than six insincere *good mornings* as he made his way to his office.

"Good morning, Doctor Chambers."

"Morning," he grumbled back. Only two faux *good mornings* when he snuck through the side door.

He reached his office and tossed the foam tubes on the floor and started his laptop. Gina stepped in and dictated his calendar for the day.

"Get me Ben and Luke Sanders," he said to her.

Ben Galvani had a corner office with a spectacular view of Avenue of the Americas. He ushered Tyler along with Luke to the round table next to his display case. He smirked as Tyler set the fluorescent tubes on the floor.

He wore his suit jacket as he usually did when he met with Tyler. Ben was in his mid-forties with slicked-back slightly receding hair. He had a formal constitution when he met with Tyler. His assistant hovered at his side ready to fetch a water or a coffee for her boss's boss. Tyler declined and the assistant let Ben know that she was just outside and available if Mr. Chambers or he changed his mind.

Harvard, Cambridge, Mass, the plaque in the display case shouted. Tyler always questioned Harvard's prestige. There were only so many ways to present the Peter Principle to students. Did their professors exude some sort of higher plane of understanding when they lectured? Did they have access to different and better knowledge than CUNY? Better case studies, better connections, yes of course better connections but the curriculum was the same.

Ben always poised himself underneath his diploma. He would then express interest in Tyler's weekend, asked about his wife, his daughter, remembered their names, sports, and sometimes a political event, although he avoided political beliefs, never quite alluding to a party affiliation. Then down to business.

"What's on your mind, Tyler?" he finally asked.

"We used these at the lake for the summer and they're already cracked."

"What lake?"

Tyler told Ben what lake, to which he recited a whole host of stories and events and friends having to do with the lakes. He was wholly unconcerned with the three pool noodles sitting on the floor of his office.

Luke Sanders poised himself with his tablet at the ready for jotting notes. He glanced at the noodles as Ben recounted a story about the CEO of Dow Chemical.

"…so they actually have various levels of quality assurance. The ISO-9000, Malcom Baldridge—"

"They fell apart mid-season," Tyler interrupted with.

"Okay. Are you sure?"

He directed Ben's attention to the three pool noodles. Luke, with the nod of approval from Ben picked one up. He bent it in half and sure enough, in the middle cracks had formed in the foam tubing.

Tyler pointed the cracks out as Ben leaned closer and ran his finger around the wared middle. Tyler noticed that Ben's reading glasses were on his desk and wondered if he could see the cracks.

"Definitely. I can see that. How much use do these have?"

"Half a season."

"Half a season?"

"Did you leave them in the sun when you were done with them?" Luke asked.

"They're meant to be left outside," Tyler said.

"Okay, let's talk about product quality. In Luke's department they've explored obsolescence. That's where we determine the customers' needs and wants and adjust product design accordingly. Luke's department specializes in quality and obsolescence models."

Luke set the pool noodle down. "That's right, Ben. Tyler, have you heard of how Alka-Seltzer doubled their sales?"

"They told people to take two instead of one."

"Correct, you've heard this story."

Apparently every school taught the Alka-Seltzer urban legend.

While inspecting the foam tube, Tyler said, "This company invented the pool noodle. This is our main product. What happened? Now we don't care about quality and they fall apart in July?"

Ben broke in. "I think Luke's Alka-Seltzer example says it all. People buy these every season, now they buy them twice a season."

"Because they fall apart?"

Ben smiled and waved his finger at Tyler. "Never change the main product, right?"

"Well, yes," Tyler said.

"Right, McDonalds never changes the Big Mac, Burger King has the Whopper."

"The Whopper, home of the Whopper," Luke added.

"I think that's a good point, Tyler." Ben turned to Luke and said in a reassuring manner clearly meant for Tyler's benefit, "I want you to get to the bottom of this. Obviously we need to maintain our brand. Find out from marketing the brand awareness effect of the other product lines. And I'm interested in what kind of product return we've experienced on the pool noodle."

Luke nodded and walked out of Ben's office.

"You know Tyler, we're releasing the boogie board in the Gulf States this week, I'm wondering if Fusion Outdoor has moved beyond pool noodles. National Guard is happy with the rescue boards, in California they love sea kayaks, easy to make, margins are still decent."

"The pool noodle built this company—"

"And now it's a commodity. Chinese suppliers can do it for less. It's not a defeat, it's the product life cycle."

"And Luke will find this out."

"Absolutely, he will. If it's affecting brand awareness he'll find out about it."

Ben set the foam tube on the floor. "Tyler, I need to ask you something. I understand that you reached out to Jerry Stritzke."

"Reached out?"

"You had a meeting with him out in Seattle last week?"

How on earth did Ben find out about this? "Yes. Well no, not a meeting. We had coffee. At Starbucks, the original one."

"Right. I just want to make sure we are aligned on our strategy."

"What do you mean aligned?"

"REI is not the kind of retail outlet we want our products in. Their markups are too high. We belong in Target and Wal-Mart with the masses."

A goddamn cup of coffee. "We were just talking."

"I want to make sure we have commonality on all our products and brands. REI specializes in quality and higher-end branding. Ours—"

"Fall apart."

"Ours are for the masses. We get four hundred times penetration with Target alone. Stritzke can eat that for breakfast if he wants. His stores are small potatoes."

"I can't have coffee with an old friend?"

"I would have liked to have been consulted. We blaze hard for this brand. We don't want it diluted or going in a direction it's not ready for. We're not interested in REI's tiny customer base."

Ben gave Tyler the Harvard MBA puppy dog look—his eyes released him from any responsibility for the professional messing on the carpet.

Tyler gave in, perhaps because of the enduring silence, "I will consult you in the future."

"Thank you, Tyler." Ben buttoned his suit. "Oh, can I ask you a personal favor?"

"Certainly."

"I need to duck out early today. I have a wake in Chicago tomorrow."

"I'm sorry."

"Thank you. My sister's nanny. They were close. She's throwing this big wake for her, which I think is wonderful."

"That's good, whatever time you need."

"Thanks, it's just that I had this charity event—MS Warrior Dash of Suffolk County. They have their annual race this afternoon in Montauk."

"Right, the warrior dash."

"All these people racing in the mud. It's quite a spectacle. We're sponsoring it."

"Right." Tyler nodded.

"Do you think you could attend in my place?"

"Of course. I'd love to."

Tyler walked out of Ben's office with pool noodles in hand. He transversed the entire forty-eighth floor of the 860 building corner to opposite corner to make his way back to his office.

He flopped in the leather chair behind his desk and looked through his mail. His Forbes had arrived and he started flipping through it.

A Stanford torus—a giant donut-shaped space station that could sustain a hundred thousand residents. It worked by spinning like a bike tire and the centrifugal force pushed everything to the interior surface, thus providing artificial gravity.

Goodness what had the Forbes people been smoking? Tyler flipped to the cover which featured a man with shoulder-length blond hair, cobalt eyes, a full grin showing off his crooked teeth and he wasn't wearing a shirt. He was the guy trying to build the first hotel in space. The donut was to be built in perhaps a century. For now, the station would be scaled down, round, and house a hundred or so people. Interesting, once the jets spun the wheel, it never needed to be spun again, barring any friction or gravitational pull.

Vacation options would include rides, spectacular views, and skydiving; and one could brag about contributing to the space revolution. The business plan was not unfamiliar. Get-rich people to do it, as the money pours in, it finances expansion for the masses. Eventually the 100,000-person resort is a reality and the crane operator in Spokane wonders if he should do Disney World or the space donut for his vacation this year.

His phone rang. Tyler put a Post-it note on the article and plopped the Forbes on the credenza.

"Charlie Mercer is here," Gina said.

"Send him in."

He shook hands with Charlie and motioned to his chair as he closed the door. Charlie pulled a folder from his briefcase.

"I won't beat around the bush with the good news. With the earnings announcement on Monday and the corresponding three point rise in the stock, your net worth has hit a milestone." He pointed to the bottom of the personal balance sheet. It read $1,000,0095,035.00. "You are officially in the billionaire club."

"Hmm," Tyler said trying not to act impressed. "What does that mean?"

"Not much more than last month. Just a bunch of zeroes like when your car hits 100,000 miles. When the stock makes a move like that and you own twenty-five percent of the company, it's going to have quite an effect on your net worth."

Charlie went through his assets and liabilities and personal expenditures in boilerplate manner. He had colorful pie charts, graphs and bullet points. Charlie pointed out the tax benefits of his wife donating appreciated stock over cash, highlights of the annual meeting, and that his property taxes had just become even more insane.

"So last week I was the world's richest millionaire and this week I'm the world's poorest billionaire?"

Charlie laughed. "I suppose you could say that."

After he left, Tyler read more about the space donut. He finished his kale and quinoa salad and tossed the plastic platter into the garbage under his desk. A knock at the door interrupted his focus.

"Yes."

"Doctor Chambers?"

Tyler recognized the man's face but had to search for his name.

"Mike Rassum if you don't recall, sir."

"Yes, Mike, how does your family find New York so far?"

"We're enjoying it. I grew up in LA so the big city isn't that much of a culture shock. I'm still learning though."

"And you transferred from the Tampa district office?"

"That's right, we lived in Clearwater Beach so I guess it is a bit of a change."

"Well we appreciate everything you've done in the Gulf Coast for the company and we're happy to have you in the big leagues. Anything I can do for you?"

"Just getting settled into that office next to Ben's." He presented a framed picture to Tyler. "Is that you by chance?"

Tyler stared at a younger version of himself on a gravel path with a canoe hoisted over his head. Next to him, Lester Wilner carried an oversized backpack. Lester displayed his trademark half-smirk smile for the camera.

"How about that?" Tyler said. "Where did you get this?"

"Found it in the back of a drawer in my desk."

"Oh, yeah. That used to be my office. I must have forgotten it."

"Why are you carrying the canoe? Don't you just pull up to the boat launch?"

Tyler laughed. "No, with a canoe you heave it over your head. It's lighter than it looks. This picture is from my college days. We camped in the Boundary Waters Canoe Area in Northern Minnesota."

"Oh you're from there, correct?"

"Minneapolis area. In the Boundary Waters you canoe across a lake and when you get to shore you heave it over your head and hike to the next lake. Portaging is what they call it. The old fur traders did it back in the 1800s."

"Well, there's not too many canoers in the Tampa area."

"Thanks for bringing this over." He smiled warmly at the picture.

Tyler wished the newest executive luck and shook his hand. He typed Lester's name into Google.

LinkedIn put him at Indian Point, the nuclear plant in upstate New York. Ten years there. Before he was a field technician and a machine operator. Now he ran his own reactor.

Gina rang him and he picked up the phone. As she spoke he opened the bottom drawer and placed the picture behind some hanging files.

"That's fine, send her in," he said to Gina.

"Mister Chambers, here's the bullets for the charity event. Are you leaving soon?" Marsha, the company's communications director, asked.

"I was about to."

"I think this is wonderful that you are taking this over for Ben. The event is going to give the company a lot of exposure and help a lot of children."

"The children. I'm happy to help."

"Well break a leg." She smiled and walked out of his office.

He folded the memo in half and stuck it in his book and phoned Gina. "I'll be in Montauk for the rest of the day."

After he hung up the receiver, he dwelled for a moment on Marsha's parting line to him. *Break a leg*—an odd thing to say…

CHAPTER THREE

A hamlet outside of Montauk served as the event host. Tyler brought his Aubrey-Maturin book to keep him occupied and relaxed during the three-hour car ride from the office. He looked out the window of the limo and realized they were in Suffolk County. He glanced at his book and in the last forty miles he managed to devour two entire paragraphs.

He clung to the book like a warm blanket. Just two hours ago he'd read the memo the company's communications director handed him. It listed the bullet points for Ben's speech. Tyler was to deliver it.

He glanced out the window—east and west, back and forth. He felt like a monkey in a cage at a research facility. What if a car pulled out and crashed into them? Nothing too major of course, a minor accident would be good. Darn, he couldn't make it.

Just tell Rogers to hail a cab home, Tyler would drive the car into a tree at five mph. No, ten. Would the airbag deploy? God what was he thinking?

He'd seen Ben give this speech before—business, dedication to the community, social responsibility, name of the company's charity, short and sweet. He never thought he'd have to do it himself.

Why would this woman just hand him a speech and think everything is taken care of? She should come out to Montauk and give the damned speech herself. She was the communications director. He didn't even think of asking about the purpose of the memo. It's for charity, do it for the children, charity is the secret word that tricks people into saying yes to something they would not normally do. Who could say no to dying children? What a sucker he was.

He recalled a similar situation where Ben thrusted him into the limelight at a board meeting. It occurred after Tyler's critic of the Seahawk Personal Kayak, a cheap piece of plastic crap which had been rushed into stores for the coming season. Sitting in it felt worse than sitting on a wooden pew for a two-hour sermon. The thought crept into Tyler's mind that Ben had engineered all of this as retribution for his pool noodle complaint or maybe his cup of coffee with Jerry Stritzke. But surely Ben rose above that level of pettiness. He tried his hardest not to think this was planned.

Rogers pulled the Lincoln stretch off the highway. They were getting close. It was time to leave the cloisters of the plush car seats.

The event handlers ushered Tyler through the backstage area. The feisty go-getter organizer spoke to her helpers and coordinators while wheeling sponsors around. She introduced him to organizers, a few victims of the cause, and some of last year's winners.

She herded him along with a few other men in suits into an area with chairs on the makeshift stage for VIPs.

Tyler marveled at the sight of the obstacle course and the excitement of the racers gathered at the start. There were cargo nets to be climbed, thick ropes to swing from, old tires, and structures built from massive logs. And mud, every obstacle had the threat of mud and the racers looked eager to get dirty. They were at the staging area behind the start line, stretching and jumping. They were dressed in shorts and t-shirts with white numbers pinned to their chests.

The organizer unclasped the velvet rope and suggested Tyler and the other VIPSs find their seat for the event was about to begin. The velvet rope clasp clicked shut and sealed them on the stage, there was no turning back. The podium with the microphone stared a hole in him. He lunged at the organizer who now stood on the other side of the velvet rope. "Excuse me, miss. Do you have an agenda?"

"I'm sorry? I don't know what you mean."

"I mean an order of events, as in what parts are taking place when."

"Goodness, Doctor Chambers." She laughed. "I thought you meant something sinister like a hidden agenda."

"Oh no, just wondering of the timing of everything so I can tell my office when to expect me back." He gave a nervous laugh.

"Nothing fancy, I'll introduce you, you can say what you need to and then Raheem will announce the event and everyone will get dirty."

He looked at the podium with dread. "Umm, when…"

But it was too late, Ms. Organizer had scurried off to put out another fire and Tyler was trapped in the velvet rope cage.

He had gone over the bullet points in his head a hundred times in the car and was tempted to pull out the memo but that would have looked odd to his other cell mates. He gauged the other sponsors wondering if they would each speak. He could go in the middle, people remembered the first person and the last but usually forgot the middle. His company was the biggest so it made sense that if only one sponsor spoke, it would be him. He could let the niche companies have the floor. What a graceful gesture. Would that be allowed? Would Ben hear about it? Would that communications director berate him for ruining her hard work?

The organizer said she was going first, didn't she? But where did she sneak off to? Tyler thought that's what she said, therefore he wouldn't go until she stepped back onto the stage. He wiped his palms against his pants, he held them open near his side so the wind blew the sweat dry.

He couldn't remember a single bullet from the memo even though he had thoroughly memorized them on the ride over. If he pulled the memo out, he'd surely cling to it like Linus and his blanket. He couldn't let anyone see him do that.

A sip from his bottle of water tempted him. No don't do that, it will just make you thirstier and then what if he has to go right during his time to speak? Even a little sip would turn his bladder into Niagara Falls.

There she was. She unclipped the velvet gate, entered the cage and sealed it back up. She went to the podium and adjusted the mic. Loud patchy noises echoed through the sound system and the racers and crowd focused their attention to the stage. She welcomed everyone.

His mouth was dry—would people notice one generous swig before he assumed his place at the podium? Would it look desperate? He would time when she would introduce him and anticipate the last swig of water. One last swig, that would give him the longest possible time between thirst-quenching relief and bladder relief.

But what if she introduced him and when he walked to the podium she just kept talking? Was she one of these people who didn't know how to finish a conversation? Was she that person ahead of you in line at Starbucks who discussed the starving children in Africa with the cashier forcing those behind her to stand in perpetual awkwardness when it was your turn to order?

Sixty degrees and overcast with humidity was a recipe for clamminess. The nerves in his back pinched, his mouth was a desert. She stepped away from the podium and motioned toward him. He stood, put on an awkward smile, withdrew his note cards, and stepped to the mic. Oh God, the water bottle was still under his chair!

Tyler returned to his seat among the mild golf-clap applause. Raheem invigorated the crowd with his radio announcer voice. With just one sentence of Raheem's steroid-laced voiceover cadence, the crowd most likely had forgotten Tyler's speech by now. Such relief to be forgotten. When he returned to his seat he blended quite nicely with the other men in suits.

A pop came from the starter pistol and the racers darted into the mud, climbing posts, falling over random objects. The frontrunners tore into the course as if the fate of the world hung in the balance. The last tier of racers lunged from the start line. They looked a bit less athletic than the others and were most likely the novice crowd.

He panted away, whispering a quiet affirmation under his breath for the speech's conclusion. Why had he never found the time for Toastmasters? He would make it his priority to join a group on Monday and never let this happen again. Of course he said that upon completion of his last speech. This time he meant it. Such immense relief ran through his body—the longest possible time before another speech.

The organizer unlocked the velvet rope and they were free to go. He wasn't sure if he should be the first to leave as it looked as though he was trying to escape. He desired an acquaintance to fill the awkwardness. He could run over to the parking lot attendant who directed Rogers where to drop off and park and pretend they were old friends. They could talk about the race and the charity and if he enjoyed his chosen vocation of parking cars. He probably didn't see his speech from the valet stand.

He walked off the stage and disappeared into the crowd of spectators. The dryness in his mouth surely caused bad breath. Dampness gathered in his underarms and BO rank crept up through his collar. He didn't smell bad even when he worked out but his stress sweat reeked like a hobo's.

He needed a shower and would brush his teeth. He'd schedule a massage to coax the knots and monkey fists out of his back. Goodness that would be refreshing, he'd be recalibrated and the stench on his body associated with this event would be rinsed down the drain.

The spectators mixed with the racers at the course finish line. They hurled congratulations and high fives and posed for selfies, and they wore their layers of mud with pride.

Tyler's eyes fixated on a blonde with an athletic build. She wore a blue sports bra exposing her stomach which had a navel piercing. She wore black jogging shorts and running shoes although he couldn't tell what color they were. She had dazzling blue eyes, bright white teeth, and her smile soothed his stress. He imagined the joy of rolling around in the mud with her. Such freedom to be with a woman who darts through mud as a pastime. She laughed with three men and another girl, all of them covered in mud. He knew he'd never break into her clique but wanted to desperately. Perhaps next year he could run in the event. He was still in top condition from his swimming scholarship days. But Ben would never allow that since it would sully the company's precious image.

"Hi, you're Tyler Chambers, right?"

A grinning man about six and a half feet tall covered head to toe in mud stood next to Tyler, slightly eclipsing him.

"I'd shake your hand but I'm kind of dirty," he said in a soft British accent.

"Oh that's fine—"

"Some of us are going for wings and beer afterwards if you're interested."

"Oh, I'm not really—"

"The Buggered Rooster. It's a place in Chelsea. Best wings on the planet. Thirty Eighth and Tenth Avenue."

"I'm sure it's good…"

Tyler paused as he regarded the man's face. Familiarity washed over him as he tried to place it. His hair was wet and dirty but blond and pulled back in a ponytail. Dried caked mud covered his face but his bright blue eyes shined through the grime as did his bold toothy smile. Half of Tyler's mind shuffled through stock invitation declines while the other half tried to place the face. It was that fella from the cover of Forbes. The guy trying to build a Hilton in space. Richard Branson was his name.

"Be there in one hour," Richard said.

CHAPTER FOUR

A G5 propelled Tyler across the length of Long Island to a muni airfield in New Jersey. He arranged for a helicopter to bus him to West Chelsea and drop him off at the heliport at West 30th Street. A car waited for him and it sped to the address Branson gave him.

The area, known for its nightlife of mega clubs, lofts, and old industrial buildings, bustled with activity. He found the door which had a faded W337 on the archway.

Old brick and painted-over windows muffled the club-mix music. A woman leaned against the façade smoking a cigarette. She was Tyler's height, wore a red dress, had athletically built calf muscles, and an Adam's apple.

"Hi," Tyler said. "Do you know if Richard Branson is in there?"

"Yeah, I know Richard," she said in a dark brown voice. "He's in back."

She pulled the industrial door open for him and he walked in. Tall women with broad shoulders in evening gowns talked, drank, and laughed throughout the bar.

"Can I help you, kid?" an old man said.

"Where's *in back*?" Tyler yelled over the music.

He pointed to an area down a hallway that looked as though it led to the bathrooms. "Back there," he said.

Tyler walked down the dimly lit corridor. A heavy black curtain blocked the doorway at the end. He stuck his hands in, found the opening, and slipped through. On the other side was an altogether different party. The men wore suits mostly without ties. A stout blonde woman in lederhosen flew past him with handfuls of beer steins. He felt sawdust under his shoes and realized it was a German beer hall.

"Tyler!"

Richard shook his hand. He had his flowing shiny blond hair back, a sharp blue button-down shirt and khaki shorts. Somehow he'd managed to clean himself up, get new clothes, and arrive before Tyler, all in under an hour.

"How are you? Glad you came, I really am. Lola dear, one for Tyler."

The portly woman who almost ran him over handed him a stein. Goodness, how on earth did she carry them all?

"Thank you, Miss Lola," he said with a gentleman's bow.

"You're sweet kid, you're a gentleman. What are you doing with this old scruff?"

"Oh listen to her," Richard said as he emptied the last of his oversized stein, another indication of how quickly he arrived.

Richard grabbed Tyler's forearm and they shuffled to a group of three men talking under a chandelier made of deer antlers.

"Gents, this is Tyler."

"Hey, Tyler, Howdy, Nice to meet you," they said.

One of them extended his hand and Tyler switched his beer into the other and shook it. He wished he had said something pleasant to the gentleman instead of just giving him an odd look but he knew that he'd seen him from somewhere. Another moment of déjà vu.

"I'm Evan, welcome aboard," the first man said.

He knew the young man, maybe in his mid-twenties, from somewhere. He shook hands with the other two men and immediately forgot their names but the name Evan stuck with him. Before he could strike up a conversation Richard tugged his arm and off they went to the next group.

Next to a framed poster of Marlene Dietrich, a man around Tyler's age spoke to a Middle Eastern fella.

"Tyler, this is Nate and this is Rishi."

They shook hands. “Welcome aboard. We’re glad to have you,” Nate shouted.

“I’m looking forward to talking with you, Tyler,” Rishi said.

“Nice to meet you.” Tyler stared at Nate since he recognized him as well. Then it came to him. He was Nathan Blecharczyk, the founder of Airbnb.

“How do you like the beer?” Rishi asked.

“Good. Good stuff.” Tyler felt the buzz taking effect.

“Well gentlemen, you’ll get a chance to pick Tyler’s brain, I have to introduce him to everyone else.” Richard pulled Tyler away to the next group as Nate and Rishi lifted their steins to him.

“This is James, don’t say anything too loud, he might be recording this,” Richard said as he gulped his ale.

James laughed and smacked Richard across the back of his shoulder splashing his beer on the sleeve of his forearm. Richard leaned back and let out a big jolly belly laugh.

Tyler laughed too, not sure of what the punchline meant.

The name James Jannard popped into Tyler’s head. He was the sunglasses fellow. Tyler remembered Oakleys, the expensive sunglasses from the late 90s that everyone had to have. They were made of some spaced-age plastic that withstood extreme heat and cold. He remembered someone lending him a pair on a skiing trip in Utah. He lost them because he didn’t strap the band to his head as his friend urged him to do. He recalled the sticker shock when he told his friend he’d buy him a new pair.

“Richard is a joker, don’t listen to him,” James said. “He still thinks the moon is the last frontier even though it’s just a big fucking rock.”

Tyler laughed even though he didn’t quite register the joke since he was recounting the article he read on James a few years ago.

James sold his sunglasses empire as Tyler recalled and developed a new camera. As in a movie camera. Some sort of higher than hi-def camera that indie filmmakers sought out. Expensive but for 80 grand you could replace your 350 grand studio monster. Somehow selling space-aged sunglasses to snowboarders in Vale translated to high-end indie filmmakers at Sundance.

He gazed across the room at the Dietrich poster that Evan and Rishi were talking in front of. Evan Spiegel—that’s his name—the Snapchat founder. Tyler realized the room was full of people from the stack of Forbes magazines in his master bathroom.

On and on Richard ushered him around the German beer hall, shaking hands, laughing, telling jokes, Lola a constant presence of galloping lederhosen and crystal steins. He had to stop placing faces before his eyes rolled to the back of his head. None of them mentioned their companies, forcing Tyler to recount the endless Forbes articles he'd read. Of course they wouldn't, would Zuckerberg tell you where he worked? He would do his homework when an opportunity to bury his face in his phone presented itself. For now he would try his hardest to enjoy the party.

Richard ushered him to a long beer garden table where two men were sitting on benches.

"I'm Dave," one of them said, extending his hand.

"Pleased to meet you." Tyler took his hand.

"This is Elon."

Tyler shook hands and introduced himself. Elon was an odd name. The only person he knew of with that name was…Tyler realized he was shaking hands with Elon Musk, the owner of Tesla and SpaceX. He tried his hardest not to be nervous, goodness he needed to get through his first beer.

"Good to meet you, Tyler," Elon said.

He had a perfect in. He once heard Mr. Musk speak at a seminar on electric propulsion. He was in the third row and came close to asking a question but the host handed the microphone to some electrical engineering twerp. The chance to finally ask his question had arrived! …God no, that would be stupid. Don't say anything stupid, don't say anything stupid. Watch your alcohol intake, but drink more to loosen up.

Richard motioned Tyler to a seat at the bench. He slid in and Richard sat next to him. Tyler was now sitting kitty-corner to Elon Musk.

David grabbed Elon's forearm and demanded his attention "…Elon this is the future, you of all people should know this." David leaned closer to Elon causing him to flinch since he spoke with his hands. "You're afraid of the boogie man, we're going to fall off the edge of the world, the sky is falling, let's burn witches. You're afraid someone will get run over."

"No, not at all."

"Then why? Explain."

Lola interrupted. "What kind tonight, Richard?"

"Ahhh, regular, sea salt, Jamaican, and how about some spicy? Tyler, does spicy agree with you?"

Tyler realized who David was, he started PayPal along with other investors including Musk. He wondered if Richard was an investor in PayPal at one time.

"Tyler, you're not afraid of the ghost pepper?"

He turned to Richard and Lola. "Oh I'm sorry, yes, spicy is fine."

"Fine, I'll bring out a dozen each and we'll see how you do."

"Tyler, Richard here tells me you invented the pool noodle," Elon said.

"Wait, we're not done here. Explain it to me. You think it'll be like Terminator where the robot cars will run everyone down and eat them."

Elon turned back to David. "You're thinking of that Stephen King movie, *Christine*."

"No, not..." David let out a sigh and threw his hands in the air.

Elon turned to Tyler. "So what's the secret? Not to undermine your success but it's just a big piece of foam, right?"

Tyler set his beer down. He would make sure he didn't make a fool out of himself talking about pool noodles to the man who dabbled in rockets and electric cars. He'd practiced his speech on making the pool noodle many times before.

"The secret of the success of the pool noodle was not in the design or materials composition or cost control, it was the distribution network."

"How so?"

"There's something called the Oreo defense in retail. So at the grocery store in the cookie aisle, there's only so much space for cookies, so what Oreo did was come up with all sorts of different types of Oreos to take up space. The double stuff, the mint ones, the minis, seasonal, pink ones, etcetera."

"The double stuff, those get me every year," David said as Elon and Richard gave a perplexed look.

"So every time they came up with a new type, it would nudge one of the Keebler Elf cookies or a Pepperidge Farm either off the shelf or to the dreaded bottom shelf. They could have come out with radish-flavored Oreos. Stores would have stocked them, they'd knock the competition off the shelf, and people wouldn't buy them, but they'd still buy Oreos since the brand name stretches for the entire middle length of an aisle, they have the Boardwalk of retail aisle space by doing that." Tyler realized he was speaking too quickly and sounded like a high-strung typewriter.

"Interesting, so pool noodles do that?" Elon asked.

"Well the thing with pool noodles is that at retail outlets such as Target and Wal-Mart, there's still a concept of prime shelf real estate and lousy shelf real estate. We offered to fill their Baltic Avenue shelf space with our product."

"What's Baltic Avenue?" Elon asked.

"That's the shitty properties in Monopoly, right past Go," David said.

"Oh right, right, right, Boardwalk and Baltic. I understand," Elon said.

"So you actually wanted the crappy shelf space?" David asked.

Tyler tried his hardest to slow his words down as to not showcase his nervousness. Did he just talk about radish-flavored Oreos? Did his breath still stink? "Well the pool noodle is long and fluorescent colored. It overcame the inherent weakness of the bottom shelf, you walk into the long aisle of outdoor equipment and it's the first thing your eyes see. Target and Wal-Mart were happy to have someone fill their bottom shelves and the noodle was in every retail outlet in America. We introduced a variety of new products after that since we had good retail and market penetration."

"The penetration, you got to have the penetration, your foot in the door, that's brilliant, Tyler." David waved his hand in the air as Lola strolled by. "Lola, four pink torpedoes," he barked. He turned back to Elon. "Simple ideas. Tyler gets it, why don't you? That's what I'm trying to do with the self-driving car. I don't get it why you're all boogie man on this idea."

"Simple doesn't not mean brilliant. And I'm not boogie man on the self-driving car."

"Then what's your problem?"

"I think your idea is a poor execution of a brilliant concept."

David's mouth hung open as Elon emptied his beer stein.

Richard raised his hand in the air in a surrender gesture. "Okay gentlemen, we can agree to disagree. David I'm sure your plan has merits, it's just that Elon brings some good points—"

"It's a terrible idea," Elon said as he set his stein down without looking at David.

"I suppose you could do better." David turned to Tyler. "Tyler what do you think?"

"Yeah go ahead and tell Tyler," Elon said. "Tell him your simpleton idea."

"So Google is coming up with the self-driving car, recognition software so the thing knows what the road looks like, it can see the lines, it knows the difference between a pedestrian and a stop sign, it knows traffic lights. My idea is a totally different concept.

"We put sensors in the road, the car is guided by a central traffic control. Where to go, where to stop is told from a central supercomputer."

"I see," Tyler said.

"You don't have to worry about a computer recognizing a stop sign or not seeing it in bad weather. Hell you wouldn't even need stop signs or traffic lights. Where the cars stop would be programmed in the central network. What do you think?"

Tyler grasped his beer. "Hmmm," he said and took a drink.

"I don't think he likes it," Richard said.

"Bad idea," Elon said.

"What, you don't like the business side of it? I'm going to make a fortune on the sensors, that's where the money is. Cities would have to buy millions of these things, maybe tens of millions."

"What would happen if someone stole the sensors and just randomly put them on the edges of cliffs, Wile E. Coyote style?" Elon said.

Richard and Tyler laughed.

"Why would they do that? You're just being cute. You could just as easily say that the Coyote could hack into the Google software and program the Road Runner's car to drive into his cave for dinner."

Elon laughed again. "It's just not a viable idea."

"What's wrong with it? Tell me what's wrong? Simple and easy."

"What's wrong is I think it's an inferior idea to Google's recognition software. You're not simplifying the concept, you're stupefying it. And you're bringing government into it so you'll force it down people's throats whether it works well or not."

"Government? This from the guy who runs taxi service to the International Space Station, who's your biggest client?"

"What I'm trying to get at—"

"What's your demographic again? Who rents space on rockets? Is that females, ages 22 to 38?"

"Let's get back to your—"

"Baby boomers? Midwesterners? African-Americans? Who's your customer?"

Elon finally turned to David. "Government. I get in bed with government. We screw seven days a week and twice on Sunday, okay."

"Okay, then if I take a shot at your dirty little government money whore are you going to look at me funny every time I see you?"

Richard raised his hand again. "Gentlemen, it's a reality of business these days that most have some sort of government contracts. It's a perfectly viable customer and no better and no worse than the coveted 18-35 male demographic—"

"Oh listen to you mister *holier than thou*." David interrupted. "Are you trying to stick it to us that music and travel are some sort of free-market-capitalist-enlightened industry because you don't have to grovel to the government for revenues?"

"I said no such thing, David. Goodness, you think I just hover about how terrible you and Elon are?"

Lola set a fresh beer in front of Elon. "Thanks dear." He turned to David. "For crying out loud, I do not feel bad for taking government money. I'm proud of what I've done for NASA and the ISS. I sleep like a baby. You on the other hand seem to have some *repressed issues. Shall ve talk about zem?*" Elon said in a faux German accent as he stroked his chin.

David turned to Tyler. "Tyler, you got any government contracts?"

Tyler readied himself to jump in with something extremely witty and intelligent. "We sell some safety equipment to the National Guard. Some life jackets." He sipped his beer to allow the other three a moment to bask in his awkwardness.

"Yeah see?" David said. "And Richard I bet government employees fly Virgin."

"They mostly fly British Airways, we're not their preferred vendor because of the court case."

"Your business model seems less focused on a great idea and more focused on sticking it to Google," Elon said.

David turned back to Elon. "What? You think I have repressed feelings from my childhood? My father didn't play catch with me enough so I'm lashing out at Larry Page and Sergy Brin?"

Richard leaned back. "He's right. You're vindictive."

"What? I, ah, no, no, no."

"Yes, yes, yes," Richard and Elon nodded together.

"You're acting like nothing more than a Thomas Edison bullying Tesla," Elon said. "Who cares if Google has the better idea, you just want to slam yours through and go down in history. Go ahead and pound that square brick into that round hole. Be the Boy Scout who drags the old lady across the street whether she wants to or not so you can get your merit badge."

"So, when I…" David threw his hands in the air again. "Tyler help me out here. Pool noodle, simplicity, good channels, good distribution, the Oreo cookies. How do Oreos get me out of this?"

Tyler gulped his beer. He made a bit of a sour face trying to think of a good response that wouldn't get his head bit off by David O. Sacks, head of the PayPal Mafia.

He had read about the Google self-driving car and the technology they were constantly testing. He wondered how thousands of little sensors would be placed on roads and highways and street corners. And what if someone stepped out into the road by accident, how would the car know to stop?

Tyler turned to David. "What do you mean by boogie man?"

"We call it the boogie man effect. Basically people who are afraid of new ideas, you know, afraid of change."

"Yeah, come up with good ideas but people are complacent—afraid of technology, science, and change," Elon said.

"When digital music came about, everyone at Virgin thought we'd be redundant within months. They wanted to fight it tooth and nail when we should have embraced it and built a new model around it. They were afraid of change and the unknown. Textbook boogie man effect."

"It's still alive and well today. Columbus had to deal with it, Einstein did, even the guy who first sliced bread had to deal with people who thought bits of metal would get in their sandwiches," Elon said. "People are afraid their self-driving cars will go off cliffs."

David leaned over to Tyler. "Sometimes you got to ignore the boogie man and just go with it." He leered at Elon.

"I don't hate all your ideas, just this one."

Lola came over and set grammar school style brown paper towels in front of each of them. She set a huge platter of wings in the middle of their table.

"Gentlemen, plain, sea salt, Jamaican jerk, atomic. Enjoy."

"Where's the torpedoes?"

"They're coming, they had to get raspberry ginger ale from the front bar."

Silence finally endured as the four tore into the wings.

Tyler felt like he was back in college at that hole-in-the-wall bar on 112th Street. The Jamaican jerk had a strong pimento taste hitting his taste buds. The atomic was the perfect pinch of spicy balanced with flavor. The little muscle at the top of his cheeks stiffened up, and it was good. He drenched his taste buds with a slam of beer to cool them off.

A grand pile of bones gathered in front of each of them on the paper towels.

"Final wing?" Richard asked Tyler. "Want it?"

He hesitated.

"They'll bring more, don't sweat it, mate."

Tyler snatched the wing and tore into it.

Richard wiped his mouth with his hot towelette. "David, I hear you bought a pharmaceutical outfit with Peter Thiel."

David wiped his mouth and set his hot towel down. "That's right, we're getting the band back together."

"Lovely. What kind of venture is it?"

"It's not a pharma, it's a genetics research lab."

"Genetics? You know about genes and chromosomes and such?"

"No. You could fix one of your planes?"

"Point and match. But tell me about it. What are you up to?"

"Researching liver disease."

"In what capacity?" Tyler asked.

David turned to Tyler. "We're experimenting with…regeneration."

"Interesting, the liver is the best target for such an undertaking."

Elon's eyes winced. "Wait, is this the thing you wanted me to invest in? What was it, the Providence Country Club last year—"

"No, no, totally different concept."

"Really?" Elon asked.

"Yeah, really. Look, you wanted nothing to do with this, you got what you wanted. Thiel thought it was a great idea. What do you care?"

"You want to clone humans?"

Richard choked on his beer. He coughed into his hot towel. "Goodness, David, you're going with this thing?"

"It's not cloning." He turned to Elon. "It's not cloning."

"What would you call it?"

"Look, new business model, new everything. This time we're doing it."

Lola appeared with the pink torpedoes. She set them on the edge of the table and quickly bussed the battlefield of bones and napkins. She placed a shot of pink liquid in front of each of the four.

"'Bout time," David said.

"Pay him no attention. He's in one of his moods," Richard said.

"Oh, if I can handle the Liza Minnellis out there, I can handle little old David." She put patted David on the shoulder and walked away.

Tyler knew the rule of network drinking. Two drinks, never a third. He would nurse his beer and try to stay in the conversation. He could play his philanthropy card. No, not in this crowd, they didn't care about charity. He could talk about going public, or product line, the new production facility just outside of Taipei. No, none of those. Think.

"I think genetics is an admirable field," Richard said.

"To eugenics!" Elon exclaimed.

David, Elon, and Richard raised their pink shots. Tyler raised the beer he nursed, hoping nobody would notice that he didn't touch his shot.

Tyler swigged and the other three pounded their shots, slamming the mini tumblers on the table.

"So…" David exclaimed. "Eugenics. You think me and Peter are trying to create a master race. Well Heil Hitler, you got me."

"Wait what the hell are you lads talking about?" Richard asked.

"Go ahead, tell him," David said.

"David is trying to clone human organs, oh replicate, that's what he's calling it now," Elon said in a faux positive tone.

"Human cloning. Who are you going to do first?" Richard asked.

"No! Not human cloning. We're…replicating organs."

"Oh replicating, like with a 3D printer?" Elon said.

"Okay, look Elon, this is a much different business model."

"Is it legal in the States?" Richard asked.

"Of course it is."

"Totally legal," Elon exclaimed as he rolled his eyes.

"Look can I explain the model?"

"All right, tell me your business model."

"Okay so you replicate our own organs. They're kept cryogenically frozen in case you need a replacement later in life."

Elon rolled his eyes. Richard stroked his beard.

"Uh-huh," Richard said.

"And you can…" Elon waved his hand searching for a phrase.

"What? I know what you're going to say."

"Oh yeah, what?"

"You are searching for a way to trash my idea without sounding like a boogie man. You think it's a great idea but you fear the unknown—"

"Excuse me, I'm the guy shooting crap into space, I roll over the unknown and leave the flat-earthers in my wake."

"Oh well pardon me, go ahead and finish your thought, I'll wait, take as much time as you need to disguise your flat-earthiness."

"David, you needn't psychoanalyze Elon," Richard said.

"Why not, he Freuded me with my road sensor plan."

Tyler's beer was gone. He could nurse a third. He had plenty of wings, no way would the alcohol make him utter something he might regret. These three had way more than him, he could talk about his toenail collection and nobody would remember.

Elon shook his head in dismay and focused his attention toward Dave. "Look. Let me just ask you a question about your plan."

"Okay, shoot." David crossed his arms and leaned back.

"Is it legal?"

"Absolutely."

Richard uncrossed his arms. "Do you mean it actually is legal, or do you mean your barrister found a way around the law?"

"Okay, here's the deal. Cloning humans is against the law. You also can't own human tissue unless it's yours."

"You can't own a skeleton?"

"Not a live one. You can't create organs and keep them alive to sell them later. You can't own the patent on human genes either."

"But can't you own animal genes?"

"Animals and plants are considered property so you can own your specific genes that you created."

"Wait you mean, Monsanto can own a cow."

"Monsanto doesn't do livestock, just plants but if you breed your own cow or stalk of corn, you can file a patent on that."

"Ah you could breed a genetically superior human gene and patent it. I'm not going to compare you to Hitler but you're certainly making it difficult," Elon said.

"No, no." David waved his finger at Elon and Richard. "It's illegal under the Thirteenth Amendment based on anti-slavery case law. A genetics case back in the early 2000s used the Thirteenth Amendment when some company wanted to replicate human organs."

"Lincoln ruined it for everyone. I wonder if he knew all the terrible consequences of banning slavery—"

David shoved his finger in Elon's face. "Okay listen to me Musk. This is not owning other human tissue. This is you replicating your own tissue. You would hold the title card to your heart, liver or kidneys and they would be stowed in a third-party cryogenic warehouse. It forms a bailor-bailee agreement like when you drop your dry cleaning off."

"And if someone doesn't pay the storage fee, what happens?" Elon asked.

"Ah the rental fee. Do those Storage War boys show up and bid fifty dollars for the kidney?" Richard asked as he and Elon tried to hide their smirks.

"No, no, no." Again David jabbed a straight index finger toward their faces. "By statute, by the Constitution that is, they can't buy an organ. So I don't know, the organ is destroyed or something. We're still working on what the collections process will look like."

"But won't others start doing this since you can't patent the human organs?"

"We have lots of patents pending."

"But you can't patent human genes."

"You can't patent human genes but you can patent the technology that replicates them. That's why we would corner the market right away before they expire. Get there first with the most men as Napoleon said."

"And you think you could make money when people replicate their organs?"

"Well, that's the genius of the business plan, we actually wouldn't make that much on replication. The real cash cow would be storage. If someone has to store a kidney or heart for twenty years, that's a steady stream of income for a long time. Hewlett Packard doesn't make anything off their printers. Toner is where they make most of their money."

Richard and Elon leaned back and crossed their arms. Richard pondered David's plan as his stein, with a few gulps of beer left, hung from his fingers.

Elon uncrossed his arms and set his empty stein on the table. "Okay David. A couple of problems." He put his fingers out to bullet point his responses. "First, who would do this when organ donation is your competitor? Never compete with those that do it for free. Second, this has been done before with cryogenics. Nobody has ever successfully been revived who signed up for this before they died, not to mention that it's crackpots who do this sort of thing. Maybe Thiel is crazy enough to do it, but not anyone in this room—"

"Do you know anyone with too much money who would want to extend their life?"

Elon smiled and leaned back.

"Go ahead, let your eyes glance about the room. Let me know if extending your life for a few dollars would appeal to anyone you know."

Elon held his fingers out again and touched the end of his ring finger. "Three! And I hate reiterating this but you have that eugenics/master race/Hitler had the right idea/playing God stench attached to this whole idea. And four, and I'm going to say it, to make this idea work you have to sell it to 300 million boogie men believers. People who are creeped out by stem cell research, cloning humans, and landing on Mars."

"You know what your problem is?"

"Do not say I'm the boogie man. I believe in genetic technology but the public doesn't and that's your target audience."

"It's hard not to call boogie man on you."

"Again, good concept, crappy business execution."

David flopped back in his chair and Elon did too, letting everyone know their fight ended in stalemate.

"I appreciate your candor. I'll let Thiel know you think he's Himmler."

"Himmler?"

"I'm majority holder which makes me Hitler so he's Himmler."

Elon shook his head at David's witty Nazisms.

Tyler picked up his pink torpedo causing Richard, Elon, and David to notice that he had not yet partaken his shot.

He drank it down in a long elegant lunge and gently placed the glass at the center of the table. "David I think you have a good idea but there's something you need to do to make it work. You need to set the narrative with a good marketing campaign and PR firm."

"Set the narrative?"

"Yes. Cigarettes aren't carcinogenic. They're toasty. It's not cage fighting, it's mixed martial art competition. We don't eat cows, we eat beef. You may have good answers and a strong argument as to why this isn't aligned with slavery or eugenics but even if you win those arguments, you've achieved a useless victory. The naysayers have set the tone and put you on the defensive. Nobody's talking about the benefits of your product, they are debating human cloning. A good PR firm can set the public narrative for you."

Elon, David, and Richard nodded slightly.

"You could highlight the health benefits, you could highlight the individuality of how these are *yours* not some big company's organs. Play the health card, align it with responsible living, like life insurance plans. Covering the future for you and your loved ones. If you can get that out first, then the tone is set and the naysayers are the defensive ones. They look crazy because now they are comparing health insurance plans to Nazism."

"I like that. Now people like Elon are the nut jobs."

"Exactly. I'd lose the term cryogenic since that's been hijacked by the wacky crowd already. Maybe something the common man can understand—you have a spare tire in your trunk for emergencies, why not a spare liver? Don't highlight extending your life since that falls into the crazy fountain of youth mentality, highlight enjoying your current life. A seventy-year-old man running marathons with his spare heart.

Really highlight the fact that it's about you taking control of *your* body."

"Interesting, Doctor Chambers. Very interesting." Elon finally smiled.

"That's genius," David said.

"People will have it in their mind that this is the future of medicine, they won't think of the traditional ethical debates of cloning. But don't call it cloning. Replication evokes rational thinking."

David leaned back, crossed his arms and rubbed his chin in a philosopher-proving-God-is-dead manner. This caused Richard and Elon to roll their eyes.

"That's brilliant, Tyler."

"Thanks, David."

"You got any ideas on my road sensor model?"

"Hmmm." Tyler glanced at the ceiling for inspiration.

"He's too much of a gentleman to tell you it's awful," Elon said.

"Hey, the man is thinking."

"I kind of enjoy driving," Tyler said. "Think everyone will want to give it up?"

"You enjoy getting stuck in traffic waiting for your turn? You could be reading a book or watching TV or making love to your girlfriend," Dave said.

"Well, I have a few fun cars, we have a Ferrari and a Lambo."

"A Lambo?"

"That's right."

"A Lambo, just one?"

"Actually, two."

"Mighty impressive. I'm going to go talk to Bezos."

"Well these wings were great, weren't they guys," Richard said.

"Oh, wonderful," Elon said. "It was good meeting you, Tyler."

"Ty, come do a short with me at the bar," Richard said as he wiped his hands clean.

"A short?"

"A shot as you boys call it in New York."

Tyler wiped his hands and tossed the towel on the table.

"Casa Noble, Extra Aged," Richard said to the bartender.

"Am I going to regret this tomorrow?"

"Absolutely not, this is actually a sipping tequila, so you don't shoot it as if you're still at university. The good stuff doesn't give you the nightmare stories."

The bartender filled two mini tumblers with brown liquid from a stout bottle. They said cheers and sipped the smooth spirit.

"So Tyler, we don't really talk about toys at these things."

"Excuse me? Toys?"

"You know, boats, fancy cars, condos in Ibiza."

"Oh, I shouldn't have said I have a Ferrari?"

"Probably not. That's why Dave turned grumpy, but he's a sourpuss anyways."

"Should I apologize—"

"Oh no, no, not at all, you're new to our group so you'll figure out the rules as you go along."

Tyler sipped his tequila and he scanned the room as a U2 song filled the bar with Celtic rock. Everyone enjoyed themselves as he tried to place the familiar faces that he hadn't yet figured out. Cover of Fortune? Forbes? Barron's? He tried to think of the products that were in the room. Virgin Airlines, Instagram, Napster, Oakley, American Eagle, Red Bull, Pandora, Snapchat, all in West Chelsea to sample the best wings on the planet.

"Richard, what is this place?"

"Like-minded people coming together to drink beer."

"Like minded?"

"That's right. Everyone here has risen in their field of expertise and is looking for new directions to pursue. We come here to get away from people who follow us around. Single minded, blinders on, not willing to embrace risk. I mean don't get me wrong, I love my execs, they run my business for me and I love my friends, but sometimes I need to be surrounded by these kind of folks."

"I can see what you mean."

"That's why we have a little unwritten rule that we don't talk about toys. Nobody here cares about fancy cars or mansions. That's for the newly wealthy to brag about, we don't even think of ourselves as wealthy, we think of ourselves as free."

"I don't feel free." Tyler looked away for a moment, regretting what he just blurted out.

"I know what you're going through, mate. I went through the same thing. You can't drive a fancier car than a Lamborghini. I've scarfed down the best caviar and bathed in champagne. And the ladies, I could tell you some stories."

Tyler smirked when he mentioned the part about the ladies.

"When's the last time you enjoyed your Italian car collection out on the road?"

"Well, it's not a good winter car."

"It's July."

"I know, I know, I just mean I haven't un-winterized them. My mechanic has to change the oil—"

"More than a year?"

Tyler thought hard.

"More than two years?"

Tyler smiled at him letting him know his point made it through.

"Do you have a condo in Miami or Aspen?"

"Ours is in Vale."

"When's the last time you skied?"

"Skiing isn't my thing. Come to think of it, my wife doesn't take to it either."

"Tyler, you're not alone, you're in a room of men bored with their fancy toys, that's why we don't talk about them."

"I'm glad you told me the rule, any others?"

"Yes, no star fucking."

"Star fucking?"

"Name dropping. Don't mention any celebrities or other members who aren't here."

"No name dropping. Got it."

"Nobody here cares if you know Paris Hilton or the governor or the president. Everyone here has shaken hands with a US president. They're all a bore. Except Clinton, he was a gas to hang with."

"So what should I say?"

"Talk about your ideas. Tyler, these men build and create and have visions. It's difficult to be around naysayers. I mean somebody decided to break the sound barrier once, plant a seed to see what happens, and said what if we build a social media site where you blog 140 letters at a time. These were stupid ideas at one time that were easy to rip to shreds by people who know nothing of boldness and who sit on the sidelines and criticize, laugh, and point."

Richard finished his tequila. "Sorry, I get worked up—"

"No that makes perfect sense, Richard. I know what it is to be laughed at for ambition and creativity."

"Don't get me wrong, these men are big personalities and aren't intimidated by anyone, they trudge forward through the critics and ignore the naysayers, but still…"

The bartender came back over.

"Another?" Richard said.

Tyler nodded.

The bartender retrieved fresh glassware and poured another shot of Casa Noble, a spirit whose name Tyler hope he'd remember tomorrow so he could send Rogers to get a bottle.

"…still, Tyler. It's good to be around like-minded people every once in a while before we jump into the gauntlet known as a startup."

Tyler's dress shoes slipped off his feet and dropped to the floor of the limo. He slouched down in the back seat letting his tie bunch up. He lounged his feet on the sofa bench running the length of the side. He spread his arms along the top of the cushions and allowed himself a deep breath.

A successful night. The horror of the speech that afternoon fell away from him like dead skin. He would drift off to sleep as the car would arrive in Scarsdale in about an hour.

He would look up every person he crossed paths with that night. Tyler suffered from a common social condition where he forgot names two seconds after introductions. He did well that night though. Every name lingered in his frontal lobe. Maybe he had trouble remembering names of his wife's friends because they didn't matter to him.

No wives were there tonight. Tyler knew Rachel would ruin his new social club if given the chance. She would not stop talking about toys and celebrities she's rubbed elbows with. The club rules were silly at first since toys and name dropping were the only subjects Tyler knew. But on the other hand, it was liberating to talk about crazy ideas instead of just pondering them in his head. He thought hard about the last engaging conversation he had at a benefit at their home but couldn't come up with one.

Trendy restaurants they had gotten into, a mention of a private island, breakfast with the president. Tyler had to grin at Richard's president comment. Standing next to Barack Obama mesmerized Rachel. He wore the same suit he always wore, he smiled the same smile he always did, perfect posture. Rachel hung that picture with such a strong sense of unique pride but the president had posed for thousands of pictures like that.

He wouldn't take any pictures of his club. It was his. He would not tell his wife of whom he met. Drinks with friends, that's all. There's no way on God's green earth that she would have any follow-up questions about Tyler's whereabouts or who he socialized with. She couldn't possibly be interested.

The girl covered in mud entered his mind once again. She understood what those men in there were about. Toys, boats, and fancy cars didn't impress her. Free men like Richard, and himself caused her face to glow. He wondered if Richard might have even known her.

Her look of euphoria as she gasped for breath, the shock of the cold on her body since it was chilly for July. Her skin tightened from the cold, her running shorts bunched up her thighs. The white of her teeth from smiling. Maybe she wore a suit during the day and her smile represented her getting away with something, of stepping into a different world of freedom of running in the mud.

As Tyler drifted off, the mud girl lingered in his dreams.

CHAPTER FIVE

The car service dropped Tyler off in Little Italy. He instructed the driver to circle the block and pick him up in twenty minutes. He walked up the block to the REI store on Lafayette just below Houston Street. He glided past the security guard, past the bike accessories, past the women's outdoor apparel and laid his focus on a blue 3-day backpack that had a halo of light around it since it was under the track lighting. He picked a tent, sleeping back, air mat, Jetboil mini-stove, water purifier, and freeze-dried food. The total came to just under six hundred dollars and he handed the cashier his black Amex.

"Where to?" the young man said.

"I'm not sure yet."

"Well, that's the best way to find something new. Could I have your membership card?"

"I'm not a member."

"Would you like to become one today?"

"No thank you."

"Are you sure? Ten dollars and you get five percent back. It would pay for itself with this purchase alone."

"No thanks."

"I thought I'd mention it since I've seen you in here before buying camping supplies."

"No thank you, just this."

The driver waited on Mulberry with the trunk open. Tyler tossed the camping gear in and hopped into the back and they sped off to Teterboro in Bergen County, New Jersey.

A fresh G5 waited for Tyler at the muni airport and as soon as he boarded the door was sealed and it rocketed off toward Northern Minnesota.

Tyler made camp for the night at Rock of Ages Lake in the Boundary Waters. It was one of the more remote of the 1100 lakes in the area. Not because of its distance but because it was on a hiking trail and not accessible by canoe like many of the other lakes.

Although he had been to other more majestic national parks, he yearned for the Boundary Waters. Whereas Yellowstone had snowcapped mountains and Zion had painted canyons and rocks sculpted by the ages, Northern Minnesota was plain by comparison.

The area was the gentlest of national parks, not needing cascading redwoods or purple mountain majesties but instead simple trees and modest lakes. The trees came right to the shore, a sight most people weren't accustomed to as cabins and condos usually gobbled up lakefront property.

He set his pack on the rock face and downed a bottle of electrolytes and filtered lake water. He removed his shirt and realized he hadn't broken a sweat on the fourteen-mile hike to the campground. His daily cardio regimen had paid off.

The lake he camped at was located on a 34-mile hiking loop known as the Pow-Wow Trail. Since it was not accessible by canoe, an ambitious backpacker who humped fourteen miles into the loop was rewarded with their own private lake, hidden in plain sight from the canoers.

His campground was perched on a rock face that hovered about thirty feet above the water's edge and acted as an observation deck. The lake had no ripples, it was a sheet of glass.

When he camped alone, the ideas flowed to him like a raging river. The lone backpacking kayak in Acadia, the titanium full mess kit in Mount Rainier, the self-propelled scooter for scuba diving in the belly of Dark Canyon…every idea shot down by Ben or someone else with an excuse about feasibility or price points.

He spread the tent on the ground and pushed the rods through the holes. He glanced at the clouds to gauge if he needed the rain guard but sky was clear.

The excursions always left him excited to tell Ben what products the company should explore next. The MBA execs would always patronize him and by midafternoon hawking his new ideas to people who didn't listen exhausted him.

Mister Chambers, these ideas you have are always inspiring.

Now that sounds like a good idea, how many times have I wanted one of those?

You've obviously put a lot of thought into this, but...

He was the washed-up insurance salesman who only sold a policy so people could get him out of their living room.

He gathered sticks and cracked them in half and built a log cabin style fire with dried pine needles as the tinder.

But Branson wouldn't laugh at him or patronize him. His new friends would listen to his ideas and take him seriously. After all, that was the purpose of their little clubhouse in Chelsea. If Ben walked into that clubhouse he'd shove his business cards around and try to explain product mix to Elon Musk. Bring the man trying to revolutionize energy down to your petty level.

The mini stove rumbled from the water boiling and he poured it into his pouch of chicken a la king. After a few minutes he dug into it with a titanium spork as he gazed out at the lake from the edge of the rock face.

He put the empty pouch into a Ziploc bag along with his energy bars, walked down the cliff face, and placed the bag about a hundred feet from the camp on a tall rock. Traditionally, campers bear-proofed food by hanging it from a tree. It was said that this was no longer effective since campers use the same tree a hundred paces from the campsite and the bears learned which trees were popular. Sealing and tossing food on an unassuming rock out the open was more effecting at throwing off the bears.

The sun touched the horizon and turned the water into a bright orange. His eyes drifted to the sky and the thoughts in his head relaxed.

He struck a match to the log cabin and it came to life. The tinder caught the kindling and as it engulfed the cabin he placed fuel logs on top.

Someone had dragged a log up to camp and placed it next to the fire pit. A perfect bench for years to come. He breathed deeply as the fire soothed him and was thankful the mosquitos and gnats left him alone. The soft glow of the fire and the cracks and pops hit his ears like a symphony.

He was finished thinking about Ben.

A beaver cannonballing into the lake caused him to break his concentration from the fire. He spotted it swaying through the center of the glass lake slicing it in half with its wake. So calm was the lake that a lone beaver swaying his tail back and forth caused a ripple that eventually touched the shores.

It is said that good ideas come to people in the shower, supposedly because having a comfortable place where you are alone with minimal activity is a formula for creative juices. Pacing in and out of the downpour from the showerhead met the minimal activity standard. A hot tub was too comfortable and offered no such effect.

There was not one idea in that German beer hall that Tyler couldn't have endeavored on. His wealth acted as a straitjacket, forcing him into a life that once excited him but grew stale as the years dragged on. The first time he and Rachel stepped into the vast marble entryway of their Scarsdale home flashed through his mind—the grand staircase, the fountains that poured down the sides, the indoor palm trees. Now they were maintenance headaches. The palms needed dusting, the glass guards next to the mini waterfalls needed cleaning every day or they were patched with water stains, thus diminishing their majesty. They paid a gal 38,000 a year just to keep the grand entryway crisp and clean.

No longer would money control him. Money was now a tool to him and he would do as he pleased.

Every idea he ever had flashed before him as he crouched and prodded the fire. All ideas either too expensive, impractical, or, just plain nuts. Funny how the grander the idea the less likely someone would shoot it down. The simpler the idea, the more harsh the criticism. Perhaps grand ideas were so hard and expensive that the critics didn't bother criticizing them.

The fire died down again and he decided it was time to turn in. He pulled off his shirt and pants, crawled into the sleeping bag, and inhaled one last deep breath before closing his eyes.

Another beaver cannonballed and a wolf howled in the distance. The crickets started their chorus. A relaxation undulated through his body.

The calm before the storm.

Tyler's nose was the only cold part of his body. He gathered the tenacity and motivation to leap out of his sleeping bag into the cold morning—one rip like a Band-Aid.

The cold air shot into every pore of his body. God it felt good. A fog crept over the lake and he saw his breath even though it was summer. Start packing the camp, that'll warm up everything. He tore into his sleeping bag and pulled the rods from the tent.

The camping worked. It was a new day and a new life.

He hiked out of the loop, filtering water, admiring the lakes, chanting the occasional affirmation. He was eager to get back to his rental car.

Twenty minutes speeding toward Ely Municipal Airfield, the G5 waited for him, and then three hours back to New York. He was a bullet. He managed to pack camp, hike the fourteen miles back out and get to the plane just before the opening bell.

As the jet engines hummed, Tyler scrolled through his phone contacts. *Mike Beller, broker, NYSE, 212-593-5501*. He highlighted the number and paused for just a moment to relish a deep breath. He wondered if Elon had such a moment like his. He exhaled his breath with force, spewing the last ruminants of his old life from his body. He touched *send*.

Back in New York the M60 bus dropped him in Harlem to connect with the subway on 125th and Lex. He approached a homeless fella with a cart, talking to himself.

"Hey, want this?" He referred to his backpack and camping equipment.

"Sure, boy." The man grabbed the backpack and unzipped the top looking at all the treasures inside. Tyler climbed the elevated platform stairs to the Six train as the M60 pulled away.

"Hey thanks, vanilla."

He smiled and waved at the homeless man and his toothless grin.

He checked in to the Bernic Hotel on Third Avenue and 47th around noon for the sole purpose of showering and shaving. Rogers had left a fresh set of clothes for him and by 1:00 he was checked out and hiking across 47th to Sixth Avenue.

After stepping off the elevator to his office he said good morning to the receptionist. She didn't say anything back, just held her mouth open in shock. He walked through the main door and through the executive wing. He held his chin high and had any of the executive secretaries offered him a faux good afternoon, he'd happily return the greeting. Instead he felt their awkward stares, but as he strode he kept his chin high in the air.

The noise and chatter of the office died down with the occasional whisper replacing it. The Harvard mouthpieces poked their heads out of their offices.

He walked past Gina to the door of his office. "Can we go over a few things?"

She grabbed her notepad and followed him.

"Ben's looking for you. Do you know what's going on?"

"I'll see him after we're done. I need a few things. First set up a new LLC under my name. Make sure it's an S Corp and an LLC. Contact Monica Bellway at Rockland County Trust and have her set up a new bank account—"

"Mr. Chambers, a question if you don't mind me asking, this is outside the scope of my duties. Is this something you should have a personal assistant do?"

"Ah, of course. Want to be my new corporate admin? I'll pay you double what you're making here."

"Um, I wasn't…"

"You're at eighty-three?"

"Eighty-eight five."

"Let's see, that's, one seventy-seven. Draft an employment agreement between yourself and the new LLC. Also put your notice into Fusion. I believe company policy is that if you give less than two weeks' notice you lose accrued vacation. I'm happy to compensate you for that as well."

"Yes, sir." She wrote both requests on the notepad.

"I need a few attorneys. Get me an attorney with utilities experience, specifically nuclear power. Also I need an attorney who's dealt in tribal affairs."

"Tribal affairs?"

"Yes as in Indians. Native Americans, I mean."

"Okay."

"I also need one that specializes in international treaties and diplomatic affairs."

"Diplomatic affairs. Okay."

"Also a maritime lawyer, laws of the sea, ports and such."

"Maritime, got it."

"A few years ago in Minneapolis they moved a building called the Shubert Theater. Largest building move ever. I want to meet with the head engineer of the project, see if you can find the firm in charge of the move and the man who ran it. Also I need a ship broker."

"A ship broker."

"Big ships, like if I wanted to buy an oil tanker or a battleship or something like that."

"Battleships, okay."

"And Robert Yellowfeather. Get me a meeting with him. He's head of business operations for the Minnetrista tribe near Duluth, Minnesota."

The door opened and Ben walked in.

"Morning, Ben," Tyler said.

"Gina, may I have a word with Tyler please."

She closed the door behind her.

Ben planted himself in the chair in front of Tyler's desk and didn't bother with small talk about his weekend. "I thought we had worked together over the years to the point where our friendship meant something. We have built a certain amount of trust in this enterprise and in one action, you've ruined this company. I want an explanation."

"I'm moving on, Ben. Bigger and better things."

"Moving on."

"Yes."

"Moving on? There's better ways than dumping your holdings. The stock dropped sixty percent from this stunt. The 8-K filing reports that you dumped all your shares at once. You wiped out two billion of equity in a half hour. Every person you work with has stock in this company and you wiped out half their holdings."

"Buy low, sell high, if they believe in what they're doing they can buy it back." Tyler threw his hands into the air. "It will recover in a few months. No harm."

"No harm? That's all you have to say for yourself?"

Ben desperately wanted Tyler to hang his head down, the little kid that spilled milk or broke a dish. But no, he wouldn't give him the satisfaction.

"I'm here to clear out a few personal items from my office and see if Gina wants to come with me."

"I'm sorry my concern for our employees and shareholders is interrupting your time to retrieve your personal effects. You know that financing deal is going to fall apart now. There's no way they are going to give us a two hundred-million-dollar line with this. The Southwest expansion is done."

"I'm not going to be in your way anymore. I know you're happy with this. Don't deny it, everyone is going to come into this place tomorrow realizing that they can finally run this company into the ground."

"Run it into the ground? We built this company for you, that's how you see us?"

"I've got work to do."

Ben snarled under his breath, buttoned his jacket, and stormed out of his office.

Tyler tossed his family pictures in a box. He opened his drawer, dug through the hanging files, and found the picture of him and Lester with the canoe and shoved it into the box.

He scanned the office one last time to see if he forgot anything and walked out.

CHAPTER SIX

Four crystal steins hit the table with a loud clack startling Richard, Elon, Dave, and Tyler. "Let me know if you boys want something to eat," Lola barked.

"Thank you, love," Richard said.

Lola smiled at Richard and trotted away.

"Tyler, you ever had Achel Trappist?" Dave asked.

"No, I haven't."

"It's the best of the Trappist Ales."

"That's up for debate, Saks," Elon said.

"Don't listen to him, it's the Johnnie Walker Blue of beers. Made by monks in Belgium."

"Hardest to get in the States, that's for sure," Richard said. "To killing the boogie man."

"Death to the boogie man," Elon and David said.

They touched steins and each imbibed in a generous swig of the blond ale. Tyler set his stein down and let out a gasp at how smooth the beer was. He agreed with Dave. How could any beer possibly taste better than this one?

"Ghee outdid himself getting a keg of this. It's going to be gone in a few minutes when the rest of these louses start drinking it," Richard said.

"Back to this artificial gravity," Dave said. "So what happens if the station stops spinning? No gravity."

Richard took another gulp from his stein. "No gravity, but there's nothing to stop it from spinning. An object in space will spin indefinitely."

"But nothing has to keep it spinning?"

"You would have a set of boosters that start the initial spin. The spin would slow only because of light gravitation from other planets nearby, but the boosters would maintain the spin. We're talking fifty kilograms of thrust for a station the size of London."

"That's hard to believe," Dave said.

"In a vacuum like space where there's no air, there's nothing to slow you down. Your giant wheel spins and spins until you put on the brakes," Elon explained.

The table spoke science and Tyler knew he'd have a leg up on the group…Dave and Richard at least. He knew Elon likely knew more about rocket science than he did. He hoped to get in a few good comments.

"Still…" Dave stroked his chin as if he had a philosopher's beard. "…I can't get past this concept of necessity. What's the point of a giant space station?"

"The ISS is important. Governments can't support it enough," Richard said.

"Right, but that's peanuts in scale and just some research through government. Not one penny of consumer money. A space station the size of New York City with 200,000 inhabitants has to produce something."

"They could produce research on effects of space, study interstellar stars, and discover new planets through advance optics that would put the Hubble to shame."

Dave squinted his eyes and shook his head. "The thing is though, there has to be something of value in the end."

"Exploration of space isn't valuable?"

"No, not beyond government saying it is. There's no such thing as a private space company."

"Really?" Elon said as he slanted his head in a sarcastic manner.

"You know what I mean. Consumers don't go out and buy space stuff other than the occasional celebrity that wants to be shot into space."

"So we toss aside the notion of space exploration?" Richard said

"Let's say a government digs holes in the desert and then another government agency fills them up. Both are doing something of value. The holes need to be filled because they're there and new holes need to be dug so the government program has something to do—"

"Oh come on Dave, that's a pretty vain analogy," Elon interrupted.

"But you're going to have two hundred thousand people in space working to learn more about living in space so more people can live in space? They need to produce something otherwise it's just a pyramid scheme involving a unique piece of real estate for people with the means to live there."

"It wouldn't be a hundred thousand, we'd build a more modest station first. It would be the size of a couple of soccer fields. Fifty people perhaps," Richard said.

"And government funds it and Elon is your biggest customer?" Dave said.

"No, it would be a luxury hotel. There's a market big enough to support a fifty-unit hotel in space."

"And you're going to build one on Mars?" He turned to Elon.

"Someday."

"What are they going to produce?"

"Our product is exploration."

Dave threw his hands up, "You guys have turned into a couple of charity cases since we last spoke. What happened?"

"I'm sure a business model will present itself once we get going," Elon said.

Dave stuck his hand in the air in an aggressive manner. "So you're going to invent Smell-O-Vision—invest, design, promote and then worry about feasibility as a last detail? Tyler help me out on this."

Tyler opened his mouth and raised his finger to speak when Lola interrupted. "You boys ordering dinner?"

They were no longer talking science, they shifted to business. Tyler couldn't play his nuclear physics card. He had to think of something good to say about business.

"Sure, what's popular tonight?" Dave asked.

"Irish style, regular breaded," Lola said.

"Sounds boring."

"You've never had boring wings by Jean Georges."

"Is he back there?"

"Slaving away."

"Okay, four dozen. And do you got anything with cognac?"

"I can do a French tickler with Remy Martin, Louis the Fourteenth."

"Sounds good. Four French Ticklers then."

Dave turned back to Elon. "Colonizing Mars would be posturing, not a business plan. I mean you hope to mine iron ore and fly it back to earth for two cents a pound with a trillion-dollar overhead?"

Dave leaned into Richard. "Your boat races and your air balloon rides—you broke records but it's not like it opened the gate to air balloons or fast boats as a new mode of transportation."

"That was a personal venture and I didn't ever say I was going to start a zeppelin company."

"Elon, help me out, did you build rockets because you enjoyed it or was there a business plan?"

"Space exploration is a product that's in demand. People do want space explored and they're willing to pay for it, it's just that it's done through taxation and government rather than a traditional customer-to-business purchase. Why can't it be turned into something monetized like the green movement has done?"

"Don't get me started on green enterprises." Dave waved his finger in the air. "You think people would pay say a subscription to find out the scientific studies they are doing on Mars? That's far-fetched, to somehow monetize what they do on Star Trek. Star Trek was a socialist utopia where nobody cared about money and the government spent all of Earth's resources on space exploration."

"It doesn't matter if it's a socialist utopia or free enterprise. Under either system, the people demanded space exploration and if they stopped finding value it would eventually trickle up to Starfleet's budget, even under a controlled economy," Elon exclaimed.

"Give me Star Wars and its freedom and capitalism over Star Trek any day," Dave said.

The beer slid down Tyler's throat like a calm stream—like drinking heaven. Achel is what Dave called it. Tyler would have to research it when he got home. Don't forget the name, he told himself. Achel.

Richard raised his finger toward Dave edging his way back into the conversation. "But there is this concept of creating demand out of thin air once the product has shown itself as useful. If it were 1960 and I asked you if you wanted an oven that cooked food by spinning water molecules by zapping them with microwaves, you would say 'no, I already have an oven.' And there actually was a time when the most beautiful communities on the coasts of Florida were swampland. They developed them and people flocked by the millions to retire there. Build the product first and demand appears out of nowhere."

Richard turned to Elon. "Elon, how would I build the 50-unit hotel in space? Not interested in why, but how?"

Before Elon answered Dave blurted, "Oh so I'm just out. How you're going to pay for it is a stupid detail?"

"Let me try to sell this to you, Dave," Richard said.

"Yes, sell it to me."

"No, I need open-minded Dave, lower your shields."

"Shields down. I'm ready. I'll be good."

Richard turned to Elon. "Elon, how?"

Elon wiped his lips of the Trappist ale and set his stein on the table. "Our biggest strength at SpaceX was that we didn't steal the old model of rockets that Boeing and the government utilized and attempt to improve them. No, what we did was start from the ground up and built something that would be twenty times better. Boeing built rockets for a hundred million, we built them for a tenth of that, plus we made lots of money on them even at that price. That's because we ignored the lumbering design that always had endless government money behind it."

"Okay, go on," Dave said.

"You follow me?"

"I follow you."

"The ISS cost around 150 billion to build and install in space. Richard, you would never want to copy anything they did otherwise a simple toilet will cost you millions. You would want the most creative engineers in the world to design you a simple space hotel from the ground up. The ISS has thousands of subcontractors working on one tiny aspect of the space station and a huge bureaucracy puts them together. My advice, stick your engineers in one big room and tell them to design the thing. And as a bonus, that model will attract the most brilliant people in the world who are tired of working as fourth-tier subcontractors. You can even pay them less and they will still jump on the opportunity to work in that big room without lumbering government red tape."

"You haven't sold me," Dave said as he guzzled his ale.

"I'm not done. Here's the thing. The ISS is 150 billion. We're going to do it for one twentieth of that. That's…"

"Seven point five billion," Tyler jumped in with.

"Seven point five bil. If I did that, would a hotel in space be viable?"

Tyler was proud of his quick math skills that saved the day. He'd garnered their attention and respect!

Dave turned to Tyler for approval and Tyler gave him a subtle nod. "It's getting there, I guess," Dave said.

"Look at that," Elon exclaimed as he threw his hands in the air. "Halleluiah, I sold Mr. Cynical, where's our titty sprinkles, wait what are they called?"

"French ticklers."

"French ticklers for everyone," Elon yelled as he put his arm around Dave.

Lola set the shots on the table and they toasted Dave's temporary lack of stubbornness. This time Tyler downed his with everyone else.

"Ty, big Ty, help me out." Dave put his arm on Tyler's shoulder. "You're the smartest of us four, what do you think of building hotels in space and on Mars? Where's the business plan? Do you even need one?"

Tyler took a deep slam of the Trappist Ale and cleared his throat. The others awaited his response with curious patience.

"Dave, I respect your dedication to a business plan but there's a concept you guys are dancing around. It's called synergy.

"Elon, the name of your company is Tesla. Surely you drew inspiration from Nikola Tesla?"

"That's right."

"And I know you were the type that played with model rockets growing up."

"Right again."

"I bet you could name every astronaut ever to have entered space."

Elon smiled.

"And Richard, you've broken records with your sailing and your balloon rides. Although that didn't contribute to Virgin's bottom line directly, I think doing that made you a better businessman. There'd be no

Virgin if not for your bold sidesteps."

Richard nodded.

Tyler had the floor and he was on a roll!

"Somehow when bold individuals step forward, the chips fall into place. You can follow a path through the woods but you know the path is there because someone else was there before you. So you blaze a new trail and see where it leads. Even if it has no clear business model, sometimes it needs to be done and the model presents itself. And a funny thing happens. You inspire. Maybe you fail but others follow and that's your contribution to the community of science, boldly trudging forward."

The three men nodded at Tyler's inspirational speech.

"Amen Tyler, that was beautiful." Richard slammed the rest of his ale.

"Thank you Tyler, that was good." Elon nodded in approval.

"Ty man, I think you get it." Dave rubbed the back of Tyler's neck as he smiled.

Dave turned to Richard. "Richard, you're my friend. I won't give you any more shit about this. I think you should build it."

"Thanks, Dave."

A rewarding quiet settled at the table. The four men rested their hands across the crystal steins with their fingers wrapping around the glass.

"Hey…" Dave broke the silence and turned to Elon. "…tell me about this girl the papers are talking about."

Elon lifted his hand in a surrender manner. "Oh God, that girl has caused me so much grief. She's a freaking intern but I let her tag along at that tech convention in Atlanta and someone said we're together."

"Someone? How about everyone?"

"No, not everyone, some San Jose rag, SI quarterly or something. They do articles on the latest startups in San Jose. They did an exposé on me and implied that she's my girlfriend. I mean an industry publication and they're doing National Inquirer material. That's why I left Silicon Valley. They used to be about changing the world. Now they're about 140 characters and clicks."

"So not true?"

"Not in the least. But God she's hot, I had lunch with her once…with like six other people. I don't know how the media put two and two together and called us a couple."

"Isn't she a Russian lass?"

"Yeah, Nina's her name. Sexy as hell. She made it to my company through Vadim Petrov, the guy who is the son of Vladimir Petrov."

"That's the...phone guy. The service provider for Russia," Dave said.

"Yeah, little phone tsar. Kind of a snot but when I visited Moscow he seemed the reasonable type."

"Well his daddy set him up nice."

"I'm okay with old money, especially if the kids are nice. I know I said snot, but he's actually a pretty good kid."

"So what are you up to with him?"

"We talked about the ISS, he has a few connections with the contractors doing the Russian part of the effort."

Lola shoved a huge platter of wings in front of the four and laid out paper towels and wet naps. "There you gentlemen go, forty-eight of Jean's finest."

"Wonderful, Lola," Richard said.

Elon laughed and turned to Tyler. "You know, Ty-man, your name came up when me and Vadim hung out."

Tyler looked up. "Oh?"

"Yeah. Vadim, we were shootin' the shit and he mentions your name. He said you bought a battleship from the Russian Navy. I don't know where the hell he got his info but I told him I knew you. He clammed up when I said I knew you."

Tyler laughed as he guzzled the rest of his Trappist Blond. "No, that's crazy. Russian Navy doesn't even have battleships anymore. It was a nuclear aircraft carrier."

Tyler grabbed a handful of wings and dropped them onto his brown paper towel. He experienced a lightheadedness from the shot and the beer attacking him simultaneously.

"Why would you buy a nuclear-powered aircraft carrier, mate?" Richard asked.

"Going to sail it through the Great Lakes to Duluth and then drag it across Northern Minnesota to an Indian reservation where I can hook the nuclear plant to the power grid."

Tyler sunk his teeth into the crispy wing. Goodness it was heaven.

The succulent meat melted in his mouth. The breading was so light and fluffy, not thick and grease laden. Somehow Jean Georges managed to create the perfect wing even if it wasn't some weird concoction. He elevated boring and regular to the next level. His taste buds danced to a fast-tempo choreography.

He set the clean bone on his paper towel and was about to dive into number two when he looked up.

Elon Musk, David O. Sacks, and Richard Branson hadn't touched the wings. They stared at Tyler in disbelief, their mouths hung open.

Shit.

Did he just blurt out what he thought he did? *Two drinks, never a third. Two drinks, never a third.*

Tyler resembled a deer on an old country road with its eyes frozen in the high-beams. He searched high and low for something witty to say to deflect their shock.

Lola slammed four fresh steins on the table which caused the four to jump. Tyler stood causing the chair to scrape violently against the sawdust-covered floor. He wiped his hands on is pants. "Excuse me gentlemen, I just recalled I have a prior engagement."

He disappeared to the back hallway near the bathrooms. He glanced at the three as he walked away trying to gauge if they were still looking at him with dumbfounded looks. A humming exit sign and a beat-up fire door. No "emergency exit only" sign. Imagine setting that off and bringing more attention to one's self. He took his opportunity.

Tyler walked briskly through the alley trying to not appear drunk. *Two drinks, never a third.* He had forgotten the old networking rule. Three beers and a shot, and the beers were huge, not pint glasses, what was he thinking? Hopefully they would forget his comments, they had just as much to drink as himself but they excelled at downing beer and remaining coherent. Surely they were talking about the craziness he just laid out on the table. Or maybe they switched back to space stations.

He could never go back to that group. Forever he'd be a laughing stock. No use, they would forget him soon enough, he was very forgettable.

He emerged from the ally and turned the corner onto 10th Avenue, peered down the block, and eyed the front of the bar, just a few patrons in evening gowns smoking cigarettes. He turned back toward 11th

Avenue and hiked toward the Hudson to avoid the risk that someone might come out the front of the bar and spot him. Oh God, what was he thinking?

He could never go back to that club again.

Tyler walked into the parlor and handed Rogers his suit jacket.

"Evening, Rogers. Is Mrs. Chambers in?"

"Good evening, sir, she waits for you in the master bed."

"How is she?"

"Angry."

He walked through the foyer and ascended the grand staircase. On the plane he constructed a perfect rhetoric for Rachel and went over it in his head a few times and anticipated every possible question she may have. He was prepared for this.

He stepped into the anterior room of the master bed and removed his shoes and loosened his tie. He opened the door and Rachel tore herself from the view of the reserve. She had a tumbler of wine in her hand. She set it on the vanity and charged toward him.

"What's going on?" she demanded.

"On with what?" Tyler asked.

"I spoke to Lana today and she wanted to know why we sold the company without consulting her. She said it was important for philanthropists…Tyler, why did I have to learn about this from a publicist?"

"An investment opportunity came up and—"

"You sold it right from under me, our company, the company we built from scratch, how could you have done that without talking to me, behind my back? How could you humiliate me like this, how could you betray me..." She fought back tears.

He glanced at the wine on the dresser and hoped that she'd step back and take another drink, but she stood her ground, demanding an answer.

"We're moving into a new chapter."

"Why would you not tell me?"

"I didn't think it mattered to you."

"Why would you think that?"

"You haven't even been to the company in over a year. They don't know what you look like except if they read Page Six."

He won that round but wasn't proud of it. Her tears stopped and she stared at him as if waiting for a better explanation. He wished she would just grab the wine glass and throw it, break something, storm out of the room, throw a tantrum, anything but direct confrontation.

"I'm not involved in the day-to-day operations so you thought it didn't matter to me and you dumped it?"

He clenched his hands. None of his prepared responses matched to his wife's logical inquires. New directions, opportunities abound, ROIs, and paradigm shifts were the weapons he stocked up on for this battle. He failed at setting the narrative. Maybe if he called her to his home office and had this conversation at his desk instead of wine in the bedroom…

"I'm tired of people stepping on me all day long," he mumbled with his head hung down.

"Stepped on? Stepped on where?"

"At work."

"Tyler. That is why I left that company years ago and you should have too."

"They think we're idiots, even though—"

"Yes I know, they look at us as bumbling aristocrats who get in their way of running a company. I sensed that every day I stepped off the elevator and walked into that place since the IPO. That's why I stepped back and let Ben Galvani run it. If they want to think us snotty kids who got lucky, let them. The fact is, those snickering executives show up to work every day with one goal, and that's to make money for you and me. Let them suck on that when they want to sneer at our excesses."

"So you understand what it's like to be laughed at." He looked up ever so slightly. Another pyrrhic victory.

"You sold the company that we built and then you kept it from me until I found out from some offhand remark at a luncheon. What did I do to you to make you treat me like this?"

He hated it that she was so reasonable in her discourse. So logical, she didn't even interrogate him or hurl insults. Her questions were reasonable and he yearned for a slipup in her demeanor that he could capitalize on. For God's sake throw the wine glass.

She waited for an answer.

"I just feel walked on."

"Where? Where do you feel walked on? You sit in your library, you don't come to functions and when you do you're non-existent. You chose to retreat from this family."

He walked over to the dresser—a strategic retreat.

"Tyler, where do you go when you leave town? I know it's not company business."

He looked back over his shoulder realizing the connotation of her question. "I've never stepped out on our marriage."

"I know you haven't, but you go out in the woods alone. That's awful. I wish you did have an affair, it would at least be normal."

How on earth could she know about that? He felt embarrassment at such extravagance of lone backpacking.

"I don't know," he said.

She grasped his two fingers and leaned her head against his arm. Tyler couldn't look up at the mirror to see her face. He didn't deserve her affection.

"Where's the money now? I spoke with Henry at Madison Trust and he says there's no wire from the sale."

"I have an account with Rockland County Bank. The money's there."

"I want access to it."

"Your name is on there. It's our money."

She let go of his fingers and turned him to face her. He finally lifted his sulking head.

"You hurt me with this, Tyler. You hurt me."

His condemnation to the guest bedroom brought him relief and he made himself comfortable for a possible long stay. But instead of staying in the guest bed, he asked Rogers to set up the portable airbed in the library.

The breaking of the news had not gone as planned.

He felt squirmy. His wife held her own well, as she always did.

His library offered him sanctuary from the world, just like the lesser-known canyons of Utah or the remote, undeveloped area of Northern California. Tyler had been to Great Basin in Nevada, the most remote place in the US. Surprisingly it was the busiest campground he'd been to in recent years, stumbling across many souls like himself, trying to seek refuge from the world. Did she have him followed? Maybe he should have paid cash for his camping equipment.

He needed confidence. Confidence in his decision. This was the part where he would second guess everything. He needed to knock that devil off his shoulder and listen to the angel. When they started the company Rachel propelled his ideas from the bowels of indecision. He would still be considering dimensions of the pool noodle if Rachel hadn't pushed him to make a decision. He could use her right now since his greatest enemy, procrastination, lied in wait to rear its ugly head.

The lights were out in the library and he had locked the door. An array of accent lighting gently haloed the top shelf of the otherwise dark room. He cowered under his silk covers and resisted the urge to help himself to a nightcap from the decanter.

His wife had pulled the dagger from her back and plunged it right back into his stomach. She used to hold his first two fingers tightly in hers. He had long fingers and she had petite hands. She squeezed them like a child, someone who needed the security only a loved one could give. That part hit him the hardest. She delivered her message of pain with love.

God what an asshole he was.

As he drifted off, a small detail crossed his mind. Selling of the stock fueled her intense anger, but one would think she'd mention the aircraft carrier. If one sells one's fortune and buys an old rusted warship, one would mention that.

She didn't know about the carrier…

…yet.

That was to come.

Goodness.

CHAPTER SEVEN

Three weeks later

The alarm in Tyler's phone woke him. The effects of the sleeping pill were still in him and grogginess lingered in his veins. He knew that eating breakfast would push the chemical through his system and he resisted the temptation to lull in the warm bed.

A knock at the door forced him out of bed, 4:03 in the morning, right on time. He opened the door and a man in a white jacket walked in with a covered plate of food and a pitcher of coffee. Tyler thanked him, sent him off, and tore into his omelet and toast.

He walked over to his suitcase and pulled some binoculars out and looked northeast out his hotel window which overlooked the tip of Superior Bay. He squinted and adjusted the focus on the eye piece.

There it was.

A tiny gray dot way off in the distance. That was his dot, right on schedule. He warmed the shower and gobbled more of his breakfast, watering down his coffee with creamer so he could drink it faster.

He jumped in and quickly scrubbed himself down. By 4:23 he was packed and out the door.

He screamed up the highway next to Lake Superior toward his little gray dot which became bigger and bigger. He sped through the area of

Northeastern Minnesota known to the locals as the arrowhead region.

Six AM, he pulled off the highway about a hundred miles northeast of Duluth and parked at the helicopter landing. The gray dot had grown to the size of the Titanic.

Tyler tossed the keys to a young valet. The rotors roared as he rushed to the helicopter. He climbed in and slammed the door shut. The pilot handed him a helmet and he fastened his restraints and they took off.

It was a short flight to Carrier Tolkov. The 700-foot Tolkov boasted six stories from the water line, a flat deck, and a control tower that most carriers in the modern world utilized. It had a displacement of 60,000 tons, 10,000 of which had been removed and left somewhere in Russia's Eastern port of Vladivostok as the equipment would never be needed. The beast still tipped the scales at 50,000 tons.

The helicopter landed ship's aft and Tyler stepped out. The pilot waved and Tyler gave him a thumbs up as he flew off. He walked briskly toward the tower, admiring the vastness of the flight deck.

The helicopter weighed around one ton and would bring the displacement of Tolkov to 50,001 tons which was unacceptable. Everything that could be removed from Tolkov was removed and no unnecessary weight was allowed aboard.

He ran through a door at the base of the tower and leapt over several bulkheads. He ascended the stairs which were so vertical, they might as well be called ladders.

The sixth deck was as chaotic as a palace kitchen during a royal wedding. Engineers and technicians were seated at several consuls around the bridge. Every station was a frenzy of activity. Seventy-two-inch flat screens displayed a dizzying array of diagnostics—terrain maps, tables of air pressure measurements, tension nodes, and several icons of tractors connected to lines. Each line had a color readout with an indicator ranging from green to yellow and bright red.

The comm was seated with headphones and a mic. She had three displays in front of her with a terrain map showing flat green terrain and a body of water separated by a highway.

One display had around fifty thumbnails squeezed together. The video camera feeds showed the front of the ship, the sides, closeups, and faraways of what lay ahead.

He joined a man standing near the front of the deck gazing through the window. “Morning, Captain Chambers,” the man said.

“Morning, Archer.”

Jack Archer was as tall as Tyler with thick black hair, a lantern jaw, brown eyes and a barrel chest. He was clean cut and in his 50s and stared out the window like a man about to take the first step on a different planet.

“Everything is ready, we’re in fifty feet of water right above the first log.”

A worldly reputation in unique engineering projects followed Archer. When a man had a vision to build the tallest building or the longest bridge or dam up the biggest of rivers, they called Archer to manage such a feat. Archer was the tactician that bridged visions from the minds of great men to the physical world.

When engineers warned that a sky bridge connecting the Petronas Towers wouldn’t work because of wind sway, Archer found a way. He managed the design of the Great Belt Suspension Bridge, a bridge so long, the towers had to account for the curvature of the earth. He found a solution for Venice’s constant fear of tidal waves.

Now Tyler stood inches from him as he was about to give the order to bring the operation underway.

“Inflate number one,” Archer announced.

The dispatcher relayed the order. He and Tyler stepped back to the monitor with the camera feeds.

“Bring up cameras forty-two and forty-three…thirteen and sixteen.”

The technician clicked on the thumbnail screens and they exploded to larger views, each filling a quarter of the monitor. The screen showed the water line on each side of the ship as well as underwater areas.

A flat blob filled the underwater camera’s field. The technician zoomed 13 and 16 back, one showing the stern and one showing starboard. The blob assumed a round shape.

Cams 42 and 43 showed the round object fully inflated and protruding through the water.

“Ninety-eight percent, integrity at strong,” the log technician yelled.

“Engines fifteen percent,” Archer ordered.

The boat vibrated from the propellers powering up.

“Moving forward, six meters, eight meters…” the helmsman reported.

Cameras 42 and 43 showed the round end of the inflated logs rotating indicating they were rubbing against the seabed. If they weren't the boat would float until the log underneath forward ran aground and then started rotating.

"...thirty meters!" the helmsman announced.

"Engines zero," Archer shouted. "Log two, inflate."

Archer walked to the front of the bridge and watched the log diagnostic monitor. Number one glowed a rich shade of green and number two morphed from black to green as the log inflated.

Tyler pulled out his phone and scrolled through his Facebook feed. There were several pictures of famous landmarks in compromising positions. Air Force One had its wings removed and several sets of tractor trailers hauled the fuselage. Several large wheeled vehicles dragged the Flat Iron building through Lower Manhattan.

A container ship with the Statue of Liberty turned on her side with wires securing it floated in the middle of the ocean. It had a North Korean flag flying. That one received the most up-votes, 86,000 in two hours.

A barge with the Eiffel Tower upright floated by the Brooklyn Bridge. Tourists on the walkway near one of the suspension towers posed in front of the famous gray girders.

"Five logs, sir, that's all engines are good for."

"Go ahead with the line," Archer ordered. The technician displayed several camera feeds overlooking the bow of the ship. A crane near the edge of the bow lifted a huge block and tackle with dozens of wires protruding from its mouth. The Liebherr mobile crane could telescopically collapse to an oversized semi and drive on most roads, although it needed an escort. It had eighteen oversized wheels that resembled six-foot diameter donuts. When the telescopic arm was collapsed, the tall tires and low-profile cab made it resemble an industrial crocodile cruising down the highway.

They had to transport the crane in pieces by chinook helicopter and reassemble it on the runway. When the beast finished attaching the block and tackle, the crew sat at the ready to tear it back down and parse its weight off the boat. It would be needed again at their destination but that was a worry for a different time.

The crane slipped the rod of the block and tackle into the giant clasp at the front of the ship. The clasp was fourteen meters wide, cast to solid steel and had a ten-meter opening to accept the giant rod.

The crane rested the rod into place and men dangling off the front of the boat received their signal to move in. They swung to the clasping device and disengaged the crane hook. The crane lifted away and the giant boom started its telescopic collapse. As the men secured the block and tackle trapping it into its place, the crane performed a massive U-turn at the front of the flight deck and headed aft to start its disassembly. The crane weighed 200 tons, including counterweights, and they needed to get as much weight off as possible, making 49,800 tons Tolkov's new weight.

"We're ready, comm," Archer said.

"Yes sir." She flipped twenty switches from left to right on the communications relay hub. As she flipped them the lights above each turned green indicating an open channel to the team of tractors. "Ladies and gentlemen, this is Tolkov. Start your engines!"

Archer walked back to the video monitor. "Feed one and two please."

The technician pulled up two cameras. They were both aerial views from drones.

A hundred tractors starting their diesels at once surely must have sounded like the Indy 500 on steroids.

"Tolkov to spike team. Report," the helmsman yelled through the com.

"In position, locked and loaded. Spike is a go," the spike team leader yelled over the com which was broadcast to the bridge.

"All tractor teams, ahead, ten meters," she barked.

From the aerial cameras Archer and Tyler watched as the tractors inched forward. Twenty teams of five, each pulling one of twenty inch-wide steel cables. As they moved forward, the slack tightened on the aft block and tackle causing tings and twangs to reverberate through the air.

"Cam eight, please," Archer requested.

The camera technician obliged and Archer looked closely at the two trucks parked near the beach.

Down on State Highway 61, two flatbed semi-trailers had metal frames which held the twenty heavy cables in place until they'd be lifted six stories in the air as the tractors tightened the slack. They were parked on each side of the four-lane Highway 61 and the morning commuters and vacationers drove under the array of cables completely unaware of what they were for or what significance they'd play in America's energy future.

As the com ordered the tractor teams to pull, the wires lifted themselves off the trailer frames of the two trucks and floated in the air, inching to the sky as the slack tightened.

Archer walked over to a technician who monitored the tension diagnostic units attached to each end of each steel cable. "Report."

"Sir, GPS reports that we are moving. Ten meters. The wires are as tight as they're going to get and all are in the green zone."

"Excellent. Com, forward. Initiate log six inflation."

The side cameras showed log six inflating, logs seven, eight, and nine were poking out of the water. Concrete weights on log nine barely protruded from the water. The weights were needed just in case the waves tried to grab the inflated logs before they were ready to be crushed by Tolkov. As she lumbered along, the logs kept inflating until the carrier lunged fully on the beach.

Tyler watched the bow cam on the monitor screen. The water splashed around against the bottom of the bow as the twin propellers poked out of the water. As Tolkov cleared the beach the propellers became completely exposed and the entire boat had cleared the waterline.

"Mr. Archer, we are out of the water," Tyler shouted. He felt just a bit of embarrassment from his childlike excitement, but everyone was too busy to notice and damn it, he had earned it!

Archer leaned over the com and inspected the tractor team formations. He grinned at Tyler and gave him a thumbs up and returned to the tractors.

Tyler buried his nose in his phone as an excuse to bow out. He stepped through the bulkhead into the hallway and put his phone back into his pocket and walked into the bathroom or head as navy personnel referred to it as.

Inside he rinsed off his hands which were covered in sweat. His hands shook, not from anxiety or nervousness but from a jolt of relief and happiness that his crazy plan was actually happening and working quite well. He smiled at himself in the mirror promising that he wouldn't spend any more time in the head unless he really had to go.

He returned to the bridge as they were about to cross Highway 61. The state troopers had diverted the traffic to the west on a temporary road built by the ground construction team in preparation for the journey. There were already people taking pictures at the site of a giant ship crawling from the beach on a bunch of gigantic Lincoln Logs.

He scrolled his Facebook feed again. The Onion article popped up and there it was, a giant aircraft carrier in a corn field and a headline that screamed "Navy carrier grounded in central Iowa due to reliance on Apple maps."

He switched to Twitter and scrolled through pictures of landmarks on barges and ships which were retweeted at an exponential rate. The photoshopped images of landmarks and buildings traveling by sea buried the images of Tolkov even though it went viral as well. His phone vibrated as a call interrupted his Tweeting.

"Tyler Chambers," he answered.

"Tyler, this is Hailey."

"Hi Hailey, just saw the retweets and the shares. Where's the Taj Mahal?"

"We had trouble with that one, it just didn't go viral like the others. We could bump it up if you wanted to, but I think the other images covered what you were looking for."

"I'm happy with everything else. I think everyone likes the North Korean Lady Liberty one the most."

"That's my favorite too!"

"Great, I think I'd consider this SEO campaign a success, Taj Mahal notwithstanding."

"I'm happy you like it."

"I got to run, Hailey, thank you for everything, send the invoice to our accounting and we'll get a check to you by Friday."

He hung up and turned back to the helm. His aircraft carrier would be hidden in plain sight for at least a day or two, thanks to a well-executed social media campaign. He walked over to the camera monitor and the tech displayed the feed of the aft where the first log had slipped from under the ship and was free. The log tech zoomed into it and a utility boat lunged toward it. A man with a pole at the front of the motor boat attached a wire to the clasp at the end of the floating log. The boat zoomed out of the way. From the beach a colossal utility vehicle pulled the log ashore.

The vehicle would have no problem dragging the three-ton log from the water, over the beach, over Highway 61 past Tolkov, and back to the front where it would be reused.

The logs each weighed about three tons but since they were thirty feet high and two hundred feet long, they glided like balloons dragged through a backyard picnic by a child. High winds could threaten to roll the logs back into the sea but the day was calm.

Tyler walked out to the starboard balcony and glanced down the side. The vehicle dragged the log past Tolkov and made a wide turn bringing it into line with the other logs for the ship to roll over.

He squinted to see Highway 61 in the distance in what would have been the boat's wake had they still been in the water. Several road crewmen in orange vests ran out to the highway. They checked the damage caused by the logs. They expected some cracks but the damage would be minimal. Any damages would be fixed with the crews working into the night, ensuring that Duluth commuters weren't too inconvenienced.

Archer walked out onto the balcony. "What do you think, Captain Chambers? Everything is going to plan so far, don't you agree?"

"Absolutely, I don't think I could have asked for a better leader on this project."

"How long are you staying aboard Tolkov?"

"Not long, I need to meet with several people back in New York, plus a few loose ends at the reservation. And I'm sure lots of folks from the government are going pay us a visit."

"What if they board us?"

"I'm sure they will at some point. Just do as they ask and leave the rest to my attorneys. They won't delay us by much when I'm done with them."

"Can I tell you something in confidence, Captain?"

"Of course, Jack."

"I must say, this is the most exhilarating thing I've ever done outside a bedroom."

"Me too, Jack."

Tyler patted him on the back and the two grinned at each other and returned to the bridge as Tolkov creaked along.

Tyler descended several floors below deck to the hangar. As he slid down the ladders a pounding echoed through the corridors and it grew louder. When he neared the hangar Kanye West's voice greeted him.

He opened the bulkhead door leading to the hangar and stopped as the music popped and went silent followed by a loud hum from the giant speakers. He paused for a moment to admire the hangar's vastness.

He was careful not to step on any of the dancefloor paneling. A man flew by him with a case of beer and loaded them into the fridge behind the bar.

As Tyler passed by the DJ booth two young men argued in Russian as a loud feedback noise echoed through the hangar. The one Russian slapped the other one's hand and pulled a plug causing a loud pop and the feedback to go silent.

"Morning, Kapitan," the DJ said.

"Morning, gentlemen," Tyler said as he passed by the booth.

At the far end of the hangar he disappeared into another bulkhead. As he made his way to the admiral's quarters, he passed by an enticing woman in a red evening gown. She glanced at him with a sour look and continued down the hallway stumbling in her high heels over metal seams in the floor. Tyler knew this woman was Russian. She had that round pouty face that Russian women had and Russians never smiled at strangers since it came off as insincere and goofy.

He pounded on the metal door loud enough to overcome the music.

It opened and Sergi greeted him. "Tyler Chambers! Enter!"

The admiral's quarters were plush and carpeted with traditional Russian artwork and wood paneling. The ceiling had exposed pipes and beams painted black to hide their intrusiveness.

A flat-panel TV displayed the Netflix logo along with several categories. The minibar featured about twelve kinds of vodka. Tyler smelled a sweet, pungent odor he recalled from his Columbia Frat party days. Since Sergi had diplomatic status, he did as he pleased. True, marijuana was probably not legal in Russia either, but Tyler didn't dwell on this.

"You too stiff, Tyler. I fix you drink. I know Martinis, Americans still drink Martinis?"

"Oh none for me thanks, but help yourself. How are you and your friends doing down here?"

"Natalya angry at me. She think there's pool. I told to her to look but she going to get lost."

"Oh, I hope she doesn't. We marked everything with yellow tape, hopefully she understands the tape."

"Tape? You tape this?"

"The yellow tape, so you don't get lost," Tyler pointed to the walls. "It's a big ship."

"Ah the tape. I'm going to go see Tasha. I show her the bridge, where I command the boat from."

"Sure, just make sure you stay out of everyone's way. It's crazy up there."

"Do they have more caviar? The girls only eat Persia or Black Sea."

"We'll fly some in, don't worry."

"Maybe we go to casino tonight."

"No, no going to casino, you have to stay here."

"Oh Tyler Chambers, you hold me prisoner on me own ship."

"My ship, you're just renting for a few weeks. But anything you want, if you want to play poker, we can have a dealer and a table flown in from Black Bear. Remember our deal is that you don't leave the ship or your father will have both our heads."

"I love Daddy, he so strict sometimes though."

"We'll get you good caviar. Want some American vodka?"

"Blackkkk," Sergi let out.

Tyler laughed.

"What if I get lonely? What if Tasha and Natalya get lost on ship and I never see again?"

"Then we'll fly in a couple of new gals. Minnesota has lots of Scandinavian girls. Could you get by with blonde, blue eyes, and huge racks?"

Sergi let out a sigh. "I will do what it takes to serve the Motherland. You coming to welcome party tonight? More women will descend on Tolkov. We have Russia's best DJ. It be wild party. You in?"

"No party for me. I have my wife's fundraiser to go to otherwise I'd love to stay."

"Oh Tyler, you big pushover for wife. Stay here. Lots of women and beer and hip-hop."

The Onion
Washington – An anonymous source at The Department of Homeland Security has reported Russian naval movements in the Midwest. "Satellite images have located a Russian Carrier group moving through Northern Minnesota." The source, who confirmed this on condition of anonymity, said DHS is taking the threat seriously and is ready to deploy the Third Fleet along the West Coast as a show of force.

DHS officially has no comment on the Russian fleet movement but stressed that high command is always on heightened alert.

Retired CIA analyst Jack Ryan reported to The Onion that the Saint Lawrence Seaway has always been under-protected and the Russians could just be testing how far the US Navy will go to protect the Midwest since they traditionally focused on East and West Coastal defense and have left the heartland relatively unprotected.

Ryan also pointed out that this isn't the first unconventional invasion by Russians. Back in 1984 the Soviet Union installed a Marxist government in Mexico and successfully invaded America by usurping the coasts and invading through Texas. This attack was repelled by a band of teenagers with the war cry "wolverine."

"Americans who forget their history are doomed to repeat it," Ryan added.

President Trump called it "fake news."

Tyler set his tablet in his lap and glanced out the window at the quilt pattern of farms filling the landscape of Eastern Pennsylvania. His phone rang.

"Hailey, how are you today?"

"Good. Did you see The Onion article?"

"Just read it. It's got quite a few shares."

"Hey I wanted to make you aware of something, did you see the Energy Department's response?"

Tyler glanced at his newsfeed. "No, I didn't."

"Are you near a computer?"

"Sure."

"Just Google *energy department aircraft carrier*."

Tyler tapped the search into his tablet and clicked on the first news item. "They already issued a memo. Damn, I thought the article would delay their action for at least a day or two. That's not much but it's a ton of time to us."

"Did you read it?"

"Not yet." Tyler tapped on the memo and scrolled through it. "Wait, what is this? This isn't the memo."

"The one issued from the Chairman of the Nuclear Regulatory Commission? Is that what you're looking at?"

"Yeah but I think it's someone's idea of a joke. This can't be it, this is some sort of news parody site."

"Tyler, that's their official response."

"Are you certain?"

"NRC dot gov?"

"Yeah, that's their website. Wait a minute while I read this thing."

MEMORANDUM FOR MISSION OF USS NAVY CARRIER FLEET

FROM: Robert L. Rutledge
Chairman of Nuclear Regulatory Commission

SUBJECT: Response to request for information regarding fleet movements in Northern Minnesota

The longtime journalists of the news site, The Onion, have brought to our attention the transportation of monuments, battleships, and aircraft carriers over land and sea to various international ports. The NRC wishes to clarify a few points on the subject of the nuclear aircraft carrier currently traveling through Northern Minnesota.

The US Navy has deployed ships in America's Heartland. Fleet movements by our longtime ally, Canada, are of concern. We have confirmed reports of ship movement throughout Saskatchewan, Manitoba, and Alberta by the Canadian Navy.

While we respect Canada's right to defend itself, we must too defend our boarders and not allow a naval imbalance along Northern Minnesota and the Dakotas.

We appreciate the timber, maple syrup, and stand-up comedy passing through customs daily and the United States guarantees the flow of automobiles, farm equipment, and Big Macs. However we cannot look past the aggressive naval movements through Manitoba's soy fields.

Although our Navy has yet to find a navigable route for our ships, we will continue to drag them across the land until a permanent maritime route can be established.

Until the Third Fleet is fully deployed, we recommend that Park Rangers increase their patrols along the border and stay alert for naval craft.

"Hailey, what the hell is this? Is this real?"

"Tyler, do you remember back a few years ago when the White House received an online petition to build a Death Star?"

"Yes, I vaguely remember that."

"The White House actually did issue a memo addressing it. Since it was obviously a joke and they were required by policy to respond they released a cheeky memo talking about the cost and how there were better alternatives."

"And so this is a joke from them to us?"

"I think what happened is the Department of Energy assumed the pictures of the ship were a hoax and issued a joke memorandum in return."

"Well, I guess then the article did work pretty well."

"And the memo is from Robert Rutledge."

"Right, Rutledge, he heads the department."

"I wanted to bring this to your attention because I think you made some folks at the Energy Department extremely angry since you got one over on them twice."

"You're right." Tyler pondered the implications of an angry federal government as Hailey remained quiet on the other end of the line.

"I almost feel bad," he finally declared.

Hailey laughed as a huge grin formed on Tyler's face.

"I guess I might need you in the future to deal with the fallout."

He thanked Hailey and hung up. He dropped his tablet on the floor and leaned back in the seat of the G5 as it flew through Upstate New York.

A shiver fluttered up his spine as he realized he had gotten away with something. It bought Tolkov two extra days and fully justified the fee he'd paid to The Onion for the article.

Someone was going to lose their job. They had reacted to the social media by being a comedian. Tyler was stirring the pot and making a wondrous mess of things. He leaned back in his cushy chair and told the flight attendant that he wanted a scotch to help him sleep. He would surely be on someone's hit list by the end of the day.

CHAPTER EIGHT

"Your evening attire awaits you in the anterior closet."

"Thank you, Rogers. Please alert me when it's twenty of."

Rogers pivoted a perfect hundred-eighty-degree arc, adjusted his nose upward, and stepped with his usual tortoise-like swagger and pulled the double doors shut behind him.

Tyler reached for his phone from his silk robe pocket. He thumbed his code and opened the Tolkov app. A dizzying array of tiny buttons opened and he tapped on each one. The tension on the wires read steady at medium orange, the tractors displayed a full green traveling at top speed, the boat averaged a brisk 3.37 miles per hour. 22.47 days to destination—the number of days always displayed at the top. No major issues, Archer had the situation well in hand. He pressed the power-down button since the temptation to check it every five seconds overwhelmed the OCD part of his cerebrum. He slipped the smartphone back in his pocket to focus on his book.

One of the ground rules his wife laid down was that he attend her fundraisers and pretend everything was fine, although she said it in a much more roundabout manner. No conversations on the stock dumping, just deflect toward the foundation if asked. Wear the penguin outfit, stand up straight and be pleasant and boring which he excelled at anyways.

Quietude. He was sealed in his library. He ran his fingers along the spines of the books. He inhaled and relished the smell of the books, an affirmation of these few precious moments before the party. He reflected on how a time and place once existed when he found little value in reading beyond academia. Why read fiction which contributes nothing to your knowledge when a universe of fact existed to further yourself? Tyler wondered how he could have ever thought that way.

He climbed the wrought-iron spiral staircase to the upper level. The second-level ledge wrapped around the interior and at just a few inches deep with a thin railing it afforded only a slim individual like himself the ability to explore the titles of the upper level.

He reached for the second book in the Aubrey-Maturin series, a collection of stories centering on a swashbuckling ship captain and a ship's doctor during the Napoleonic wars. In its place he slid in volume one.

He admired the view from aloft. The Tsarist chic rug lent such majesty with its hand-woven traditionalist patterns. The chandelier gave off the perfect shade of light that lent everything a touch of gilded glow.

He descended the spiral staircase and set the book down on the end table. His robe had come open exposing his silk boxers and he tied it back up. The antique leather chair squeaked and creaked as he nudged himself into a comfy position. He reached under the lampshade to pull the little chain.

Tyler spun the antique globe. Siam, Ottoman Empire, and Asia Minor passed through his fingertips until he came to South America. The Americas were mapped out of proportion since the territories on the antique globe were not yet explored in depth by Anglos.

He exhaled the smells of the library and dove into his book.

Was Maturin the "correct" character to cheer for and did the author intended that? Surely anyone who read the books would love the swashbuckling Captain Jack Aubrey. Doctor Maturin rambled on about philosophy and nature. Whereas Captain Aubrey was clearly the main character, Tyler found himself bored by the captain's hero antics and Maturin filled the void when he jumped back on the page.

He recalled seeing *Jurassic Park* in the theater. Richard Attenborough and Laura Dern enjoyed ice cream and he remembered having to go to the bathroom from the supersized pop he guzzled down and that this was the time to do it—character development moment. Spielberg knew audiences came for dazzling dinosaurs but would need a bathroom break. The character development part occurred at the exact moment when a bladder would reach its capacity.

Truth be told, when Tyler saw the movie a second time he skipped the gargantuan bucket of pop and stayed for the character development moment and enjoyed it.

He respected Captain Aubrey but Maturin rendered the book unputdownable and inspired him to purchase the entire series and assign it the most prominent place on the mezzanine shelf. He hoped and prayed that Maturin wasn't killed off in the third or fourth book. That would have been wrong. Of course the title Aubrey-Maturin Series implied that he made it to book twenty.

As the author described 19th century Europe, he fantasized about turning his home into one of those English countryside estates with gardens, servants, and old furniture. What if they did away with contemporary décor? The gaudy art, the stainless-steel kitchen, the designer furniture by some trendy German interior designer. The old-world globe was a good start. Modern books made his shelves a rainbow-speckled color palate. Gone were the days of old grey and navy-blue books that smelled of paper mills and cobwebs. He wondered if Harry Potter could be printed on an oversized hardcover with old Greek lettering, uneven pages. Maybe the publisher could add an old English library stench to the paper.

Surely others rooted for Maturin, they had to be out there. Did kids get in trouble if they talked too much about Huck instead of Tom? Were there nerdy, awkward trekkers that admired Spock over Captain Kirk? Chewbacca instead of Han or Luke? Chewy did turn the tide at the Battle of Endor.

A knock at the door caused him to look up.

"Yes."

Rogers opened the door and stepped in at full attention. "Sir, the time is 6:40."

"Thank you, I will meet you in the bedroom."

"Meet, sir?"

"I'll sneak through the back stair. If Mrs. Chambers sees me undressed, it will upset her greatly and that won't be good for either of us."

"Ah, yes, very good, sir."

Rogers closed the door behind him. Tyler placed a gold-leaf bookmark on page 42 and set the book next to the crystal decanter. He tied his robe again and snuck one last smell of the books and left through the discrete servant's door in the corner.

The servant's stairs were a hotbed of commotion. Loud voices, the occasional yelling, pots and pans shuffled around, the staff, both full time and temporary for the night were running up and down the stairs yelling out instructions, bussing supplies to the kitchen, boxes of linens, the rattle of silverware, cases of wine, a bin of shaved ice, floral arrangements, tea lights.

He reached the top and peered out of the hallway from a door disguised as a wood panel. Lupe feather-dusted a plant next to the panel and was startled when she noticed him.

"My dear, where is Mrs. Chambers?"

"She is in the kitchen. Shall I ring her?"

"Goodness no. Where's Rogers?"

"Mr. Rogers is waiting for you in the bedroom."

"Ah, he beat me. Thank you."

He scurried across the hall and into the master bed. He closed the door behind him and took his robe off and tossed it on the vanity chair. He walked into the closet and Rogers motioned to his tuxedo. It hung on the valet stand, pants perfectly pressed, shoulders square, black shoes stowed in the bottom.

Tyler observed the universal code that women took months to get into evening wear and men tossed it on ten minutes before the formal event, whether a wedding, ball, or funeral. He had generously allocated fifteen minutes.

He tucked in the white shirt and buttoned the pants. He tied his bowtie and looked at it in the mirror. Rogers affixed his cufflinks and presented his shoes one at a time.

"Can you fix this?"

Rogers inspected the bowtie. "Sir, you no longer need my assistance with this. You've become quite skilled."

"Really?" He turned back to the mirror to evaluate Rogers's statement. "Don't you think I should go with the black?" The baby blue reminded him of something a gangly teenager might wear to prom.

"No, sir. Mrs. Chambers was specific about this outfit down to the shade of black of the socks."

6:59. Tyler was ready.

"Sir, one pressing issue. Mrs. Gertrude is having trouble putting Miss Thora down for the night. She specifically requested your presence. I don't believe this excursion will cause Mrs. Chambers any undue ferments since she is still managing the catering staff."

"Thank you, I'll take care of it."

He walked with the stride of a mummy. The jacket felt engineered to encourage good posture. He opened the door to Thora's room and Gertie turned on all fours to him. She put a foot on the floor and hoisted herself from her knee as her joints cracked.

"Looking for monsters, Mister Chambers."

"Didn't find any?"

"No, never. Never found any. I think it's because you and Mrs. Chambers always finish your vegetables and say your prayers so the monsters stay away."

Thora watched with skeptical eyes.

"Are you going to stay late?"

"I can read in the guest room until the party is done."

She walked out of the bedroom and Tyler sat on the edge of Thora's princess bed.

"Why do you look like a pastor?" she asked.

"It's not a pastor outfit, it's a groom outfit. That's the man who gets married to the bride in the princess dress."

"Are you getting married?"

"No, but sometimes grownups pretend someone is getting married. That's what Mommy is doing with the party. Lots of grownups pretending to get married."

"Gertie is lying to us," she whispered.

"How is she lying?"

"The boogie man doesn't live under the bed, he's in the closet."

"How did you hear about the boogie man?"

"Skyler in Mrs. Brenhold's class told me."

"Did Skyler see him?"

"She didn't say."

"Have you seen him?"

"No."

"Then how do you know he's there?"

"I don't know."

"Want to play treasure closet?"

"Okay."

Thora kicked the covers off and jumped off the bed and ran to the closet.

The walk-in closet had her collection of princess dresses, toys on shelves, and stuffed animals lining the walls.

"Okay you sit there and I'll sit here," Tyler said.

Thora crawled to the spot under her hanging dresses. His carefully engineered tuxedo became untucked as he got comfortable sitting on the floor cross-legged.

He reached for the light switch. "Okay, ready?"

She nodded and he turned the lights off and the closet was pitch black.

"First reach up and tell me what dress is above you."

"Ariel!" Thora said.

"How do you know?"

"The frilly thing at the bottom."

"Are you sure?"

"Yeah!"

He flipped the lights back on. Thora looked up and laughed at the little green and aqua blue dress.

"All right, let's do it again. Ready?"

"Yeah!"

He flipped the switch and the closet went dark again. He reached to his left and felt around for a stuffed animal and put it in Thora's lap. "Now who's that?"

"Draggy."

"How do you know it's Draggy?"

"His wings and the spike on his tail. And he has a long neck."

He flipped the switch back on. Thora held a green dragon with his red tongue hanging out in her lap.

"Not bad. Now it's my turn."

He turned the lights out again. He reached over and put his hand on

Thora's head. She giggled as he touched her ear. "Is this an elephant?"

"No!" she said.

He moved to her face and ran his fingers over her nose. She giggled again.

"Is this the teddy bear? What's his name again?"

"No, it's not."

"But she has a little button nose like a dog. Is it Snoopy?"

"Daddy, it's me."

He turned the lights and Thora giggled. "It is a little puppy." He patted her on the head.

She yawned and hugged her dragon tightly.

"Are you ready for bed?"

She jumped back under the covers.

"I'm going downstairs now. I love you."

"I love you too, Daddy."

He gave her an Eskimo kiss and turned out the light as he left.

He inspected himself in the hall mirror, fixing anything that became untucked. The tuxedo cooperated when he maintained good posture. He descended the grand staircase to the main hall and headed to the greenhouse.

Upon entering he had an odd feeling that he'd never been in this room before. The greenhouse had lost its red, white, and blue color scheme from the last fundraiser in early July and exchanged it for more summery tones. The dancefloor had been moved away from the garden, the bar spanned the south side this time, and indoor trees with hanging candles lined the edges of the grand room.

He spotted his wife near the fountain. She wore a deep blue evening gown with gold earrings, a pendent with a ruby, white gloves, and black high heels. Her hair was done in big loose curls. He realized the shade of his bowtie was meant to match her dress. He stared for a moment at her shoes to gauge if they matched his socks.

She furiously scrolled through a list on her tablet. Denise and Lara chatted in each of her ears describing guests in a last-minute cram session, tapping the screen with fury.

He approached Rachel causing one of Lara's assistants to rush over to him.

"Mister Chambers," she exclaimed. "My, you look dashing tonight."

She addressed him with a huge red smile with perfectly bleach-white teeth. She put her arm around his. "I want your opinion on something."

She ushered him to the entrance of the greenhouse. "Which of these do you prefer?"

One of the framed posters showed the logo for the Lupus Foundation and displayed a group of perhaps fifty children standing in front of a hospital. The other featured a single little girl.

"This one conveys the foundation's vision whereas this one highlights the individuals whom the foundation helps. Isn't she a cutie?" She motioned to the little girl on the second poster.

"She certainly is."

Tyler knew why she asked him this. Her job involved keeping him away from his wife for the night, until an official meet was needed. She would be his guide, beard, and keeper for the evening. She had seen him approaching and launched toward him lest he was able to get in a word with his busy wife and distract from her hosting duties.

He didn't catch Lara's assistant's name. Maybe she thought Tyler should know it by now. As she spoke she shook her head from left to right as if to convey more importance to her words. She talked about herself but always allowed a moment for the listener to jump in with his own story. She was good.

"So fission is what we do now but fusion is what we should do?" she asked. He wondered how on earth they arrived at this subject.

"Yes, but the technology is just out of our reach. Fission is when you take away particles, fusion is when you add. An old joke is that nuclear fusion is the technology of the future and always will be."

Hahahahahahahahahahahahahah, she cackled as she gently smacked his arm. Ah, yes, Miss Cackle—he remembered her laugh from two events ago.

The sound of formal heels clacking against the marble floor in the main hall grew louder. The guests were shuffling in.

He and Miss Cackle strolled around the greenhouse arm in arm. Lara Farnsworth had an unlimited supply of outgoing young women at her PR firm to handle people like Tyler. Last time a tall redhead handled him. She also had a high-society cackle but not this bad.

As she introduced him to guests, party cliques formed and people fell into two categories. Those who Rachel invited and those who were dragged to the event by those Rachel invited. He was to converse with the dragged-to crowd but he was happy with this arrangement.

Miss Cackle pulled him past young socialites, past members of the media, past the artistic types, and the hip crowd until she corralled him with the dragged-to crowd. One herd was the decision maker, the other herd signed the check.

Mark Johnson of Citibank, husband of Lucy Lynn-Johnson, the reporter on New York One. John Steiner, husband of performance artist Penelope Steiner. "Pleased to meet you," Tyler would say, extending his hand. A few kind words for his wife, some self-deprecating comments about wives wearing the pants in the family. A curator of the Frick Collection, some producer for Focus Features, they made artsy fartsy films (films not movies). Their dates hanging from their arms were their polar opposites. Miss Cackle introduced him to each 'dragged-to' person. She acted as the societal glue, lest the 'dragged-to' crowd found a lull in the small talk. And every one of them were dressed as a carbon copy of himself.

Miss Cackle looked across the room and caught Lara motioning to her.

"Mister Chambers, I think it's picture time," she exclaimed.

"I look forward to hearing more about this as I'm sure we'll cross paths as the night progresses." Tyler's go-to exit strategy. Miss Cackle from the first event taught him that closing line.

We're refocusing our philanthropy efforts and Fusion Outdoor has been instrumental in our transition. That was the other line he was made to memorize. Refocusing and instrumental were the premiere buzzwords surrounded by a couple of second-tier buzzwords. One of Lara's assistants went over this with him, even giving him a business card-sized flash card. She didn't write it though, he recognized Rachel's corporatey prose style that she was so good at.

Miss Cackle cradled his arm and nudged him through the crowd to where there were flashes from the photographer. Tyler stopped and locked eyes with a man who stared straight at him with a grin. The slightly balding plump man wore a cummerbund that looked ready to launch if he happened to inhale a deep breath. The déjà vu forced Tyler's memory to shuffle like a rolodex. Finally he found the name under "W." It was Lester Wilner, his dorm mate from Columbia who he used to canoe with. He recognized his half-crooked smile and noticed he'd put on a few pounds in the last decade.

Miss Cackle pulled him from his flashback down memory lane and they blazed through the throngs of New York's philanthropic elite to get to the photo-op staging. Oh God of all people, why was Lester Wilner here?

A short woman with an apron full of makeup supplies examined his face. She stepped on a chair to bring herself to Tyler's level. He closed his eyes as she dusted his forehead, cheeks and chin with a powder to hide the shine that would otherwise be highlighted with the photography lights.

He stepped in front of the background which featured sponsors' logos pasted in a repeating pattern. Some children's hospital, FedEx was involved and the SoHo ArtStart program, whatever that was.

Why would Lester be there? He wasn't married to anyone famous, was he? He would fall into the dragged-to clique which meant Tyler would have to talk to him and *catch up. What have you been up to?* He dreaded these kinds of inquiries from people he hadn't spoken to in a long time.

Rachel and Lara chatted as they scrolled through her tablet. She tapped her finger on the surface as she instructed Lara with her hush voice.

The photo assistant escorted a little girl in a pink dress to the photo op area. Rachel shoved the tablet to Lara, handed her her glasses and rushed behind the little girl. She gently placed her hand on the little girl's shoulder. Tyler placed his hand at the small of Rachel's back. He smiled and leaned his head in slightly. Rachel had painstakingly taught him how to smile for an event picture. Always lean the head in slightly to eliminate waddle neck. Even slim people displayed a double neck if the shutter snapped at an inopportune time.

Rachel's iron fist attitude dropped for just a moment as she smiled sincerely for the camera.

The lens clicked. Tyler glanced down at the little girl. She had some sort of thick padding under her dress. It looked like a type of back brace to help straighten her.

Lester lurked out there somewhere. Tyler squinted and found it difficult to see with the lights blinding him.

"One more," the photographer said.

He and Rachel smiled even harder.

"Come on Lizzy, one more, you can do it, smile big." He snapped the picture. "Good work!"

Rachel dropped her smile and rushed over to Lara. Tyler breathed a sigh of relief as his work for the night was over. Miss Cackle came over to fetch him again. She leaned over the little girl.

"How are you doing, Lizzy?" she asked.

"Tired," the little girl mumbled.

"Oh why are you so tired, honey? Did you stay up late?"

"I had surgery today."

Tyler stepped over to his wife. "Are we done?"

"You're done. Go enjoy the party." She glanced at Miss Cackle who clasped Tyler by the arm. Lara tapped a box marked *Tyler Chambers – husband* on the tablet and a check mark filled it in.

"Who's next?" she asked Lara as Miss Cackle dragged Tyler away.

Go enjoy the party – That phrase spelled relief for him. It meant his work was done and he could now imbibe on alcohol.

The pair wandered past the ice sculpture and she planted him at a plush circular style couch with a few other members of his clique.

Miss Cackle performed what could be described as a standup routine for the men sitting at the round sofa near the bathrooms. The men laughed at her self-deprecating humor as Tyler endured the awkward boredom.

A server handed out champagne flutes from a silver platter. Tyler slammed the drink, kicked back, and tried to enjoy Miss Cackle's deprecating humor.

She huffed up her strapless dress as though it was a good pair of Levis. She had her audience in her grips as Tyler grabbed another flute of champagne. He glanced around the room trying to feign interest in the East Coast Philanthropic Elite. He spotted Lester again, in the corner, about as bored as Tyler. He looked as though he was about to strike up a conversation with the fichus tree. He turned and looked Tyler's way. Tyler focused back on Miss Cackle, pretending that he didn't see Lester.

"One you mount, the other you throw back." *Hahahahahahahahahahah*, she cackled again with the men laughing.

She managed some sort of standup routine about fishing and having one-night stands causing hearty laughs from the dragged-to crowd. While these check signers got drunk off Tyler's liquor their dates were wooing his wife and begging the opportunity to give her a check and a possible invite to the next event. Miss Cackle could herd cats if she wanted to. Goodness, could she ever fathom the importance of her role in philanthropy.

He gulped another slug of Dom and a scale appeared above his head. On the one side was this party, on the other was catching up with Lester and answering a slew of *whatcha been upto* style questions. With every loud cackle and stupid joke, the awkwardness of "catching up" made the scales tip toward Lester. He'd have to explain how he invented the pool noodle for the thousandth time and try to make it sound interesting. On the other hand—

Hahahahahahahahahahah,

….another burst of laughter from Tyler's babysitter.

Enough. He stood and focused his attention toward Lester. Their camping trips were so much fun. Dammit he would bring those up and not give Lester a chance to bombard him with questions on the pool noodle or Fusion Outdoor or lack thereof.

"Tyler, you all right?" she shouted.

"Just need a pit stop."

"Hey me too. We'll go together."

She saddled his arm in hers and they headed toward the bathrooms. She was to babysit the men but Tyler was the problem child.

"You're funny as hell Tyler. Don't ever change." He sauntered to the men's room and she toward the ladies'.

When she disappeared into the ladies, he noticed a security officer near the entrance to the greenhouse ballroom. He approached the stalky gentleman with a spiral cord protruding from his ear.

"You security," he yelled over the music and crowd noise.

"Just enjoying the party, Mister Chambers."

"You got cuffs?" Tyler said.

"No, just enjoying the party."

"I'll give you two thousand dollars for your handcuffs. You got cuffs, right?"

"Mister Chambers, it's a wonderful party, I think you should go back to it."

"But you'd sell me your cuffs? Right?"

"I don't know what you're talking about."

Tyler pulled a wad of Franklins out of his pocket. "But two grand, whoops, there's like three grand here. You would give me your cuffs for that?"

The man looked around to gauge how many people were looking at him and Tyler. He leaned into Tyler. "That's some serious bank, Mr. Chambers. What you going to do with them?"

"Just for fun, if you know what I mean."

The man grabbed the wad and stuffed it in his front pocket. He reached to the small of his back and pulled a pair of handcuffs out and handed them to Tyler in a discrete manner. "You need the key?"

"No," Tyler said as he made his way back to the round couch clique.

Miss Cackle emerged from the ladies' room and Tyler clutched her hands. "Hey have you seen the antique phone booth in the parlor, it actually works."

"Oh I saw that, can I call my mom?"

"Absolutely."

They stepped into the booth.

"Wow, my sister had one of these at her wedding. Fun. I love it."

"Okay we're going to play a little game," Tyler said. He removed the phone from the receiver and handed it to Miss Cackle. Then he affixed the cuff to her wrist. "And now we attach the other end to the receiver."

Hahahahahahahahahahah, she let out, only this time there was just the slightest drop in her cackle tone.

Tyler left the phone booth and went back to the greenhouse. The cackle faded away until Tyler heard it no more.

He wandered through the greenhouse until he spotted Lester still standing next to the fichus.

"Doctor Chambers." He smiled and they shook hands.

"Doctor Wilner, what have you been up to?"

"Living the dream. You?"

"Same here."

The two grinned at each other searching for what to say next.

"Where do you work, Lester?"

"Indian Point, Reactor Two."

"Reactor Two? What do you do there?"

"Head Engineer."

"So Reactor Two is your baby."

"My baby, monster really, but it purrs like a kitten when I have it at ninety-five percent capacity." Lester chuckled.

Tyler made the right choice. There were a million questions he wanted to ask Lester. The more he talked to his old friend, the more he felt he could handle the pool noodle jokes. Tyler made eye contact with Rogers across the room and he stepped lively toward them.

"That's great you have your own reactor," Tyler said.

"Looks like you did pretty good for yourself too."

"Eh, I get to dress up and come to these things. You still play pool?"

"Yeah, little, here and there."

Rogers appeared next to Tyler's side. "Rogers, would you mind opening the billiards room? What are you drinking, Les?"

Lester glanced at his Miller Lite bottle. "How about scotch?"

"A bottle of Macallan 30," Tyler said to Rogers.

The billiard room ceilings stretched high with a tiffany light array hanging above the pool table. Those waiting for their shot were given the choice of lounging on the Chippendales or a seat at the minibar in the corner. Since it faced north the windows displayed a majestic view of the neighboring park reserve.

The quiet of the room offered relief from the chaos of the party. They agreed to a friendly game of eight ball with Tyler taking the stripes. He poured Lester a dram, handed him a cue and chalk, and offered him the chance to break.

"Heck of a flop you have here." Lester sent the balls in all directions but missed sinking any.

"Yeah the company has been good to us. It's kind of a pain at times."

"Pain? Wish I had those kind of problems."

"It's impossible to have privacy with the servants, and Rachel doesn't let me wear jeans or sweats, it's like living in a zoo habitat, only no forced mating."

Lester laughed as he gulped his scotch. "Still, it's better than that apartment on a hundred and fourteenth."

Tyler paused, not allowing his smirk to ruin his shot. He sent the eleven into the corner. "Remember the cockroach you tried to stomp that sent the pasta sauce everywhere?"

"Oh man, that was homemade from Hampton Tomatoes my grandma sent me."

Tyler chalked his cue, shaking his head. "We simmered that for two hours, everything was ready, we had the cheap jug wine—"

"Seward Vineyard's."

"Yes, Seward, from the Lower East Side, made by Hassidic Jews."

"That cockroach ran out and scared the crap out of you and you knocked the hotplate over."

"It wasn't me, you tried to stomp it with your size twenty-twos and you hit the table leg," Tyler said as he made the thirteen disappear into the center pocket.

"No, *you* hit the table leg, I remember that."

Tyler shot the cue ball at the stripe ten bouncing it off the edge of the corner. "See you're making me laugh and messing up my shots, I could have sunk that."

"How is Rachel?"

"Good, did you see her?"

"Yes, she and Judith gabbed away. Did you think Rachel was stressed? She looked stressed."

"I don't know, I haven't spoken to her today. This is work for her so I stay out of her way."

"So do you guys enjoy hosting these soirees?" Lester shot the three into the side pocket.

"Not us, it's mostly her party, my job is to make an appearance and get my picture taken. How did you get roped into this?"

"I remember she loved organizing dinner parties at Columbia. I'm here because Entergy donates money to the Children's Lupus Foundation. Our plant head handed me the invite and thought I'd check it out."

"Dinner party? That's a stretch for those parties. Kegger is more like it."

"Those girls at the keggers though. She was good at getting me laid. I mean meeting women. Good women like Judith, jeez did I say laid?" Lester chuckled.

"Yeah, she always had a way at brokering people together. Those MBA women were sexy as hell. Us with our pocket protectors and them with their power suits."

"Goodness, the silk stockings on some of them…they came to the parties and your eyes were glued to those short skirts. God those legs…now, you're going to make me mess up my shot." He sent a solid in the corner pocket and missed. He had given Tyler the perfect opening to put the nine away. Just aim for the bottom of the cue ball so it would spin and come back from the pocket.

Tyler leaned over to sink the nine.

"Why did you just up and leave the Hadron Collider?"

He plucked the cue ball and it completely missed the nine.

They were past the small talk and reminiscing and Lester brought out the big guns. Tyler readied himself for pool noodle inquiries but not the Hadron Collider.

"Combination of circumstances, you know—midterms, dissertation, Rachel." Tyler regaled himself and stepped back. "Well, it was Rachel," he shyly corrected.

Lester held his pool cue like a staff and nodded as if Tyler's answer lacked sufficiency. He set up his shot and sunk the six into the corner.

"I just needed to be with her. Tough decision but she's my girl. I knew she'd go off to somewhere and that's that. I couldn't let that happen."

Lester chalked his cue and aimed for the number one. It bounced around the corner but didn't go in.

Tyler felt the awkward moment and searched for more small talk but he found none. Now nudging the conversation to pool noodles tempted him. He leaned over the table to line up his shot and wondered what scowl Lester threw in his direction. Was he still glaring at him as though his answer was not enough? Did Lester show up just to ask him that question? This part of the conversation would tilt the scale back to Ms. Cackle's company.

Tyler stared the fifteen down—a perfect opening. Just knock it in.

"Yeah, you guys were pretty hot and heavy," Lester said as if he let Tyler off the hook with a copout answer.

"Hot and heavy." Tyler smiled as he lined up his next shot. He found it difficult to concentrate on the fifteen.

His old friend caused nostalgia to flow through his mind like a good wine buzz. Lester fought in the trenches. While he monitored Reactor

Two at Indian Point, Tyler took his daily massages and hot bath treatments. Lester stuck with it and Tyler invented the pool noodle. Lester made the motor of the world function and provided the energy that fueled Manhattan while Tyler invented a foam tube. Maybe Lester's job was a daily grind but he was at least doing something.

The temptation was strong to pull out his smartphone and show Lester his boat. Would he approve or would he just stand there with wide eyes, mouth open, tongue hanging out with a 'I'm standing next to an insane man' look on his face?

The fifteen went in and Tyler moved to the last stripe, number fourteen.

"Ty, where did you go after you checked your messages?"

Tyler righted himself from the table. "What?"

"Where did you go after you checked your messages and disappeared from that bar near the Collider?"

Tyler shook his head mildly. "Checked my messages and then I went back to NYC."

"Why did you just go? We didn't even get our meatballs, you just bailed?" Lester grinned shyly, trying not to offend the host.

"I told you, Rachel was going to just move, I spent every waking hour with her when I came back to New York. Now I'm married to her." Tyler gave a crooked smile with a nod to Lester as if that response put an end to the questions. The question forced him to wonder how life would have turned out if he stayed for the meatballs and let Rachel go her own path. No Fusion Recreation Equipment, no pool noodle, no marriage. Just meatballs and nuclear friends. It wasn't difficult to see his decision as anything but perfect until Lester leaned on a pool cue in his billiards room grilling him about the past. He still preferred Lester's interrogation over the party.

The doors to the billiards burst open. It was Rogers to the rescue. "Mister Chambers, Miss Kendra is searching for you."

"Who's Miss Kendra?"

"The young woman you were with most of the evening. It seems as though she's managed to escape the predicament you put her in."

"Oh, her."

"May I suggest, sir, you return to her side as it would distress Mrs. Chambers greatly if she found you away from the party."

"Five minutes, I promise."

"Very good sir, I will keep her occupied until then."

"Thank you, Rogers."

Rogers turned and left the billiard room.

"So that's your butler?"

"Yeah, he's my right-hand man."

"And his name is Rogers?"

"Archibald Rogers."

"So Mr. Rogers is your butler?"

"I suppose so. I've never thought of it that way. He does have an affinity for sweaters in the winter months."

They both laughed. Tyler prepared a joke in his head for Miss Cackle or Kendra or whatever her name was. She would surely be mad at him but would never hurl an accusation at him—simple misunderstanding involving manacles. He sunk the last stripe in and then made the blackball his target.

Lester watched helplessly as Tyler put the blackball in its place. How he wanted to whip his smartphone out and scroll through updates on Tolkov. After the party he'd sneak out…back to Northern Minnesota, back to the Arrowhead, back to his ship. How he longed for his ship.

CHAPTER NINE

Tyler opened his eyes to the white pipes running through the ceiling. He stretched his legs and realized that Russian officers must have been short since his feet kicked against the wall while the top of his head rubbed against the opposite wall.

He reached over to the IP phone which rang a second time. "Chambers. How far? This is really it then? I'll be right up."

He nudged himself carefully to the edge of the cot and glanced at the pipes again. The ship wasn't built for tall sailors which made him cautious every time he had to stand from a seated position.

He hung up the phone and wiped his eyes. He looked in the mirror and fixed his hair as best he could. He dug through the mini compartments for pants and dove into the tiny closet for a shirt. It was hard to believe that if one navigated the Russian Navy hierarchy and achieved Captain Lieutenant a closet served as your new home.

On the bridge the mood of the crew felt heightened. They focused on their duties but everyone sensed the enemy on the horizon.

Archer leaned over the balcony with binoculars as if the extra few inches it gave him mattered. He handed the binoculars to Tyler. Several black dots hovered in the horizon and they were growing in size.

The two returned to the bridge.

"Ladies and gentlemen, may I have your attention for a brief moment," Archer announced as everyone removed their headphones and turned their chairs to him. "Everyone is to remain calm, we expected this. Under no circumstances do I want anyone harmed, safety is our top priority. When our visitors board us, I want everyone to follow their instruction. Do not answer any questions or tell them anything except to request an attorney. Your legal expenses will be covered by Captain Chambers. Captain will make arrangements to make sure everything is taken care of."

Four Seahawk helicopters landed on the flight deck. Attack helicopters hovered in the distance. Tyler could make out the missiles under the pylons and the cannons sticking out of the nose just under the cockpit canopy. They looked like angry mosquitoes.

Men covered in armor with machine guns jumped out of the copters and rushed to the base of the tower. Tyler and Archer stared at the monitors showing the tractor teams. Helicopters landed around them and one landed near the spike team several miles ahead.

The SWAT teams rushed the tractors motioning them to stop, which they did. The diagnostic readouts on the wire tension faded from orange to yellow and finally to green.

"Sir, we've stopped," the main dispatcher said.

The clanking of boots ascending the ladders grew louder.

"Everyone just calm down and keep your hands out in the open and step away from your station," Archer said.

Four masked men rushed in with weapons pointed at the crew.

"All hands on your heads. Stay where you are," the SWAT commander barked.

The crew complied. A half dozen agents walked in who had FBI insignias on their jackets and their sidearms holstered. One of them had several white plastic binders attached to his hip. One by one they frisked the crew and bound their hands behind their backs.

"I want to know who's in charge of this operation."

"I'm Captain Chambers and this is First Officer Archer."

"Oh you're a captain?" the FBI agent said in a sarcastic tone.

"Every person on this ship has legal counsel and wishes to invoke their right to representation," Tyler said, not completely sure if he'd be taken seriously by these men with guns.

"We'll make sure you talk to your attorney. Come with us."

Tyler and Archer were the first to be led out. They stepped backwards down each ladder with an FBI agent ahead to assure they didn't fall since their hands were bound behind their backs.

They walked down the main corridor toward the flight deck when a man appeared at the end of the bulkhead. He wore a blue suit with a rose on the left lapel and a Russian flag pin on the right.

"I am Ambassador Sergio Stanisavovich Rudnisky on mission for Stanislav Anatolyevich Rudnisky. This vessel has diplomatic status and you have unlawfully boarded according to the laws of your nation. You will disembark immediately."

Sergi had two assistants behind him. Both were young, professionally dressed women in skirt suits. They had their hair up and one wore glasses. They looked vaguely familiar to Tyler until he realized they were Natalya and Tasha.

The lead FBI agent and one of the SWAT officers stepped forward. The agent held his hand out and made a "come hither" gesture with his finger.

On the flight deck of Tolkov, Tyler and Archer along with the entire crew sat with their backs against the tower and their hands bound behind them. They watched as two FBI men escorted Sergi toward a Seahawk helicopter. Natalya and Tasha were escorted by two female FBI agents. They had bound their hands in the front.

The helicopter revved its idle engine causing wind to gush across the flight deck. It took off west, toward Camp Ripley, Tyler assumed. The bird became smaller and the sound of its engine died down. The crew looked on with confusion but at least they weren't terrified. Perhaps they did trust him and Archer even though he had not yet given them a reason to.

The lead FBI agent screamed over his phone near another Seahawk. He stuffed his phone in his pocket and walked briskly to the lead tactical officer. As he spoke, the lead tactical officer's face went from professional to shock. The man tried his hardest to hide his expression but Tyler knew he had the FBI right where he wanted them. He glanced at Archer who had a huge grin forming on his face.

The helicopter with Sergi, which was now a dot in the horizon, made an aerial U-turn and grew bigger and bigger. The hum of the engine turned into a thunder. The Seahawk was coming back.

It landed on the flight deck once again sending gushes of wind everywhere. Tyler squinted his eyes and shrugged his head into his shoulders since he had no other way to deflect the wind. The Feds unloaded Sergi, Natalya, and Tasha. They cut their plastic binders and pointed them back to Tolkov's tower. Natalya and Tasha scurried across the flight deck in their heels and stepped through the bulkhead door. Sergi strode by with his hair and suit jacket flapping in the wind. His lapel flower had blown off. As he walked by Tyler he winked and gave him a very dirty smile.

The FBI agent watching over Tyler and his crew spoke into his radio. The man pulled out cutting pliers as did the other agents. They pulled each member of the crew off the ground and snipped their plastic cuffs.

After Tyler's were snipped he felt his wrists, just like the bad guys did in the movies when their cuffs were finally removed at the police station.

The FBI agents collected the plastic binders as if they wanted to leave no trace. They rushed back to the Seahawks and slid the doors closed. The four massive helicopters lifted off. The wind soon died down and the noise from the rotors dissipated. It was quiet again.

"Stations," Archer commanded.

The crew ran back into the tower and scurried up the ladders.

Archer and Tyler watched the black dots disappear into the horizon.

Archer turned to Tyler with a big smile. "Orders, Captain?"

Tyler grinned back at him. "Forward."

CHAPTER TEN

Wall Street stocks tumbled amid news that American assets across Russia had been frozen. Premiere Putin spoke of an international incident involving the aircraft carrier move in Northern Minnesota. Putin claims that American authorities had ignored long established diplomatic protocols by boarding the ship. The FBI has no comment on the incident in question which happened this afternoon, but confirmed that no bureau personnel were currently on the vessel.

Stocks recovered quickly once the Kremlin lifted the freeze only forty-five minutes later—

The television went blank and Tyler turned in his easy chair. Rachel hovered over him and dropped the remote in his lap.

"It's you. That giant ship. This is what you spent everything on."

He stood and retied his robe. "Rachel, this is an investment of the century."

"No it's not, it's a stupid stunt and a waste. And I'm a fool for being married to the man who did it."

"Nobody knows that. Everything is hidden through LLCs and shell corporations. Archer is who they look at." He tried to take her hand.

"Don't touch me. I've spoken to a divorce attorney; I suggest you do the same."

"Rachel, our lives are so boring. This is the most exciting thing I've done—"

"You've done? You've done? Let me tell you about my excitement. I get to make a difference in children's lives. I run a philanthropy group that has touched thousands and you sit in your library and drink and read your stupid books. You were fat, happy and, content and got everything you always wanted. You have your cars, your butler, I give you your privacy when you just disappear on your little camping trips. Everything was perfect. You didn't want anything in this marriage except to pretend that you're still in charge of that stupid company. You let your pride get the better of you and you lampooned me in the process."

"I had to do something," he whispered.

"I will never take Thora from her father but you had better be ready to part with whatever is left in our accounts."

She picked up the remote and clicked the on button and Sue Herera came back on. She set the remote on the end table and walked out of the study.

She was right. Tyler's lot in life was to be a paper husband, a paper father, a paper king. He thought back to when he was Rachel's equal. What the hell had happened since she played that damned role as a save-the-world princess? They were in their thirties for Christ's sake. He thought it so generous of her when she first approached him with the idea. But it wasn't giving, it was giving up.

He turned off CNBC and tossed the remote on the couch. His books were calling.

He sunk into his squishy leather throne in the windowless library and stared at the top shelf of the north wall. He was flying through the last few chapters of the third Aubrey-Maturin book.

The staff had an easy time that week. Mr. Chambers opted to stay at some high rise in the city so Tyler and the staff had the estate to themselves.

Other than Thora's nanny, most of the staff stayed at the manor. He didn't make many demands of them and they seemed to enjoy this. Divorcing parents offer favors and extra treats to their children during the process. Somehow Rachel and Tyler afforded the staff the same conditions. He sprang for pizza and gave them nights off as if he were some sort of emperor giving clemency. He even spotted one of them in regular clothes, a welcomed violation of protocol.

Rogers would stay with him though. It was as if Rogers were his favorite child. What an awful metaphor, Tyler thought. But yes, it was obvious that of the staff of fifteen, fourteen of them would likely go with Rachel and he'd get Rogers. Describing the staff as objects to divvy up was not much of an improvement in the metaphor department.

A knock at the door interrupted Tyler's reading. He affixed the bookmark and balanced the novel on the armrest.

"Yes," he said.

Rogers stepped in. "Sir, there are some guests in the parlor. They have brought alcohol and groceries. They requested that I cook chicken wings. Should I show them in?"

A shock ran up Tyler's spine. How did they know he was home or where he lived? Of course they could find out. That was easy, but why did they come here? He couldn't face them, certainly not after ducking out of the club that night—

"Sir, should I put them in the lounge or will you receive them here?"

"No, yes, just…that will be fine."

"What will be fine, sir?"

"Just let them in here."

"Very well, sir."

Rogers closed the door behind him. Instant panic caused Tyler to leap out of his sofa chair. Why did he say to let them in? Why didn't he just tell Rogers to tell them that he wasn't home?

He grabbed his book and darted up the wrought-iron spiral staircase and inserted it into its place, he turned around and looked at his library scanning it for….he wasn't sure, why on earth did putting a book on a shelf matter at this point?

He scurried down the steps and stopped in the middle of the grand rug. Several exit strategies raced through his mind. The service stairwell, then to his bedroom, down the back stair to the garage, maybe going out the main door of the library but sneak through the kitchen to the garage. Did he tell Rogers to put them in the parlor or the lounge? He couldn't remember.

The service stairwell was foolproof. They wouldn't see him.

He heard a muffled laugh. He recognized David O. Sacks's big laugh. They were in his home. How would he explain his disappearance?

Why would you buy a nuclear-powered aircraft carrier, mate?

Richards's soft accent and perfectly rational question ran through his head.

Elon's dumfounded look flashed through his memory. Richard squinted his eyes. He had big eyes and Tyler's upchucking answer as he licked his greasy fingers caused Richard to squint as if he spoke in Pig Latin. Dave just nodded in confused appeasement.

The shriek of the bench legs scraping against the sawdust-covered floor when he abruptly stood ripped through his mind.

I have a prior engagement.

What an awful response—the excuse of a woman on a boring second date. He might as well tell them he needed to wash his hair.

Clack...clack...clack...clack...high-quality dress shoes against marble. He recognized the cadence as Roger's swagger. They neared his sanctuary.

He had to face them and soon. He knew what they would ask. What's with this crazy aircraft carrier guy and what's he smoking?

It must be another guy with a similar name, what aircraft carrier? No you have me confused with someone else, thanks for stopping by.

He grabbed the service stairwell door. He paused before turning the brass handle.

Death to the Boogie Man. He heard the steins smash together. Richard's hotel in space, Elon's rockets and electric cars, Dave's replicating organs. These were not men who would belittle his ideas. Richard invited him into their world for a reason. They were not his adversaries, they were his friends. They were the only ones who might understand what he was doing.

He let go of the door handle and faced the library entrance.

The doors swung open and Rogers extended his arm and motioned his guests into the library. He took a deep breath and a calm came over him.

Richard, Elon, and Dave swarmed him with their hands out, each wanting to be the first to shake his. They jeered and high-fived a few times. When Tyler detected beer breath he knew everything would be fine.

"Can your lady make these?" Dave asked.

"Sure, what are they?" Tyler said.

"Just wings and hot sauce from some hole in the wall in New

Orleans."

Tyler nodded. "Yeah, I can ask her to do something. She's from Jamaica so she'll probably know wings."

Richard put his arm around Tyler. "So Ty, we were just in the neighborhood and thought we'd swing by. We want to hear about your project. All of us are loyal readers of the Post and want to know what the hell this is," Richard said as he grinned.

"Yeah, kind of left us hanging," Elon said.

"Sure, follow me."

Dave held the bag of groceries out to Rogers. "Pardon me sir, our host Tyler says you have a lovely Jamaican gal who can do justice to wings, could we possibly press her to cook these?"

"We do sir and she will make her best effort to exceed your stereotyped expectations."

"Thanks," Dave said as he handed the bag to Rogers.

They followed Tyler to the corner of the library. Tyler reached for a book—a Vince Flynn from his Mitch Rapp series.

A distinctive click caught everyone's attention and the bookshelf gently fell back. Tyler pushed the shelf revealing a secret, dark passage. The three friends followed Tyler down the skinny hallway.

They entered a room and Tyler hit the lights. It was the same size as the library—two stories tall, no windows, but it had several expansive monitors and a topical map in the middle with little orange bulldozer models and an aircraft carrier.

Several pictures of tractors, carriers, wires, and blueprints of the carrier itself dotted the walls.

"Damn, Tyler, this is like a Bond villain layer," Dave said.

"Yes, very cool Ty, very cool," Elon said.

"Thank you." Tyler let his eyes wander around the room. "I never thought of myself as a Bond villain, but thank you."

"Tell us what this is," Richard said.

Elon set the beer on the end table.

"There's a fridge there." Tyler motioned to the wood panel on the wall.

Tyler walked over and opened the panel revealing the mini fridge. They loaded the beers and popped open four longnecks.

"So how long before you're at your destination?" Richard asked.

"Eleven days give or take."

"How fast does that thing go?" Elon asked.

"About six inches a second, roughly one third a mile per hour overall."

"A third, you mean like—"

"Point three miles per hour."

"Yeah that's slow, about how fast my mom walks," Dave said.

"That's right, about walking speed," Tyler said.

"What are the logs made of?" Elon asked.

"And it's all cables?" Dave said.

"Have a seat, I'll show you."

The three crashed on the leather sofa.

"So…" Tyler grabbed a remote control off the sprawling topical map and pressed a few buttons. Three screens came down from the ceiling and came to life. "…the ship itself is a Kuznetsov class carrier, looks kind of like ours only a bit smaller. It's sixty thousand tons but we managed to strip it down to fifty. USS Reagan is around seventy thousand just for comparison. Her name is the Tolkov but we're renaming her Wawasayg when we get to our destination"

"Wawasayg?" Dave said.

"Wawasayg, very good. Minnetrista for northern lights. Fifty thousand tons and we're hauling it with a bunch of tractors rigged to a block-and-tackle mechanism." He clicked the remote and the monitor displayed the crane lifting the giant pulley rig to the bow of the ship.

The three peered over the map from the couch as they drank their beer.

"The lines are wrapped through in a threefold purchase with disadvantage style giving a roughly six-to-one advantage. Come look." Tyler motioned them to get up and go over to the model of a block and tackle. He walked to the couch briskly. "Up!" he exclaimed.

"Okay, big Ty, okay!" they said.

They followed him to the other side of the map and he handed Dave a brass weight.

"Yeah, heavy," he said.

"Three pounds, now let's hook it up." Tyler hooked the cylinder-shaped weight to a paracord rope strung through a series of pulleys on a metal frame. He pulled the rope tight and handed it to Dave. "Go ahead, lift."

Dave pulled it tight with one hand while he held his beer with the other. "Yeah, easy-peasy."

"Exactly," Tyler said as he grabbed a hanging scale off the table. It had two clasps on each end and a digital readout. He hooked the clasp to the paracord and handed the device to Richard. Richard put his forefinger through the clasp at the top and pulled, lifting the three-pound brass weight. As Richard lifted, the scale readout bounced between .47 and .61 and eventually settled on .53 pounds.

"So six times the length is how far the tractors have to move in relation to the boat?" Richard asked.

"Correct."

"So it's like they're hauling eight thousand tons instead of fifty?" Elon calculated in his head.

Tyler erased a whiteboard and wrote out a formula and filled in numbers as he spoke.

"In theory it's a seven-to-one gain but you have to factor out around 10% for each purchase, a purchase is what they call it every time the rope goes through a pulley, six loop de loops so this is a three purchase pulley system with disadvantage; disadvantage and advantage refer to which way you pull; pulling away requires a seventh loop de loop with no power advantage, just more friction so it's called *with disadvantage*."

Tyler managed to fill the entire whiteboard with red marker during his short description of block-and-tackle friction calculations causing Dave, Richard, and Elon's mouths to lull open.

"Over here now!" Tyler ushered his guests with mild forcefulness back to the map. "Each little orange dozer represents a team of five tethered to one of twenty main lines to the block-and-tackle system. So a hundred tractors pulling twenty cables." He picked up a model tractor. "Caterpillar, model D11. Weighs about a hundred tons and can pull around fifty."

Tyler turned on the second monitor and it displayed the diagnostics screen of each tractor team from the feed aboard Tolkov. "So twenty lines, each with tension data from the diagnostics devices on the tractors and the lines themselves. See that team six on the right? It's dark orange because we've been having problems with that one since yesterday. They're still moving but they're going to replace the line they think—"

"Wait, is that live?" Richard asked.

"Yup, I have live feeds on everything." Tyler tapped a few more buttons and the other screens lit up with live footage, most of it with a heavy shade of green since the cameras utilized the night vision feature. "Let's see, bow, stern, aft, port, tractor team one, team two, logs—"

"Yeah, wait, go back to the logs," Elon exclaimed as he pointed.

Tyler flipped back to the screen showing the sides of the logs. The three friends moved closer to the monitor and watched with unflinching fascination as the sides of the logs rotated at a snail's pace.

Dave felt a jab in his back. He turned from the monitor and Tyler held a tube about eight feet long and a foot thick. Dave planted himself on the couch and inspected the big brown log in his lap.

"Just what it looks like, it's a big inflatable tube. The real ones are two hundred eighty feet wide and forty-eight feet tall and we got thirty of them. They aren't just empty on the inside, it's an array of chambers, and each one has a pump and diagnostic devices throughout to monitor the pressure."

"And they won't pop?"

"My buddy from DuPont helped our engineer design it. It's made of next-generation Kevlar. Look!" Tyler pulled a gravity knife out of his pocket and flipped it open. He turned the knife down and stabbed the log in Dave's lap in a murderous fashion. The blade bounced up and down off the surface as Dave sat petrified hoping his genitals would endure the evening.

When he stopped, Dave placed the log on Elon's lap.

"And even if tiny cracks form, the inflators will adjust and maintain the pressure levels. It's actually expected that small fractures will occur and that certain terrain and conditions will require some air to be let out. The inflators cover that."

The four stepped over to a buffet table in the corner with a model of an aircraft carrier about four feet long. It rested atop several scale model logs, each about the size of a rolling pin.

"As the boat is pulled and the log is free at the back of the ship, they are grabbed by a vehicle that hauls them to the front to be used again."

Tyler picked up an army vehicle that had ten oversized wheels and handed it to Richard. "That's an LVSR transport. It can haul twenty tons through mud and dirt at sixty miles per hour, monster of a workhorse.

That's kind of overbuilt for our purpose since the logs only weigh a couple tons each. We've got three of them hauling the logs from the back of the ship to the front constantly."

Tyler clicked on the remote and the center screen showed the starboard of the ship from above as a ten-wheeled vehicle sped along the side hauling a log. It resembled an ant dragging a twig ten times its size.

Dave experimented with the block and tackle, pulling the string in and out and lifting the weight up and down. "Tyler. Don't you need to tie the strings to something other than the boat or the tractors? Like a stationary object or something."

"Correct." Tyler pressed the remote and another NV green image glowed on the screen. The angled obelisk jetted out of the ground with a cluster of wires attached to the top. "We call this the spike team. They bury a giant spike into the ground every five miles. The spike is about a hundred feet long and ten feet in diameter. It's made of several layers of steel tacked to each other. Like a bundle of arrows tied together, it's actually designed to bend a little but not break…" Tyler turned to the three men. "…hopefully, that is."

"A tunnel-boring machine makes a ten-and-a-half-foot-wide hole in the rock. We found a couple of spots where the bedrock is either close to the surface or exposed. That's where we put the various spike points, every five miles or so. We have two spike teams, so when one is installed they start drilling the next. When the carrier gets close to the spike, it's pulled out and the cables are reconnected to the next spike five miles farther. The old spike is hauled ten miles ahead for the next spot and so on."

He pressed the remote again and the footage of the boring machine displayed along with a 3D map of the device's progress. The device had burrowed a third of the way through its bedrock road trip.

"The tunnels are near completion, the bore has been used 24/7 and is ready to hunch over and die."

The three were quiet, holding their beers, not quite willing to take a drink as it may ruin their fierce concentration on the volume of information Tyler unloaded on them.

Rogers knocked and entered from the bookshelf. "Sir, will you take the wings in here or shall we place them in the library?"

"In here, please."

Rogers stepped in and held the shelf door open. Three cooks walked in carrying silver catering dishes and a serving cart. They placed the cart near the carrier model, set plates, and laid out three different kinds of wings.

"Gentlemen we have a Jamaican jerk which Mr. Branson was gracious enough to provide the base for. We also have barbequed with a homemade sauce in the traditional Tennessee style provided by Mr. Musk. And lastly a Creole-based sauce called 'brown woman coochie' provided by the gentleman to my left who's name I'm afraid I did not catch…"

"David, David Sacks"

"…yes, provided by Mr. Sacks. There are hot towels and napkins for your conveniences. Will there by anything else Mister Chambers?"

"No Rogers, thank you."

Rogers walked out and closed the shelf door behind him.

Tyler loaded his plate with each kind of wing. "Thanks for bringing these, guys," he said as he sunk his teeth into a barbeque sauce-drenched drummy.

The four crashed on the couch with plates in their laps and chowed into the greasy delicacies.

They feasted away in silence demonstrating the universal trait among men that great food usually silenced conversation lest it distracted from the experience.

Dave balanced his beer bottle in both palms of his hands since they were the only part not covered in sauce and grease. He raised the bottle and emptied its contents.

Richard emptied his bones into the garbage and wiped his hands with a warm, wet towel. He ripped a paper towel from the roll and blew his nose in a vast honk since the hot sauce caused his nasal juices to flow. He tossed it into the garbage and dove into the buffet table for round two.

Elon had finished his plate and set it on the end table next to the couch. He wiped his hands and walked over to the topographical map and looked over the layout of Northern Minnesota.

"Tyler," he said. "How you going to get over this river?"

Tyler set his wing down and wiped his fingers. "I'm going to redirect it."

"You can do that?"

Tyler pointed to the Talmadge River with a croupier rake. “Sure. We just dig a new path about a mile west, turn north, then back east to upstream of the original river. The water is redirected in a loop and we bury the section we need to cross. Once we cross it, the closed section is reopened and the redirected part is reburied. Hopefully in time for when the tractors get to that point, we don’t want to delay the boat for un-redirecting rivers.”

“And everybody from the harbor to the reservation are okay with you doing this across their land?”

“Sure, we have permission from everyone. It’s a mix of private land, state land, and some municipal land. We can use right-of-way easement laws my real estate lawyers tell me if we need to but nobody has raised a fuss. It’s kind of poor up there so everyone is happy with the rental money. And we have a team of developers following the ship and repairing any damage the beast does to the landscape. We’ve replanted quite a few trees and repaved roads that were roughed up.”

The three nodded in agreement as though the subject was second nature to them.

“Tyler, I thought I heard on the news that you were arrested,” Elon asked.

“No, just detained.”

He recounted the FBI raiding the ship and their prompt departure and the sexy outfits Sergi’s assistants were wearing at the time.

“So Putin did what you said?” Elon asked.

“Well, it wasn’t that easy but the Russian government owed Sergi’s father a favor, and he said Putin enjoyed defying the US government.”

“I suppose and they can’t touch you even on American soil?”

“Well, sort of. A portage of a maritime craft, that’s when you move a boat over land, is covered by maritime law, but it has to be seaworthy at all times. That’s why we can’t just rip the power plant out and move it on its own, and why we can’t strip everything from the ship, I mean we stripped about ten thousand tons of equipment that weren’t required to meet the minimum requirements of seaworthiness under international law, but it still leaves us with a buttload of weight to haul.”

“Couldn’t you just put the power plant into a schooner and haul that?”

“No, then it would be cargo instead of a fixture of the ship, so a whole different set of laws."

"And why is this Sergi involved?"

"As an insurance policy in case the portage claim didn't work, we have Sergi on board claiming the ship as a diplomatic vessel. Under international law, they can't stop a diplomatic ship passing from nation to nation unless there's extreme circumstances. And the reservation is considered a sovereign nation."

"Wow, you thought of everything," Richard said.

"Our goal is just to make like crazy for the destination before the government can figure out a way to stop us. That's why we're a 24/7 operation. The government wants a lengthy court case about portage law, but Sergi is helping us avoid that."

"You're like Smokey and the Bandit!" Dave said.

"I suppose so."

"You're Burt Reynolds!" Richard yelled.

"Actually I'm more the beer truck. My lawyers are the Burt Reynolds, distracting the sheriff so I can sneak over the border."

Richard stepped over. "Tyler I nearly died in the Atlas Mountains twice, I'm the first person in the world to make love in space, but I must say this is the craziest thing I've ever heard of."

"Thanks." Tyler smiled.

"Ty man, can I ask you something?" Dave asked.

"Sure."

"Do you got any really good booze? Some Remy or Blue or something?"

"I've got a Dalmore 50 year."

"You mind if we break it out?"

The staff had cleared the bones and dead soldiers from the Bond villain lair. Rogers laid a silver platter with four crystal mini snifters on the buffet table. He laid out a bucket of ice with tongs and a pitcher of water and uncorked the bottle. He gently poured The Dalmore 50 into the four snifters and handed each of the men a glass.

"I will leave the bottle, sir. Will there be anything else?"

"Thank you, Rogers," Tyler said.

Richard raised the glass in the air. "To my mate Tyler, may you never lose your edge and always defeat the boogie man."

"To Tyler," Dave and Elon exclaimed.

The four lifted their glasses and emptied the $20,000 bottle of spirit down their throats, celebrating their friendship. Tyler promised himself he'd never feel embarrassed or ashamed around these gentlemen again.

CHAPTER ELEVEN

The president stepped to the podium with the plaque of The Great Seal displayed below. The flicker of the lenses and flashes illuminated him.

He raised his hand letting reporters know it was time for him to speak and that the flashes had better die down.

"Ladies and gentlemen, today I dismissed a gentleman I've known a long time. Mister Rutledge is no longer part of the NRC. That's the Nuclear Regulatory Commission. The recent activity regarding this ship and the NRC's response has not been up to par for what I expect from my cabinet. I feel very badly for Rutledge, I feel badly for him. He's an accomplished man and a good family man and has done a lot for energy in our country, a lot, but someone decided to play a joke on him. They ruined his career over a prank. He's a man with a sense of humor and you people in the media destroyed him by overblowing this whole thing. I will say this, Obama sometimes took things in a light-hearted manner and the jackals in the media never pounced on him like you people did this week. It is very sad what our media has become. Very sad. And what you people have become."

"Mr. President," a woman yelled. "Is it true that there's a Russian connection to yourself, Mr. Rutledge, and this aircraft carrier?"

"They have not provided one scintilla of evidence, not one scintilla, that we had any connection to any Russians for the freezing of American assets or this whole fiasco. Thank you very much."

The president turned his shoulder and gave a thumbs-up solute as he walked off the podium. The flashes bombarded him as he disappeared from the stage.

Men in suits walked across the hotel lobby to the conference room as dings from slot machines buzzed in the distance. Tyler recognized a few of the faces from the White House press conference. They were from the government. They were the men who would have Tyler's head on a lance in the town square. Or maybe the middle of the reflection pool just down from the Washington Monument. A reminder for those who defied the government. Tyler grinned at the spectacle of such an image.

His phone rang and he glanced at the caller ID.

"Yes, Gina."

Gina's news caused Tyler to leap from the lobby sofa. He paused before giving her his response, lest she read his panic. "I will contact the bank and get to the bottom of this. No I'm sure it's a mistake. I will take care of it and let you know when you can reinitiate the wires."

Tyler hung up his phone and checked his email. There were six alerts from Rockland County Trust. All six of his wires had been rejected. Two land owners a few miles outside the reservation, Yellowfeather's money, crew payroll, and Sergi's money. A panic shot up his spine. How did the government do it? He had most of his money in a Swiss bank account. His lawyers and bankers assured him that the legend was real and not just a Hollywood thing. His operating account was in New York, they had access to that but how did they get by Rockland Country Trust? They would have surely contacted him if they had received a court order to freeze the account.

Thomas walked over to Tyler and shook his hand.

"Are you ready, Tyler?" He cocked his head and glanced at him. "Are you okay?"

"They froze the accounts. Can they do that?"

Thomas winced his eyes as he pondered Tyler's question. "That's odd. That's something they'd likely do after this meeting, not before."

"What do we do?"

"Nothing now. If they bring it up, we shrug it off. You still have access to your accounts in Zurich?"

"I don't know, I just found out about it."

"Don't sweat it for now."

Tyler regarded the Indian art. A headdress made from old leather and feathers was stretched flat behind glass. A painting of a totem pole with grotesque animals hung behind the government attorneys. Tyler's five attorneys flanked him—a tribal affairs lawyer, a maritime lawyer, an attorney specializing in nuclear power plant litigation, immigration attorney with a concentration in immunity cases, and Thomas Killian, lead council. He resisted the temptation to cost the meeting out in his head.

Three NRC attorneys and the new head of the department regarded his legal team from across the table. He was unsure of which were which since they wore matching suits and displayed the same calm demeanor.

"We intend on halting this project. The US government does not look fondly on those who flaunt our laws as your client has," Norring said as he shot a sour glance toward Tyler.

Tyler had attended plenty of meetings with lawyers representing him. He knew to sit tall and not say anything and never display emotion. Resist the temptation to jump in even when the opposing party makes it personal. Lawyers were about winning, not saving face. That old saying that everyone hates lawyers until they needed one.

"My client has broken no laws. You on the other hand boarded a diplomatic vessel," Thomas said.

"Which we vacated as soon as…" Norring shook his head. He already slipped into a trap, practically admitting the government broke the law. "It's not a diplomatic vessel!"

"Your government thought so when the error of its ways were pointed out by Putin."

"You held billions in assets hostage in Russia. The government's withdrawal was purely an economic consideration. Your client colluded with Russia. We know that for a fact."

"We can't speak to that."

"Our attorneys are filing suit as we speak. Dragging a ship across land is not a legitimate mode of transportation."

"Yes it is. It's called portage. Ships sometimes have to travel across isthmuses and there's a whole set of maritime laws which we've abided by."

"The ship must be fully seaworthy—"

"Which it is."

"The Nuclear Regulatory Commission requires power plants—"

"Again, not a nuclear reactor. It's a Russian sea vessel, it doesn't fall under NRC's jurisdiction."

"Not for long, when you get to your destination the ship is no longer in transit and loses its diplomatic status."

"True, but we'll be on the reservation which is sovereign land. The NRC doesn't have jurisdiction over Indian territories either."

$500 an hour for Thomas, $600 for the tribal attorney, $650 for maritime, $700 for atomic energy…funny how the lead general council charged the lowest but the more specialized the attorney, the more astronomical the rate. The length of the meeting times each rate and add the totals…or just add the rates together and multiply by the length of the meeting, yes that was easiest. But no, Tyler wouldn't do that math in his head.

Norring sighed and glanced down at the table surface causing a touch of discomfort in the room. He had the appearance of a typical bureaucrat. He wore a plain suit, spoke softly, and displayed a mild manner…and he had just the slightest of receding hairlines. He reminded Tyler of the men at Rachel's soirees who blended with the decor while their wives were the hit of the party. Tyler recognized him from the press conference on CNN where his boss had resigned. Norring lingered at the periphery of the monitor, sometimes in the shot, sometimes hovering half in and half out on the edge of the screen as Rutledge spoke about his abrupt departure.

Norring finally looked back up. "We ask that you do the right thing and turn—"

"You will turn around and bring the ship back to Russia." The voice filled every corner of the room causing Tyler and his attorney to affix their attention to the corner.

Rutledge was a stocky man with the face of a bulldog. His eyes were daggers as he spoke. He didn't speak with a submissive bureaucrat's tone like his protégé. His words carried a lead weight.

"I don't think you are in the position to demand anything," Thomas said to Rutledge.

Rutledge's eyes were still fixated on Tyler. Tyler knew the man would never forget The Onion article and the memo he issued. Men like Rutledge didn't appreciate being made a fool of…twice.

Tyler focused his attention back to Norring but let out the slightest of smug grins at that goofy memo the NRC issued in response to his Onion article.

Norring attempted to speak again. "The way we see it—"

"Aren't we? You really don't think there's a thing I can do?" Rutledge barked reminding everyone that he still occupied in the room. "We will commandeer the boat and drag it back to the Great Lakes and send it back to Russia."

"Why is he even at this meeting? My understanding is that the president dismissed him," Thomas demanded of Norring.

"He's serving in a consulting capacity—"

"We're going to arrest you after the ship is commandeered if you don't turn it around and send it back to Russia," Rutledge barked again.

"Is that so?" Thomas said as he shot his attention to the corner. "Let me explain something to you Mr. Rutledge. As soon as you remove my client and his Russian guest from the boat, it is no longer a diplomatic vessel. Instead it's a huge hulking piece of scrap with a nuclear plant on American soil. Only then will it fall under the NRC's rules regarding radioactive devices. You will have to go through a regular decommission costing your department hundreds of millions."

Norring tried to speak again. "Would you be willing—"

"We're through here." Rutledge stormed out. There was a feeling on the other side of the table as though his underlings had better do the same.

Norring buttoned his suit and followed Rutledge out along with the rest of the NRC's attorneys.

"Well Tyler, not the first time I ruffled a few feathers," Thomas said.

"You still think we're on solid ground, legally?"

"The Feds think we are otherwise they would have arrested you by now."

"And the frozen account?"

"Odd that they didn't mention it. You sure you it's frozen?"

"I need to contact my man in Zurich."

“Nothing says you can’t pay people out of that account. The Feds have no hand over there.”

“I know, just saves on wire fees to do it from the States and transfer over what we need each day.”

They opened the conference room door and the pings and buzzes from the casino bombarded their senses.

“Are you heading back to the ship?” Thomas asked.

“I need to meet with another attorney in New York.”

“I wasn’t aware. Tyler, I’d prefer if you’d meet directly with me and allow myself to manage our legal team. May I ask who you’re you meeting with?”

“Martin Sonnenfeld.”

“Oh, Martin. Great litigator. How’s he going to help with our case, I thought he practiced divorce law?”

Tyler gave a crooked glanced to Thomas.

“Oh,” Thomas said with a gentleman’s embarrassment. “I guess that would fall outside of my team’s jurisdiction. Sorry to hear that, Tyler.”

Tyler scrolled through his phone as he read the updates on Tolkov that Archer logged as Sonnenfeld rambled on about New York State marriage law. Martin Sonnenfeld was the best divorce attorney in Manhattan implying that Rachel’s was number two.

“So we’re on solid ground?” Tyler said as he shoved his phone in his pocket.

“I think we are.”

A man in a hotel uniform approached Tyler and his attorney. “Sir, the conference room is ready, you may go in at any time.” The concierge turned and shuffled up the marble stairs to the front desk.

A gentleman in the main entryway of the Four Seasons spotted Tyler and Sonnenfeld and walked over.

“Martin,” he greeted and gave a gentleman’s bow.

“Barry. Where are we meeting?”

“We’re in the Sutton Room.” Sonnenfeld motioned down the grand entryway.

A blur of fire-engine red swept by the three men. The carpeting muffled her angry heels otherwise they surely would have made a ruckus. Rachel didn’t acknowledge any of them.

In the conference room Rachel and Barry Lazarus teamed on one side with Tyler and Sonnenfeld on the other.

"Mister Chambers failed to meet his fiduciary duty under the basic marriage contract laws of the State of New York. His sale of the company is prima facie evidence."

"The Chambers made their financial decisions together and that's well documented."

"Not this one."

"We can show they cosigned on mortgages and capital restructures. It goes to show that they spoke of this arrangement."

"Consent by osmosis, Martin? A judge is going to want to see a piece of paper with both their signatures, not an alleged handshake over breakfast."

Tyler tapped the various apps that showed him the diagnostic information. Logs eight and twelve were showing some slight overinflating but the relief valves compensated for the excess pressure. The line of tractor group four glowed a sharp green due to underutilization. Was the team lead taking a nap? Tyler switched to his Twitter account to see what his nuclear follows were trending.

Lazarus leaned forward and tapped his finger on the table. "Your evidence of two signatures on material financial decisions actually works against you. This shows that the couple cosigned for major financial decisions and the reason there isn't paperwork for this one is because it wasn't mutual."

"There's also the issue of spousal neglect—"

"Oh come on Martin you're kidding me."

"Mrs. Chambers was emotionally nonexistent in this marriage. We have several of the help staff—"

"That's rich, of course they'll say negative things about the person they worked for. Mr. Chambers was friendly with the staff and she was the iron fist that motivated them to do their jobs. A common situation. Means nothing."

Tyler followed Michael Douglas. Mr. Douglas had several negative Tweets about nuclear power and had jumped on the anti-nuclear bandwagon since he made that movie back in the '70s about a meltdown. Tyler was tempted to respond with scientific evidence to Douglas's chicken little Tweets but resisted since he loved The West Wing and

Wall Street.

"Just for my memoirs, what did you have in mind for a settlement?" Sonnenfeld asked.

"Everything my client is entitled to, half plus fees," Lazarus said.

"My client built the company from scratch."

"No he didn't, Mrs. Chambers did. We can provide boxes and boxes of data showing her involvement. Her signature is on pizza delivery receipts from ten years ago when they opened their first office. It's on the lease. She signed the rep letters for the financial statement audits. She prepared press releases. There's that picture of her ringing the bell on the NYSE when they went public. Implying she's a trophy wife when she accomplished the legwork is incredibly disingenuous."

Tyler tucked his phone into his pocket, satisfied that Archer had everything well in hand. He noticed that Rachel's eyes were fixated on him and angry. Her arms weren't folded but they might as well be.

Lazarus pushed a thick binding of papers to Sonnenfeld. "This is our settlement offer. I'll let you comb over the fine print but it's five hundred million."

"Five hundred million? That's more than half," Sonnenfeld said.

"The stock plummeted due to Mr. Chambers's dumping activities bringing the proceeds down to six hundred fifty million. But that's not our denominator, we're starting the clock at a billion which was the net worth before Mr. Chambers's transgression."

"But where do you think my client has this money? It's all been committed." Sonnenfeld tossed his hands in the air.

"Committed where?"

"He paid cash for the boat. Any construction such as rerouting roads, or rerouting rivers, replanting trees, the rental of the tractors, the rigging units, those inflatable logs, the engineers, the land rights..." Sonnenfeld counted the points on his fingers. "All of that's been paid for up front. There's very little uncommitted funding left."

Rachel's attorney made an obvious and unprofessional transgression. His eyebrows went to the top of his head as he realized that his fee might be in jeopardy and Rachel wasn't the whale he thought her to be.

After the shock set in, his eyebrows returned to their normal place. "We could issue an injunction on this project and stop everything."

"The most you could do is freeze his bank account. The ship itself is under the jurisdiction of Russian law since it has diplomatic status. New York divorce courts can't touch anything."

"Then Mr. Chambers will consent to closing the project down and reselling the ship."

"The thing about the ship is it isn't worth anything on the open market. It's worth a dollar."

"A dollar?"

"Yes, if you bought the ship for scrap or to use in your navy, you'd have to decommission the nuclear plant first. The moment the Russian government decides to abandon the ship it becomes a giant hunk of metal on US soil. That means it becomes the Atomic Energy Commission's problem. And my understanding is that they don't mind taking years to go through this process."

Rachel had not yet torn her stare from Tyler. He allowed just the tiniest grin to escape before she stormed out of the conference room.

Goodness, Tyler had earned that. He had so earned that. Maybe he didn't deserve it but he had earned it.

Sonnenfeld stood. "Sorry Barry, you had a solid case going into this thing. Sometimes collections is the kicker."

The two lawyers shook a professionally awkward handshake which left Lazarus with a sour look on his face. Tyler knew that opposing attorneys were civil toward each other and sometimes even good friends but Lazarus's and Sonnenfeld's rapport alluded that a round of racquetball was not in their immediate future.

Lazarus scurried out of the room and through the lobby to catch up with Rachel.

Sonnenfeld tucked the settlement offer under his arm.

"What are you going to do with that?" Tyler asked.

"Shredder."

CHAPTER TWELVE

Tyler and Rogers raced down the West Side Highway in the Hyundai Equus. Tyler was one of the few people who bought the Equus. The base price of the luxury Hyundai hovered around $61,500. It had every luxury that the Mercedes S-Class had from leather, to a fold-out tray, to a rear reclining seat. Hyundai designed it for a man who would sit in back and allow his driver to usher him to work every morning.

He purchased the Hyundai out of appreciation of their marketing strategy. Victoria's Secret had a million-dollar bra that nobody would ever buy, steakhouses had the old 48-ouncer, free if you finish it, but rarely purchased, and Hyundai had their Equus. Marketers called it the halo effect, a flagship product that raised the bar of the other products in the minds of the consumers.

Hyundai needed to lift their image if the Sonata was to compete with the Corolla and the Camry and Tyler felt good for doing his part to help the ambitious South Koreans.

An evening at the theater with Rachel necessitated the stretch, a brassy boardroom meeting with vendors, the Caddy SUV with the flat-panel TV and mini-fridge, and when haste was a must, the zippy Hyundai sedan with no more room than necessary.

They crossed the Central Park Transverse and south to a liquor store near Grand Central.

Rogers dropped Tyler off at the corner of 40th Street and Madison, outside Park Avenue Liquors, a store renowned for its single malt collection. Although Rogers was an older gentleman and one could even describe him as elderly, he knew how to perform a bank heist drop-off and pick-up. Rogers attached his phone to the dash with alerts on full, ready to receive instruction from Master Tyler. He would circle the block as Tyler ran in.

Tyler leaned over the counter to the manager. "Can you recommend a single malt in the three grand range and I'm in a hurry."

He stepped out to Madison and scanned down the avenue. The Hyundai darted out of a parking spot and pulled to the curb.

He jumped in and placed the cedar collector's box next to the bottle of Minnesota Vodka. Goodness, what was he thinking buying that thing? When dealing with someone foreign it's a common practice to give a gift from one's home country as appreciation. Tyler followed this protocol by purchasing a Minnesota-made organic potato vodka. It cost twenty-one dollars.

Giving a Russian a potato vodka that was made in the northern plains of the Midwest was akin to giving a Floridian a basket of Idaho Oranges.

Morning joggers circled the reservoir as they drove across 91st Street. They turned onto Madison.

The Consulate-General of the Russian Federation occupied a four-story building that resembled many Madison Avenue buildings with their French-inspired façades. A modest red, white, and blue Russian flag was the sole indicator of the building's occupant.

Two brawny men in suits guarded the entryway as Tyler walked to the reception desk.

"May I help you," she said in a Russian accent that tried it's hardest to be welcoming.

"Tyler Chambers for Andre Luskutin."

"I will call him."

"Mr. Chambers!" A big voice came from the anterior room.

"Andre Igorevich, it's good to see you again." Tyler extended his hand.

"Oh very good, you have our surnames down. I appreciate your knowledge of the goofy patronymics that make our literature confusing for college students."

"Yes, I remember Brothers Karamazoz in college. I hope Ralph Waldo Emerson caused equal confusion among MEPhi students."

The big Russian laughed a good belly laugh and ushered Tyler to the anterior room.

Tyler handed Andre the cedar box containing the 40-year-old scotch. "Ah wonderful, I thank you for this Tyler, it will have a good home."

The armrests of the chairs had antique-style wear. A Persian rug covered the hardwood floors. The room showed off creamy brown décor alluding to old Russian nobility.

"Thank you for everything. I hope none of this caused a disturbance for the Premiere."

"Oh goodness my boy, it certainly did, but Premiere loved every minute. He enjoyed putting your president in his place. He and Ambassador Rudnisky watched the Wall Street plunge and everyone jumping around. They crucified Mr. Trump. He loved it."

"Oh that's good, it delayed our operation by about an hour, so not too bad."

"One hour, Tolkov now stranded somewhere in heartland. Heartland, that is right?"

"Yes, we are the heartland, wheat and grain. Not stranded, still crawling along. I must ask a question, Ambassador. If there is another incident with the US government, can we count on the Premiere's help again?"

"Absolutely."

"He doesn't mind sticking it to our president?"

"Eh not your president so much, he gets along great with The Don. It's your government he hates. Remember Premiere Putin worked for KGB and did battle with CIA and FBI back in the day. We're officially friends now, but he still loves to muss the feathers of the bald eagle. Is everything okay in your boat movement?"

"They've been quiet the last few days since The Russian Federation froze the assets. I think they have something up their sleeve."

"Your government is extremely sharp. They will stop at nothing. Premiere remembers cat-and-mouse games well. He's no friend of the Federals in your government."

"Sergio's been invaluable. When you see his father please give him my gratitude for his help."

"I will. The world would be a younger place if there were more Americans like you, my friend."

Tyler stepped out of the car on Third Avenue and 52nd Street, a straight shot down toward Midtown from the quietness of the Upper East Side.

He walked into a plain office building with a modest entrance and a sparse lobby. He stepped off the elevator on twenty and walked into the reception. Snakes, nebulas, aliens, the Amazon, and sharks greeted him—sharks everywhere, life-sized sculptures, posters, and even a hologram splashed across the waiting area and a great white jetting toward the entrance designed to scare any visitors.

Tyler asked the receptionist for Marylyn Lopisky.

Marylyn came out and shook Tyler's hand, she ushered him back to her office.

She had a swift stride as she showed him to her office. She understood the concept of rushing for a client.

"They upload footage constantly to the cloud. The editors are working round the clock and we've had close to a final version ready to go for some time. Just tweaking here and there."

"Will it be ready for tomorrow night?"

"Absolutely."

"Can I see it quick?"

Tyler crossed his arms as he watched B-roll of Natalya and Tasha walking around in their bikinis and lounging in the hot tub next to Sergi.

"You're leading with this? This isn't what we talked about. This isn't the Playboy Channel."

"I understand that, Tyler."

"You'll change this?"

"Well can I explain first?"

"Explain? Explain how you're changing everything we talked about and why I'm paying you?"

"Can I just walk you through it?"

"Yes walk me though this sex romp, I want to hear it." Tyler chuckled.

"We can garner a huge audience if we toss a bit of racy into the mix. The girls provide that."

"I get it that sex sells but why am I here, this is Discovery. I could have gone anywhere else, I came here for a reason. I'm here to promote science, not sex—"

"Okay, okay, let me explain this. We have something called the forty-five mark."

"Forty-five?"

"Yes, forty-five seconds is the magic metric so to speak. If we can hold viewers to the forty-five mark, they'll watch some or most of the episode, anything before that and they switch channels, or click on a different video feed."

"Forty-five, well, I can buy that. You interviewed Jack Archer right?"

"Of course, he's intercut throughout the piece. I still think we should have interviewed you."

"Nope, not me. Archer is the face of the operation. Does the footage mention me at all?"

"I was just joking, Tyler. No mention of you or the company. We'll just mention a group of investors from New Jersey. So boring that nobody will care about anything beyond that."

"Good."

"I think this is exciting that you are doing this. Why wouldn't you want credit?"

"I just don't want my face all over the TV. I'm fine with Archer stealing the credit."

"He's quite dashing for an engineer."

"And you think having the girls in it is a good idea?"

"We need the hook that reels the viewer in past the forty-five mark. We have the shots of the carrier…" Marylyn forwarded the scrollbar on the screen quickly. "…the tractors, the wire lines, and then the girls. The VO, that's the voiceover, talks about science but by the twenty-two second mark he's switched to the girls. Understand, it's only three more seconds of Natalya's bootie but it'll lock the viewer in for the full episode."

"I suppose that'll work."

"That Archer is dashing but not as dashing as that little Russian beauty. Look at that, I wish I had a bikini butt like that. Tyler, we're good at this. I promise we'll get you your audience, but this is the way we need to do it. Sciences never leads, do you know what does?"

"I think the answer is violence."

"It does but shark week is coming up and we're banking our *bleeds it leads* for that."

Rogers parked next to a hydrant and Tyler jumped into the car. They drove by the iconic Flatiron Building; Tyler wasn't sure why such a short stubby triangle-shaped aberration garnered such a distinct title when there were so many more spectacular buildings to cast a title upon.

Rogers drove down 20th Street and pulled up to another plain Midtown building. The ten-story building displayed a green iron façade and housed a branch of the New York Public Library. Tyler retrieved his laptop from the trunk.

The receptionist situated him in a conference room on the eighth floor and plugged him into the flat panel on the wall. Tyler joked with her about manning the front desk but she assured him that a girl in back answered calls if she needed to attend to the organization's guests. Joking with her relaxed him.

He practiced long breaths. There would only be a few of the NRDC elite attending. He managed to get an appointment with the head of the group, the vice president of leadership and development, and their chief public relations officer. He'd present his proposal seated from behind the safety of his laptop monitor. From the far end of the conference room the audience would be staring at the flat panel instead of fixating their eyes on him. There were enough chairs for ten but they told him that he'd only be meeting with three.

Tyler had this.

He had been told that delivering speeches to a large audience was easier than a small one since it was less intimate. He tried not to dwell on this as his heart raced. He focused his attention on the photographs framed on the wall.

Mount Rainier he recognized. The Joshua Tree with sprawling branches extending over rocks alluded to a certain dignity an elder might possess.

Tell a story, a helpful website said when giving a speech. Don't memorize and recite. What did you have for breakfast? How did you meet your significant other? What was the first day of college like for you? Just answer the questions with a story from beginning to end, that's how a speech should be.

They said 3:30 but the clock on Tyler's laptop showed 3:37. The tardiness tortured him. He focused more deeply on the lake with the mountain in the background. It garnered majesty from its simplicity and minimalism. How did they fit an entire mountain in a 36 by 24-inch frame? Surely the first person to see this photograph asked that question.

The buzz of the fluorescent lights grew louder. The air-conditioning kicked in and filled the room with even more humming. The simplicity of Ansel Adams's photography made distraction difficult. They embodied beautiful and lacked the busy-bodiness that other modern art boasted.

The doorknob rattled and Tyler fixed his attention back to his laptop. He stood, ready to shake hands and forget names as soon as they were hurled at him.

A woman walked in and introduced herself as vice chair of the group's legal counsel. "Thank you for taking the time to meet in our office. After careful review of your proposal we are declining an alignment of our two groups."

"Is Jean Macomb here?" Tyler asked.

"I can speak for her. The decision is final."

She shook Tyler's hand, handed him a business card, and walked out. Tyler packed up his laptop and a wave of relief came over him. He didn't have to give a dreaded presentation after all! Of course the meeting was a bit abrupt, wasn't it?

In the reception area he had his laptop bag slung on his shoulder and the receptionist came out.

"Mr. Chambers?"

"Yes."

"How did your meeting go?"

"Good." He smiled as he scanned her voice for sarcasm. But no, her pleasantness shined through.

"She wanted me to give this to you." The receptionist handed him a window envelope.

Tyler opened it and pulled out the document. They made out the $200,000 check to his Rolling Thunder Corporation, the shell that owned the carrier. The memo said 'refund of donation.'

"It was nice meeting you Mr. Chambers."

"It was nice meeting you too." He tried his best to be sincere.

On the elevator down Tyler smelled the check, curious if he could determine if it was printed in the last few minutes while he waited in the conference room or if had been laying on someone's desk for a week indicating they made the decision long ago. The check smelled fresh and crisp. He ran his thumb over the printing to gauge its smudgability. The fresh printing indicated that the NRDC hesitated on their decision to do business with him until the very last minute.

He recalled his days at Fusion where he would go from office to office trying to sell ideas. He was in the way. His execs snickered and laughed at his ideas when he left. They listened because they had to. The NRDC felt parallel to that experience. Of the people he'd met that day, he either paid them or did favors for them. Did any of them understand his mission or did they just smile, nod, and happily accept his money and favors?

He strode by another vast stretch of an Ansel Adams black and white glacier before stepping out to Rogers holding the car door open. He gazed at the Flatiron Building again. Did Ansel ever take pictures of Manhattan buildings?

Tyler and Archer stepped through several bulkheads as they made their way to the bridge.

"So how was New York?" Archer asked.

"Busy times. The Russians are still on our side, the NRDC hates us, but the Discovery documentary will feature lots of scantily clad Russian women."

"Those girls are quite a distraction. Not that I'm complaining."

"I suppose they cut through the bridge to get to the hot tub in the nest."

"Correct." Archer grinned.

"The pool Sergi wanted would have weighed too much so we compromised with a hot tub in the penthouse. The Discovery producer tells me the girls are an important asset for promoting nuclear energy to the world."

"I'm always nervous about interviews. Did I come off as arrogant?"

Tyler stopped at the base of a ladder to the bridge. "Arrogant, no I don't think so."

"They wanted to film more of the hangar area with the nightclub and dancefloor but they didn't have time. They left this afternoon."

"Yeah, they're rushing to get it edited and done for 8PM Eastern Time tomorrow night."

"That is pretty quick."

"So you said the ship hasn't stopped moving because of these protestors."

"That's right, still on schedule."

Tyler and Archer climbed the ladder to the bridge. The crew were glued to the main monitor as the night vision filter lit everything in a bright green.

The navigator noticed Archer and Tyler and quickly briefed them. "Three arrests. They snuck past the security perimeter by wearing body suits that masked their heat signature. We didn't expect something so elaborate."

The engineers were cutting the protestors' metal braces from the tractors which sent bright green sparks in every direction.

The navigator switched cameras and showed a closeup of the cutting tools. "We invested in some abrasive saws and circle grinders that cut through anything. A smart move."

"But no time has been lost?" Tyler asked.

"The other tractor teams picked up the slack but we shouldn't run the tractors over their capacity for extended periods of time."

Archer opened his laptop and displayed a map of their path. "Captain, my concern is the state land about three miles ahead. The state troopers can't protect us there since it's public and they can't impede law-abiding citizens—"

"This isn't law abiding," the navigator snapped.

"Just the messenger, Mike," Archer said.

He shook his head and returned to the Nav station.

Archer pulled a map up on his laptop with an orange line diverging from the more direct green one. "We may need to employ one of our alternative routes and navigate around the state land. It adds three days to our journey."

Tyler inspected the alternative path on Archer's screen. An array of mathematical equations went through his head. He knew three days would stretch his resources thin. And for each day they delayed, it afforded Rutledge and Norring another day to develop a strategy for stopping him.

"Captain, three days sounds like a long time but on state land we'd be sitting ducks for those protesters. They could easily have ten people chaining themselves to each of the Caterpillars and bring us to a halt. They also might have more sophisticated manacles to attach themselves. The engineers said it was difficult to remove them without injuring the protesters' limbs. These people are nuts."

"We still have the support of state troopers?"

"The payment in full contingent on us getting across each tract of land was a good measure. The landowners are screaming to the state troopers to protect their lease rights so if we go through private land we should be covered."

"But they might try to renegotiate."

"The higher fee is better than full stop. I mean that's your end but a full stop would spell disaster."

"This is why we had Discovery rush the documentary. We need to get the narrative out before these people can mobilize with theirs."

"We're lucky this happened at night where news cameras can't see them. If this happened during the day, the news helicopters would be filming everything."

Tyler's attorneys cost him $80,000 a day and goaded him into a frenzy of expensive safeguards. He was thankful for the lavish alternatives—leasing land around the planned path, added security, diamond-studded grinders...

The night vision cameras showed one of the freed protesters dragged away by state troopers as he thrust his fists high in victory. He thought of that Dalai Lama quote about sleeping in a tent with a mosquito.

Tyler glanced at the TV in the lobby of the Blackhawk Hotel as CNBC blared a story about his boat.

"...we have several courageous individuals who disregarded their own personal safety and expressed their First Amendment Rights toward social disobedience and stopped the ship in its tracks. Everyone should know that you have a voice and if three people can stop a battleship, then

we can work wonders if we band together."

Um, they were resetting the spike so they were stopped anyways, Tyler thought. And it's a carrier not a battleship. The banner across the bottom of the CNN interview identified her as Lotus in quotation marks, which made Tyler shake his head.

"...imagine an explosion that covered the entire Midwest in radioactive waste like Chernobyl has done to Russia..."

Ukraine, Tyler thought.

"...nuclear bombs in our own back yard. Radioactive waste in our rivers for millions of years."

The waste is recycled into new fuel, once that's spent, dry storage casks for 300 years at most. Her statements were so simple to dismantle. The reporter let her off easy.

"...yes, you can donate to Green Earth First or a variety of environmental causes that have teamed with us..."

Wonderful, she mentioned her group's name in. At least the dolt did that right.

The receptionist put her phone down. "Chief can see you now, Mister Chambers."

The leather squeaked and oinked as Tyler sunk into the couch. Native American décor and kitsch decorated the icy office, although it might not be a good idea to call it kitsch.

Robert Yellowfeather walked in from the restroom. He wore a dark suit with a glimmering white shirt and onyx cluster cowboy-style bolo tie. He usually tied his long black hair in a ponytail. He switched his Stetson to his left hand and extended his right to Tyler. He hugged him with the left, patting Tyler on the shoulder with the Stetson.

"Really good to see you, Robert."

"Good to see you big Ty." He tossed his hat on the corner of his desk and flopped into his throne-style chair, the longhorns protruding from the top bobbed back and forth as he sunk and made himself comfortable.

"Tyler, this is quite a pickle. You led me to believe everything would be fine."

"It is, it was. It's just that word's getting out and people are getting squirrely about what we're doing."

"I see."

"Look, I want to alter our agreement."

"Oh." Robert's face winced.

"Not in a Darth Vader sort of way, I want to alter it to your benefit. Land rights, property tax, all that stays of course, but what do you think of this. A physics scholarship for full-blooded Indians. Any institution in the nation or the world as long as they agree to come back to the Minnetrista rez and work for five years at Wawasayg. Tuition coverage vests after five years, twenty percent a year."

"Full-blooded Indians? Do you even know what that is?"

"Of course—people who grew up on a reservation. People like you."

"You think I'm FBI? I've got a wretch of Minnetrista, touch of Ojibwa, smidge of Yiddish, but mostly Dutch-Irish."

"I want to give back to this community and I realize how tough things are for your people."

"My people. Look Tyler my people are happy with the royalty check each month. As long as that check comes, nobody cares about scholarships."

"Nobody wants free college for an engineering degree?"

"No." He chuckled.

"Come on Robert, you're telling me—"

"Look Tyler, those cocksucking Ojibs build casinos, they do commercial fishing and hide behind treaties. The Minnetrista don't do that because they don't have the brains, will, or capital. That also leads to despair, alcoholism, unemployment, blah, blah, blah. You understand these people don't want a job. They want a check and to watch *Price is Right.*"

"*Price is Right*? I thought Bob Barker retired."

"He did, I think he's dead. Drew Carey hosts it now. Tyler, you think Indians are going to run your power plant? That's not going to happen, maybe you'll get a fellow from Minneapolis or Duluth with a touch of

Cherokee in him, but if you want real nuclear engineers, you're going to have to import them. Do you have a crew ready?"

"It's not that easy, we need core technicians, plant operators, neutron diagnostic miners."

"Not too many of those on the rez. You're going to have to fly them in."

"Exactly, that's why I'm going to Geneva tonight for a conference. This year it's located near the Hadron Collider if you know what that is."

"Sounds like a wrestler."

"No, not a wrestler. We're still looking for a head safety engineer. I need a big name since it'll help qualm people's fears. I figure there will be some big names in nuclear at this thing that might listen with the right offer. Hell who am I kidding, when I tell them I'm the guy hauling the aircraft carrier around Minnesota they will turn and run as fast as they can."

"Don't short change yourself. People admire a man with a vision who acts on what he thinks is right."

"I have to figure out how to broach that subject during the networking part of the convention."

"Hey speaking of Drew Carey, he's big in this area. The Ojibs got him to do two shows a year at Mille Lacs Casino. He's over there doing two shows a year while my people are getting drunk off radiator fluid."

"And your people wouldn't want to take a break from radiator fluid to learn physics?"

"No." Robert crossed his arms and Tyler did the same. "I know why you're here Ty, you want to do some good. We always talked about this at Columbia. Someday we'd help minorities starting with the rez. But they don't want that kind of help, it's hopeless."

"There must be something."

Robert stroked his chin and nodded his head. "Can you book Drew Carey to do a show on the carrier? You know, you throw a big party when you get here?"

"For what? It's not a hotel."

"I don't know, he can do his act for five minutes or whatever before the keynote. You're doing a whole kickoff sort of thing I hope. Formal event on the flight deck maybe? I can call his agent and get him for a few grand. Ten thou' or so. Matt Osceola told me that's what they forked out him for."

"They want Drew Carey over scholarships?"

"Hell yeah, if he gave a speech or did his act for the Minnetristas these Ojib elites would go crazy. I mean every Indian on the rez thinks you're a hero for sticking it to the Feds. Every pure-blood Indian hates the US government, but Drew Carey would be the watchman on the top of the totem."

"That would make them happy?"

Robert reached across his desk and placed his hand on Tyler's. "Yes," he said in a most reassuring manner.

Tyler grinned and shook his head.

The phone beeped and Robert hit the speaker button. "Yes?"

"A Miss Lotus is here."

"Send her in."

"Lotus?"

"Yeah, we have a quarterly. She's one of our beneficiaries."

Tyler stared at Robert for a moment. "Of the Green Earth First Group?"

"Yeah, Earth First movement, good people. They put out a good name…wait, how the hell you know her?"

"That's the main group that's been protesting us."

"Ahhh…" Robert put his hands over his head and leaned back in his chair. "Well…*awkward*." He chuckled.

"Her group opposes all of this, you're telling me you're in bed with her?"

"In bed? Well not yet. She teams up with us on federal issues. Her group protests landfill expansion on the reservation and we can leverage a bigger price from the government when we expand it. She's a useful idiot. And she's smokin'. I'm into those granola chicks."

Tyler winced. "That woman has done so much—"

The door flew open and a tall, lean woman walked in. She had long brown hair with a few dreadlocks hanging from the top of her head. She wore camo pants and a brown tank top, or perhaps sleeveless T-shirt, the kind wife-beaters in trailer parks wore as they guzzled cans of Coors.

"Chief Yellowfeather, once again it is an honor to be in your presence." She held Robert's hand, bowed and kissed it. As she did, Robert glanced at Tyler and gave him a pompous grin.

"May I sit?"

"Of course. This is Tyler."

She turned and extended her hand. "My apologies, where are my manners? It's nice to meet you, Tyler."

"Tyler is one of our social workers on the reservation."

She squeezed Tyler's hand just a bit tighter. "Sir, thank you for your service. We appreciate all you do."

Exploding power plants, Chernobyl in Russia, a battleship. "You're welcome," Tyler said as she finally released him from her grip. He gave her a faux smile.

"Chief, our people are in trouble. I know you've heard of this man who's bringing nuclear weapons to the Original Nation Dweller's Territory."

"Oh the aircraft carrier guy?"

"You make him sound harmless but he's no less harmless than Trump or the mad man they have in North Korea who have their fingers on the button. Our system protects men like this but they deserve a public execution."

"Of course, my dear, he is a mad man when you think of it that way."

Tyler rolled his eyes as Robert glanced over Lotus's shoulder to gauge his reaction.

"One nuclear plant alone could explode and make the entire Midwest uninhabitable as it did in Japan. The waste will be poured into our rivers, all for the insatiable appetite for cheap power of the white man."

Tyler used every ounce of resistance to not strangle this woman for no less than three factually inaccurate statements in less than ten seconds.

"We have hundreds of supporters that are recruiting people from around the world, but our efforts are focused in the Twin Cities since there are so many Original Nation Dwellers."

"Excuse me, what is Original Nation Dweller?" Robert asked with a curious look.

"Well Chief Yellowfeather, the word Indian or even the word Native American is something thrust onto ONDs by white men and the establishment. The term Indian is an epitaph to our great nation."

"Our great nation?"

"Yes, ours. I'm one sixty-fourth Ojibwa."

"Oh that's nice. Two percent. I'm glad we're kin."

"When I talk to other ONDs and I come here I feel it. We're connected by a kinship that others can't understand."

Tyler had his arms crossed at this point, staring over Miss Ojibwa's shoulder at Chief Yellowfeather.

"Well that's wonderful Sister Lotus. Splendid. L'chaim."

"L'chaim to you too, Chief."

"Where are you getting these protesters from?"

"We're going to the local tribes in South Minneapolis.'

"Are you getting lots of dirt worshipers to sign up?"

"Ahhh, dirt…"

"Yes, how many dirt worshipers do you have?"

"Um we get signatures and we hand out literature on how to get up here and what to expect…are you sure that term is appropriate?"

"What term?"

"Dirt…worshiper? Isn't that kind of a derogatory phrase?"

"Oh not at all. Original Nation Dwellers is actually kind of passé. It's so 2010."

"Oh, I didn't realize."

"Yeah, you remember back in the '90s when the gay rights movement was up and coming right?"

"I think so."

"Well, people used the word *queer* as an epitaph but gay folks got together and hijacked the word. They called themselves that and made it their own. Once they did that, nobody could use that word against them anymore."

"Dirt Worshiper. Do we really say that?"

"Absolutely. It's the new queer. So make sure to use that when you go into those tribal neighborhoods in South Minneapolis so they know you're one of them."

"Hmmm, I might try that."

"Do you have a tattoo, maybe a feather or a dream catcher? Please say yes."

"How did you know?"

"Let me see."

Lotus turned to Tyler and turned a blush red. She scooted over in the chair as to not offer Tyler a sight other than her back.

She leaned in to Robert and pulled her tank top down.

Robert smiled at Tyler. “That’s a good start Sister Lotus. I’m sure you’ll do well in your recruiting efforts.”

She leaned back in the chair tucking her tattoo back into her bra.

Tyler averted his eyes to the Indian folk art on the wall finally rewarding Robert with a sly grin as he shook his head from side to side.

CHAPTER THIRTEEN

"Droit par là, salle de bal B à la gauche," *Right through there, Ballroom B to the left*, the security guard said in French as he motioned with his arm to the grand concourse.

"Je vous remercie, monsieur," Tyler thanked the guard.

He walked through the crowded grand concourse. A hot-pink Darth Vader towering six and a half feet swayed by him with its fuchsia cape whooshing by his leg. Tyler smiled at Lara Croft. The woman with her twin sidearms pulled the outfit off perfectly, including filling out the tank top. Two burly men dressed in leather with huge ZZ Top beards sauntered past him. Both carried metal cases the size of cigar boxes. A piano from a side salon played the theme from Mario Brothers.

Three more men dressed in Hells Angels fatigues were talking next to a table. One of them unclasped the metal case and Tyler poked his head high above the crowd to satisfy his curiosity—a set of darts. What kind of men carried darts in such a sleek and formal case?

He glanced at the monitor on the wall:

Ballroom A – Comic Con - Switzerland
Ballroom B – International Nuclear Physicists Symposium
Ballroom C – Dart Convention & International Competition

At the end of the concourse a marque read “Ballroom B.” Full speed ahead. The husky leather men armed with darts and the cosplay celebrators gave way to fortyish balding men with an affinity for pocket protectors and short-sleeved dress shirts. Tyler hated stereotyping but knew it existed for a reason.

A man leaned into his colleagues and conjectured with his arms, his lanyard badge flailing about as he got his point across. Was a pocket protector necessary in this age of information or was this a fashion statement similar to doctors who still wear stethoscopes? The man’s cranium had a V-shape on the front of his bald head which somehow accentuated the plastic protector.

Several men surrounded a woman, a rare sight at the symposium. Six of the men watched in vane as the seventh explained a thorium isotope to her. She had black hair, thick glasses, skinny with a white dress shirt too big for her. She nodded as though the portly man convinced her, but the nodding could easily be mistaken for appeasement.

To the left, several more portly men were chomping on some sort of appetizers—they were pizza rolls, the staple of physicists that hadn’t yet earned their doctorates. Tyler remembered the heartburn taste as he choked them down in his dissertation years.

He found the entrance to the symposium—a grand table covered in white cloth flanked by energetic convention girls hustling back and forth to find the participants’ names.

Tyler approached the A-F girl. He told her his last name and she paused for a moment.

“Excuse me for just one moment,” she said in a submissive whisper. She stepped away and talked to another organizer who typed furiously on her laptop. The organizer peered over her reading glasses at Tyler. The A-F girl and the laptop woman both stared a hole through Tyler.

“Your registration and badge were canceled by the organizers,” the security guard said this with a thick French accent. He leaned his massive weight on the high table near the windows of the concourse informing Tyler in a very welcoming way that he wasn’t welcome. Did the man wake up that morning, shave, shower, and put on his crisp uniform to comfort Tyler’s ejection from the symposium?

“May I ask way?” Tyler said.

"The organizers are happy to refund your registration fee. They'll just reverse it on the credit card on file."

"Why?"

"May I see your credit card? It is just to make sure it matches up." The man smiled.

Tyler felt as though the security guard attended the Harvard school of dodging direct questions. He relented and handed the man his Amex.

"Thank you, monsieur. You should see the debit on your card within a few days. Here's my card, you can call me if it doesn't appear."

Tyler plopped himself on a stool at the Andorra Lounge just down the street from the convention hall. A glass of Boudeaux lingered in front of him, so far he'd taken one sip.

The Andorra had seen better times from its glory years, or rather Gamma, Beta, Alpha's glory years. The decrepit building it occupied would probably be razed soon since it contrasted with the modern convention hall. Tyler recalled a soccer field where the convention complex was. Above the corner booth the painting of Prime Minister Pierre Messmer still hung acting as a chaperone to the patrons.

Messmer was a hero to him back then, a haggard, unwilling hero who paved the way for nuclear energy throughout France during the oil crises of the '70s. Today the painting looked faded.

News of the crazy aircraft carrier had gotten out of course. The Discovery primetime documentary made no mention of Tyler but surely some ambitious reporter had done their homework and found Tyler out or maybe Rutledge and the Atomic Energy Commission leaked his involvement to the press. But Tyler was just boring enough not to warrant a story over the dashing Archer or Sergi the Russian playboy.

What kind of person would want to work for Tyler anyways? The great minds down the street under the giant convention dome would never have their good names sullied by working with a disgraced physicist who invented the pool noodle. He sipped his Bordeaux and glanced again at the painting of Messmer above the corner booth and reminisced when he drank there just fifteen years ago…

"À votre santé, cheers!" The Gamma-Bates boys touched wine goblets and tossed back generous glugs.

“Camille,” Lars yelled as he held up his hand.

The busty blonde came over to their table. The four sets of fraternal eyes bobbed up and down between her tight sweater and her baby blues. The conversation on fusion could wait.

“Do you know meatballs?” Lars asked in broken French.

“*Oui,* very good, very American *et* Italian,” she said in a charming French accent. They laughed as she sauntered off to put their order in.

“See Tyler, we shotgunned the corner booth. Prime real estate. See it’s round, but we could squeeze a few more people in. Specifically females. And since you can only slide in and out from the ends, they’d be trapped.”

“You think women are going to just throw themselves at us because of our ugly American charm?” Lester asked.

“That’s a good point,” Gary said.

“See those two girls over there?”

“The ones flirting with the Swedish guys from Uppsala chapter? I don’t think we have a chance.” Lester made a scowl at Gary.

“Les, let me explain something to you. Remember in the ’90s when computer guys like Bill Gates got all the girls?”

“Don’t remember nerds getting hot girls except in the movies.”

“No, it’s true they did. Not anymore though. Computer nerds are out. Nuc-nerds are in.”

They laughed and swilled another mouthful of cheap wine.

“We’re going to snatch those girls away. See we’re Americans. We’re exotic over here.”

Gary dabbed his eye drops and screwed the cap back on and tucked the bottle into his pocket. He waxed his glasses with his T-shirt. “You know I’ve never thought of it that way. I guess we are exotic if we go to Thailand or something.”

“No, not Thailand, here,” Lars exclaimed.

“But we kind of look the same as everyone in Geneva.”

“Hey around here, they hear you talk with an American accent about nuclear physics, they think you’re with the Collider.”

“But we aren’t. We’re just getting a tour—”

“No. You don’t tell them every little thing. Just puff it up a bit. Tell them we’re consultants.”

“Won’t they ask about our Gamma, Beta, Alpha T-shirts and figure out we're just students visiting?"

Lars stopped for a moment to think of a response. He glanced at Gary's T-shirt for a moment. "Ah, we turn them inside out in the bathroom."

"Why do you think a couple of French sex kittens would be into us, again?" Lester inquired.

Lars motioned with his hands commanding everyone to huddle over the table. "Guys, let me explain something to you. We are the future. We are what Bill Gates was in the '90s. We're going to design the motor of the world. It won't be run by dead dinosaurs or windmills. It will be fusion."

"And you're sure those girls know what fusion is?"

"We're going to eulogize the PC and celebrate the bar mitzvah of fusion." Tyler did raise a glass to that toast.

"I don't feel right stealing women from our Gamma brothers," Gary said.

"It's in the bro-code. We're allowed to do that at parties and social events. Tyler back me up."

"Sure go for it. Steal away." Tyler threw his hands up in a surrender manner.

"See? Here's what we do. Ty, you go over and introduce yourself."

"Okay."

"Then ask them to come over here."

Gary, Tyler, and Lester were quiet.

Tyler finally spoke. "That's it? That's your plan?"

"You're the best looking of us."

Tyler glanced at Erik and Bjorn, the two Gamma Beta brothers from Sweden. There were also some fraternity brothers from Canada sitting at the bar. They were talking to the Germans. Stanford and Berkeley, representing the West Coast chapter, were doing shots with Croatians and Russians. Even the Indians and Pakistanis were getting along over at the pool table. The Andorra Lounge was a microcosmos of world peace through nuclear energy.

Lars was surely delusional about PhDs getting women but he was right about the future. It was right here. The research from the Collider would keep physicists like themselves busy for decades. Energy was its ultimate practical use. Countries such as Croatia or Slovenia could be powered from a single plant the size of a shopping mall. It was still decades out but Tyler knew the implications.

"...*the third world*, we don't even call them that. Mallard scolded me for saying that during lecture."

"He scolded you?"

"Yeah, called me Jerry."

"Gary or Jerry?"

"Jerry. He got even angrier at me because he thought I was ignoring him."

"Well were you—"

"Of course I was, he screwed up my name. I didn't know he was talking to me."

The group laughed and poured themselves another round from the carafe in the center of the table.

"He's got it in for you," Lester said.

"Me? He's got it for Tyler. Tyler's the jock on a free ride."

"Swimming is hardly jock material," Tyler said.

"No he's totally Dean Wormser on you. Hates you good-looking sports types. He's tight with the nerds. See my pocket protector? I wear that for his sake. He sees it and it comforts him. Lets him know it hasn't gone out of style."

"So I should get a pocket protector and thick glasses?"

"No, at this point he'd think you were mocking him. Especially since you're the only athlete in the class and you killed that midterm. That really musses his combover. It's a touchy situation."

"Gary ran around the Collider yesterday," Lester said.

"Ran around it? Why?" Lars asked.

"I'm training for a marathon."

"How long is that?"

"My Garmin said 28.2 kilometers."

"Jeez, that's like 18 miles?"

"They let you run around the tractors and cranes?" Lester asked.

"I ran just outside the perimeter fence. I saw lots of runners. It's kind of a thing I guess."

"Could you see anything?" Tyler asked.

"I think it's just a big tunnel right now. We get to tour the Muon Solenoid tomorrow. They said the unit is ready but they have to finish the tunnels before they attach it to the end."

Tyler found his thoughts drifting from colliding particles and fusion to a different subject. Rachel would be finishing her degree and she predicted that she'd make Magna Cum Laude. Her talents would propel her to faraway places, no doubt far away from him. He could have spent his last quarter with her but instead traveled with his Fissile Friends as she referred to them, to tour the Hadron Collider in Southern France.

When he arrived back in New York, he'd have dinner with her at a nice restaurant and then have the difficult conversation. Perhaps it would be easy since both knew this day would come and it was a common conversation among students graduating. He was from the 'burbs just north of Minneapolis and she was San Francisco and lived up to every expectation one would expect from a West Coast metropolitan.

She might stay in New York or fly off to London, Tokyo, or back to the West Coast. He would be offered positions all over the world when he completed his dissertation. He'd work in France somewhere, the capital of practical and sustainable nuclear power.

How exciting that developing countries were getting involved—Brazil, Czech Republic, Armenia, and Hungary jumping on the fission bandwagon. One plant to power a third of a country. The old oil tycoons used to brag about powering America and putting it on the map—America wasn't discovered, it was built! Nuclear would power the world and propel the third world into a first world.

But the particle collider and fusion reactors were academic. No company employed such ambitious science. And experts predicted the fusion reactor to be two generations away. Perhaps in the year 2100 the reaction that powered the DeLorean in *Back to the Future* would be viable. Sitting around the table were a group of boys who would never know anything outside a college campus. They would go into research, some would be professors, not one of them would ever work at an actual plant. Their heads were far too much into the clouds for practical application.

"Tyler." Lars turned to him. "Ty, here's the plan. You go over and get those girls going. The rest of us will join in. We'll leave the T-shirts as is, that'll be our shtick. They can ask us what we do and we'll tell them and that's our in."

"Why me?"

"You're the Olympic swimmer. You got those long arms and chicks dig tall guys."

"And you think they'll jump all over us when they hear we're nuc-nerds?"

"Well, we don't have to call it that but yes." Lars had a cocky smile on his face. Gary and Lester looked white as ghosts. Tyler was certain neither had yet kissed a woman.

"If that is your shtick to lure them to us, how is that unique from the two Gamma Betas they're talking to now?"

Lars raised a finger in the air and searched for an answer. His eyes bobbed back and forth. Eventually his finger curled up and his arm drifted back down to the table surface.

Tyler headed toward the hall to the bathrooms. He pulled out his flip phone and found Rachel's number.

When she said hello it was late afternoon in New York. He could hear her walking swiftly and opening doors and recognized the sound of the entryway of the Watson Library at Columbia.

When she whispered his name, anger no longer lingered in her voice. The fight they had fell away and the good memories resurfaced.

"I miss you," she said.

"I miss you too."

"I just miss you. I'm sorry how I acted, but…"

Her breathing over the line reminded Tyler of the last time they held each other and her breath touched the side of his neck as they drifted off in his dorm room.

"I'm coming home early. The tour is done and the rest is just networking BS with the other chapters. It's a blowout."

"Tyler, you don't have to do that."

She meant the opposite of what she said.

"My hotel is refundable, and there's no change fee on my flight." Both white lies. He didn't want to make a big deal of it even though it was. He would call his father for money for the change fee and have to explain the nonrefundable six nights of a $245 hotel room in downtown Geneva. He would mention Rachel and it would shoot an arrow through the old man's weak spot.

"Tyler, it's midterms for us."

"I know." 62 days until graduation for Rachel, 42 until Tyler's dissertation. She'd be around for a few more days after. She already had job offers everywhere. That conversation could wait, they both knew what needed to be said. Why talk about what they knew would happen? When Tyler flew back they would enjoy their final weeks together before the inevitable. They could plan a final trip together but both were burdened with six-figure debts. That didn't matter, they had Manhattan at their fingertips. They could lie in the park, sneak wine into his dorm, hold hands in SoHo and admire the modern art, cross the Brooklyn Bridge and the promenade, all free. What mattered is that their last months were together. Like ice cream you make last, because it's so good.

Tyler hung up his phone. A call to his father and then to the airline would be next. He would check out of the hotel tomorrow morning and gracefully bow back to Columbia. His friends wouldn't notice him gone.

…the bartender poured Tyler another goblet of wine and he tore his stare from Messmer and the corner booth. He should have stopped at one. He felt ashamed for drinking the cheap house red. He stared at the soccer game even though he wasn't really watching it.

"Doctor Chambers!"

Lester Wilner hung his suit jacket on the hook underneath the bar.

"Les!" They shook hands and he plopped himself on the stool next to Tyler.

"I wondered who I might run into if I made the pilgrimage to this place." Lester swiveled on the stool and surveyed the bar. "It hasn't changed much from what I remember."

"No, pretty much the same. They didn't even update the president." Tyler motioned to Messmer.

"That's odd. We're in Switzerland, the nation that hates nuclear. You'd think they'd get rid of Pierre Messmer's ugly mug and put the current guy up." Lester ordered a scotch and soda.

"Well France is getting pretty vicious too."

"So I take it you're attending the con?"

"No, I'm heading home after this drink."

"Heading home? It's the first day."

"They already kicked me out."

"Oh." Lester nodded in understanding. The bartender placed Lester's drink in front of him. He slurped his scotch through the stir straw. "I suppose they don't want you here."

If Lester knew about Tolkov then the whole world knew and the cat was out. Rachel would throw a fit within seconds of him walking through the front door. "I wish they had told me earlier and saved me the trip."

"They didn't even tell you?"

"Just told me at the door that they cancelled my registration."

"That's too bad."

"Yeah it was quite specific as if I'd burn the place down or something."

"You're not missing much."

"Why do you say that?"

"Just a different vibe. Remember when we visited the Collider—a resurgence in nuclear just beyond the horizon. Now it's fossil fuel's retarded little brother. What the hell happened?"

"The entire industry is up in arms about Fukushima. It's 1986 all over again. Nothing but fear and paranoia."

"The industry switched tunes. The lure of wind and solar funds dangling in front of them. Of course energy companies are going to grab that carrot. Safe government profits over risky venture profits. They can't resist. It's wild in there Tyler, between academia, politicians and corporations, everyone is split. A nuclear symposium where nobody is allowed to utter the dreaded N-word."

Tyler shook his head.

"You know at Indian Point we just updated to Windows 7 from XP?"

"Wow, 7, not Ten?"

"That's right. That announcement that Microsoft no longer supported XP rippled through the nuc industry. That was four years ago and we just recently upgraded. Nobody invests in nuclear, we're still using software from the 2000s. They are just going to let the reactors fall apart and decom as they come due. There's a bunch of decom booths in there." Lester motioned with his thumb to the convention hall. "Quite depressing."

Lester pulled the straw out of his drink, set it on the napkin, and took a sip. "So shouldn't you be manning your ship?"

There it was, the whole world knew. "I am. Got everything I need on my Android. And my engineer has the technical stuff under control." Tyler finished his wine. "Sorry to drink and dash but that's it for me. I have to be getting back to my ship."

"Aye, aye, swabbie." Lester grinned and gave him a mock salute.

It felt good to bump into Lester. Tyler pushed his stool in, shook Lester's hand, and turned to walk away. He glanced one more time at Messmer. They should update the decor in this place.

Lester grabbed his forearm. "Tyler. Why don't you use my badge?" he said with a halfcocked smile.

Once again Tyler found himself wading through bikers and Boba Fetts. He made his way toward Ballroom B and stepped behind the velvet rope to the entrance. The registration tables were nearly empty of badges since the symposium was well under way.

He affixed the lanyard around his neck with Lester's badge on the front. Doctor Lester Wilner in block letters, Indian Point, New York, USA. Luckily the laminated badge did not have a picture. He stepped past security, carefully scanning for the previous guard who ushered him away. The guard was assigned to the hall area so he wouldn't have to worry about running into him once he passed through the door.

A dome the size of a soccer field hosted the convention. Structures of round steel beams resembling three-dimensional spider webs supported the roof. Elaborate booths and exhibits spanned in nice neat rows throughout the middle and around the circumference of the ballroom. The layout resembled a village diagram of cooling towers, cross sections of dry storage casks, models of reactors, the classic boiling water reactor, a pressurized water reactor, a display for Gen IV reactors, and the decom booths Lester mentioned.

He stepped by the Generation IV display observing some of the improvements over Generation III. The display had the year 2030 in green numbers above it as a goal for implementation. Tyler knew the unlikeliness of the date.

He passed a display for decommissioning of plants—a startup demolition firm with big plans. They had efficient ideas of how to dismantle old plants. There were many such plants scattered across the world, either at the end of their life or never having an opportunity to open. Plants that cost billions only to be left rotting away because of indecisiveness. This company would be a rising star in the industry just like Lester said.

A display down row for wind turbines distracted Tyler from the decom company. General Electric lurked everywhere at the convention but it was curious that they didn't present their logo at any of the displays. They did make both nuclear reactors and wind turbines, carefully playing all parts of the field. Why would anyone build reactors with the headaches that come with them when government would be happy to subsidize wind for decades to come?

The US Navy had a display for the new Ford class carrier John F Kennedy, a boat nearly twice the length of Tolkov. The pair of A1B reactors made by the Bechtel Corporations boasted 700 megawatts which approached the capacity to power cities the size of Wichita. But did it have a hot tub on the roof?

He was tempted to strike up a conversation with the man in uniform answering questions about the newest nuclear carrier to the fleet. Lester made him promise he would keep his interactions minimal as to maintain the charade. Tyler had no problem with this arrangement although it might make recruitment of a safety head difficult.

"...Chambers..."

Tyler thought he heard his name but it was just someone talking about a reactor core chamber.

A solar panel mockup complete with artificial sunlight captured his attention—the old Polish joke about a solar-powered flashlight. The booth made a cheeky argument that solar was a clean type of fusion energy. The sun technically did produce its energy through a fusion reaction but it was a silly comparison, like comparing swimming in a bath tub to swimming in the ocean.

Tyler scanned for thorium or real fusion but even with the variety of booths, many of them didn't deal with nuclear power at all.

"...aircraft carrier..." a voice mentioned from a throng of symposium members.

The aircraft carrier display impressed everyone as symposium goers mentioned the term several times as he passed through the crowd yet no other symposium goers congregated around the Navy display when he surveyed the booth. The Navy intended to build ten of the Ford class carriers over the next few decades and Tyler envisioned himself trying to buy an A1B reactor from the government when he was in his eighties.

The wind turbine model spun at a snail's pace. Two men were whispering and staring at Tyler. When he looked at them, they stopped and glanced at Tyler with shocked faces.

For a brief moment he wondered if they recognized him. He smiled back at them politely and walked away to avoid calling too much attention to himself. He didn't want to get Wilner in trouble.

The element symbol *Th* in bold red letters—there it was in the corner. It was the Thorium reactor booth and he made his way over. It was wrong that it was wedged into the low-traffic corner. It should have been down the center in the ballroom's Main Street.

A Thorium reactor had several benefits, there's more thorium in the Earth's crust over uranium, some say enough to power America for 1,000 years. Also less radioactive waste than conventional uranium and plutonium. Nearly impossible to make into a bomb and on top of that, the design of the reactor had a plug that would melt away and store molten material in a protective slug in the rare event of a meltdown. A smart design.

"...no, he's here, someone saw him..."

He wondered who the keynote speaker was who excited everyone. Several of the salon conference rooms would host professors from around the world to present their research. Some for pride, some for altruistic conveying of knowledge, but most for grant mining.

Westinghouse had some interesting presentations on their gen IV bids for reactors in China.

"...the aircraft carrier guy..."

Nobody spoke to the lowly lieutenant in alpha fatigues at the Kennedy display, yet people talked of the 'aircraft carrier guy.'

He scanned the periphery of the ballroom for anything fusion related. Three men staring at him caught his attention.

"...no, Chambers, Tyler Chambers is his name, the aircraft carrier guy..."

Shit.

He pivoted near the solar display and headed toward the Westinghouse table which had a towering booth that would hide his height. His height, blond hair, and that fact that he had all of it, made him stick out among the physicists.

Five men gazed at him near the uranium oxide model, their mouths hung open. The crowd around the virtual reality atomic bond display looked at him. One even pulled his phone out and took pictures.

Tyler high-tailed back to the Thorium booth since an adjacent bathroom offered him a hiding place. As he stepped forward he came face to face with a man he recognized, Robert Blarimie, the organizer of the symposium. The security guard who explained that Tyler wasn't invited hovered next to him but this time he did not appear to be in such a jovial mode.

"Doctor Chambers, you will come with me immediately," Blarimie demanded.

"Where did you get this?" the security guard asked as he looked over Tyler's badge.

"Found it in the parking lot," Tyler said.

The guard put Lester's badge in his pocket.

Blarimie turned his angry eyes to Tyler. "Doctor Chambers, you are not welcome here. You've disgraced our profession and we want nothing to do with you. Leave."

In a heavy French accent the security guard said, "Sir, if you come back here, the Swiss authorities will arrest you and place you in jail for trespassing. Your picture has been passed around to the organizers and security. The organizers do not want you here and the management of this facility will respect their wishes. Is this clear?"

"Yes, sir," Tyler said.

He shuffled through the parking lot with his head hung low. He made a conscience effort not to look back at the building, but he could see from the corner of his eye that the security guard watched him as he made his way to the edge of the property.

He pressed the Uber button on his phone. He crossed the Rue de Vermont to a hotel where his Uber would meet him. The driver headed to the charter gate of the Geneva Airport.

He had several messages and missed calls from Archer that he didn't feel like returning just yet. Archer had everything under control as the man needed little guidance and direction.

Thank goodness for Blarimie catching him. Everyone burned a hole in him with their eyes, no doubt wondering why the pool noodle inventor had invaded their conference. But now they knew him as the crazy aircraft carrier guy which wasn't much better. Their judgmental stares pounded against his skin.

Blarimie served on the president's advisory board for nuclear waste management and led the charge for shutting down the never-used Yucca Mountain storage facility. Billions and billions down the drain on what was now a big hole in the ground.

A dry storage cask with walls twenty inches thick of concrete and steel would contain spent fuel rods and were scattered across the world already, but putting the casks in a cavern with a thousand feet of rock in all directions did not suffice. Blarimie disgraced the profession, not Tyler. At least that's the way it should be.

The convention was a blowout. It lacked wonderment about the future like when he attended it during grad school when Tokyo hosted. Tyler recalled fueling the world as the motif, experimental technology that would be practical in twenty years and eliminate the need for fossil fuels and usher in the electric car since energy would be so cheap and abundant that only a fool would still get to work via internal combustion.

Today, the motif was one of winding down. Alternative sources of energy made it into the conference. Mankind split the atom and discovered the very fabric of the physical world and it would be tossed aside for Dutch technology from the 1600s. Decommissioning contractors handing out free pens, they were the new rock stars of the industry, vultures circling the wounded animal limping through the desert. And everyone cheered them on.

They were part of an industry that proactively decided to cannibalize itself. They partnered with paranoia and gave in easily—Chernobyl, Three Mile Island, and now Fukushima. The age of the internet came and went, Apartheid ended, China waded towards democracy, there were still people who believed that reactors caused zombie attacks, and that radon came from nuclear waste. Homer Simpson represented the epitome of nuclear power skill.

Tyler was the first man to jump from the sinking ship. He understood how other professionals in his field could look down on him for making that smart decision all those years ago. With every wealthy excess he delighted in from inventing the pool noodle he felt just a bit guiltier. Bitterness from his peers was well earned.

Could he sell the ship for scrap? It could fetch five or six million but someone would have to deal with the power plant. He wasn't sure if he could cancel the contracts with the team of tractor drivers and the leases with land owners. They had to have known of the risks involved with such a crazy project, no reason for one person to be on the hook for all of it.

On the plane he told the pilot to head for New York and that'd he'd be sleeping most of the way. He went to the supply cabinet in the lavatory and found a sleeping pill.

He stripped off his clothes down to his boxers and crashed into the pullout bed. The plane taxied toward the runway and Tyler was confident that he'd be out before takeoff.

CHAPTER FOURTEEN

Rogers pulled the Lincoln to the awning over the main door of the Chambers's manor. Tyler didn't wait for him to open the door, even though Rogers rushed to beat him.

He walked into the main entryway and glanced at the pool out back. He never realized you could see the backyard from the front entryway. Something was very different about his home. The living room had been remodeled with walls knocked out. The surreal moment hit him as he realized that everything was the same yet vastly different.

Rogers placed an umbrella in the closet. "Sir, Mrs. Chambers remodeled while you were away."

"I see that. What…what used to be there?" Tyler knew the answer to this question.

"The library and the hidden room."

"Yes, yes, I see now." He stared into the vast atrium space where his reading nook used to be. The remodel left no trace, not even the hardwood floors and Russian rug which were now marble.

"Will there be anything else, sir?"

Tyler walked to the new atrium and rested on a long upholstered carved bench. Even his heels against the marble sounded foreign. The grand skylight where his ceiling and antique chandelier used to be caused him to squint. The octagon skylight had eight triangular-shaped panes which rose to an apex in the sky.

Sunlight poured onto a statue of a Greek goddess in the middle of the room, Aphrodite perhaps, although his wife had never expressed an interest in Romanesque art.

He took a deep breath—fresh paint, fresh masonry, and the smells of other rooms. His nose did not detect any trace of paper.

He glanced at the end table and an 8x11 envelope from Speed Couriers was addressed to him. The return address read Society for Nuclear Advancement. He grasped the tear strip when Rachel's voice in the kitchen interrupted him. He cut through the grand dining room to the south kitchen.

His muscles froze when he entered. Robert Rutledge sat comfortably at the table. He had a cup of coffee in front of him and a plate with bundt cake crumbs.

He rose and extended his hand to Rachel. "Thank you for your hospitality, Ms. Chambers."

"I appreciate your coming down here to help us with our situation."

"You have my card if you ever need anything."

"Rogers, would you show Mr. Rutledge out," she said.

Rutledge strutted past Tyler. "Doctor Chambers," he greeted with a subdued tone.

That man was in his home, in his kitchen, in his spot where he ate his breakfast.

Tyler heard the front door close. "What the hell is he doing here? Do you know who that is?"

"Of course I do. He's agreed to help us get out of this situation you've put us in."

"He wants to shut it down."

"Yes, shut it down and put an end to this silly fiasco."

"You can't trust them."

"There's nothing to trust. We're going to lose everything. At least this way we can recoup some of our money and you won't go to jail."

"I have everything planned out."

"No, Tyler, I do." She placed the dishes in the sink. "You're done with this."

"You can't trust them. They will do everything to stop us."

"He's willing to put it in writing. He's going to send the proposal to my attorney."

"They froze our bank accounts without even telling us. Do you know what a mess that puts on our operation?"

She shot Tyler a confused look. "Froze? You mean the Rockland County accounts?"

Tyler's eyes darted back and forth. Her answer was rather specific, wasn't it? "Yes."

Rachel sighed and shook her head. "Tyler, *I* froze them. Money was flying out every day for your silly adventure."

"You did that?"

"You thought the government…oh Tyler, why would you think it would be anyone other than me? Did you not understand me when I said I was angry about this? You thought I wasn't going to do anything?"

Tyler's mouth froze. His anger prevented him from speaking.

"You sweep in funds from Switzerland to cover the wires going out. I want to know where those are coming from and I want access to the accounts."

"You'll never get access to those."

"You can either grant me access or I can get it legally. Swiss banking laws are not absolute as you think, especially if a spouse is seeking access."

"You would do that to me?"

"Why are you making me out to be the monster? You did this to me."

He pulled out the chair where Rutledge had been sitting, sat down, and buried his face in his hands.

"Lara Farnsworth fired me but I have a new public relations firm I'm working with. I want to continue with my fundraising, and my new publicist assures me I can still do this even though our financial situation is dismal—"

"Dismal, Rachel, I think—"

"Let me finish. I can still lead fundraisers and be a strong member of the philanthropic community. We're working on branding our name so that we can continue along. Mary Henretti, she's the new publicist, and she assured me that as long as we stay a family and project a family image of unity, we can still capitalize on the goodwill I've built over the years within the philanthropic community."

"Okay," Tyler relented.

"Mr. Rutledge told me that this project you've committed us to is worthless other than some money for scrap metal. Since you've squandered our fortune and locked us into this there's nothing I can divorce you for. You've won."

"I'm not trying to win anything. I just needed to…" He was unsure of how to finish his sentence.

"I won't divorce you as long as you help me project this family image for the next six months until this silly ship business is finished and blown over."

"Project a family image? We don't need to engineer that, we are a family."

"We're not a family anymore, not after what you did. It will be acting."

"Fine, fine, we'll act it out for the sake of your publicist."

"She's developing a plan to transition our public image from this fiasco back to philanthropy."

"What kind of plan?"

"You're not at the center of attention. That Russian diplomat is along with the people on the ship. She can easily separate your association from them. She says the media would pounce on him since he's a more newsworthy subject."

"Just walk away?"

"If you do this I won't take away your daughter. I'm going to file for divorce when the time is right but I'll still let you see your daughter."

"Where do I live?"

"Here, but you'll stay in the east wing like you usually do. The staff reports to me, you can have Rogers. You won't interfere with anything and you'll show up to the events, and you won't tell anyone about that ship. We don't ever mention it."

He lifted his head from his hands. She stared at him with her arms crossed and a patronizing face.

"That's it," she said.

"The spine of a character is his main motivation, you figure that out and your body and mind follow it relentlessly and you always have a great performance. Now the spine, it's not what you think it is, it's more than just rescuing the princess or Indiana Jones finding the ark. It's what drives the character from beginning to end. This is really good, can I get another please?"

"Certainly," Rogers said. He picked up Nick's jar. "More strawberry lemonade, Mister Cambers?"

"No thank you, I'm fine."

"And so playing identical twins, you might think it's difficult but it isn't, just find the spine as you would any other character in any other film. It's no different than playing two characters in two separate films, it's just that they're in the same movie."

Tyler took another drink from his mason jar. There was just a bit left at the bottom of the ice. He set it on the patio table.

"So to get back to your point, I'm proud of every performance I've ever done. Even the bad ones. If actors don't have bad performances it means they don't take risks. Just throw yourself in there. The vampire movie I was in, the one with the bees, yeah I get it, the internet makes fun at me, but what do I care? When a studio has a juicy role that other actors won't touch, they'll reach out to me, they know I'm game for that kind of stuff."

Rogers set a fresh lemonade on the glass table.

"Oh, thank you," Nick said. "I love these mason jars. That's how a cold drink on a summer day should be done.

"I talked to Marlon Brando once. My uncle had him at his vineyard. I asked him how he could play such evil characters so convincingly, you know *Apocalypse Now*, *Last Tango*, he said he falls in love with every character he's ever played. Even the bad ones, even the evil ones. When you do that it motivates you to empathize with them, not sympathize, you don't want sympathy, but you want understanding. And you need to be careful not to judge the characters, otherwise you're playing to the result, you're playing evil without going through the motions to arrive at the evil. Just pretend evil doesn't exist and search for the spine. Amon Goethe, Hannibal Lector, Harry Lime, even Darth Vader, they aren't evil, they just really enjoy blowing up planets and eating people's faces." Nick laughed and guzzled a generous quaff from the jar.

Tyler smiled diplomatically and glanced at the tulip garden. He calculated in his head how many hours the money would buy.

The broker came out of the house. "Gentlemen, I think we're ready."

Nick slammed the rest of his drink, "All right, Tyler, time to say goodbye."

Tyler and Nick cut through the kitchen and the new solarium and to the front door. A semi parked in the street stretched the length of his front yard causing Tyler to stall in his step. It hauled what he learned was called a car carrier trailer.

Tyler remembered a poster in his bedroom growing up. A woman changed the tire on a white Lamborghini Countach. She poised herself on the wide tire in a tiny tank top, G-string and heels. She pulled the front of her tank top way down with her thumb and gazed upward, just as all mechanics changing tires did. The Lambo in the background was jacked up and missing the front passenger wheel and appeared just a bit submissive to the mechanic.

Do you think that's appropriate for our son? his mom asked.

Kid's growing up. Don't make a stink. Dad always shielded him from Mom's smothering.

"Listen Tyler, you ever in LA, drop me a line and we'll go to the track or something. I'll take good care of your babies, you ever want to see them, just come on out."

Nick presented his hand to Tyler and they shook. Nick walked over to the '86 Lamborghini Countach. He pulled the scissor door shut and the engine came alive. Tyler felt a slight dizziness and stepped back.

The vehicle's twelve cylinders roared like a lion and the cherry-red beauty glided into the street. Nick honked twice and the car jumped to light speed and it was gone.

The semi roared to a start and the gears grinded to first. The Lotus Turbo Esprit, the Ferrari Tesserosa, the Lamborghini Diablo, the 488 Spider, the Aston Martin Vanquish, and the Bugatti Veyron drifted down the street and made a wide right on Heathcote.

They were gone.

Tyler reached in his pocket and pulled the check out to glance at it one more time. One million, eight hundred seventy-five thousand dollars from Wicker Man, LLC. It would cover a few more yards for Tolkov.

Tyler stared at a box of books at the foot of the bed in the guest room. He didn't feel like reading. He'd forgotten what a tough negotiator his wife was. She always mentioned the concept of win-win situations in negotiations. Never make your opponent believe you've gotten one over on them, advice from Covey's book on effective habits of successful people.

Rachel didn't say anything negative such as what her lawyer planned to do to him. She didn't put him through the grinder as wealthy angry wives with good attorneys were known to do. She made him an offer he couldn't refuse which was to show up at parties and act normal for a few months. No threats, no raising of voices, no drama, she laid the facts on the table from his point of view, not hers. He recalled how nicely she dealt with suppliers and vendors when they were creating their company. Through her hard-lined negotiation she always left a little for them to grab onto.

He opened the letter that had come for him earlier:

Tyler Chambers

This letter is to inform you of the Society for Nuclear Advancement's position on the recent events involving the corporation you have initiated.

The SNA's position has always been to put the public interest ahead of industry interests. Safety is the utmost concern of the Society. Your initiation of a nuclear power plant without any of the typical safeguards, procedures, public input, and environmental impact exacted damage to the reputation of nuclear advancement the world over.

We believe your actions to be illegal and that your fragrant violation of decades of safety protocols for bringing a reactor on line are inexcusable.

The Society for Nuclear Advancement hereby revokes your membership. Further, because you have caused grave damage to the reputation of our members, we request that you relinquish your doctorate of philosophy from the Department of Physics at Columbia University in New York, New York.

Attached is a request for relinquishment, you need only sign it and forward it to their Physics Department. We urge you to take these steps immediately to minimize the damage you have done to our vocation.

Blarimie and several other members of the board of the SNA signed at the bottom.

As he scanned the rest of the document which contained a variety of polite threats Rogers knocked and entered. “Sir, there is a gentleman here to see you. A Doctor Lester Wilner.”

He gave Rogers a confused look and wondered what the hell Lester would want at this hour.

Rogers waited for a response. “The gentleman at the benefit you played billiards with—”

“Yes, Lester, show him in. Is the drawing room still there?”

“Yes, sir.”

“I’ll take him in the drawing room.”

Lester stared at a painting from the Italian leather sofa when Tyler walked in.

“Tyler, you left Geneva in a hurry.”

“They sort of kicked me out and threatened to throw me in jail.”

“Yeah, I know, you caused quite a stir.”

“I know. I just want to crawl into a hole right now.”

“What do you mean crawl into a hole? You should have seen the rest of the symposium, nobody could stop talking about you.”

“Oh God.” Tyler fell into the couch and buried his head in his hands. “What have I done?”

Lester rushed over to him. “Tyler what do you mean *what have you done?* You caused a wondrous mess of everything. Everyone is talking about nuclear power.”

“But everything thinks I’m some crazy wackadoo.”

“No, they think you’re a genius.”

“Genius? But Blarimie…”

“Doctor Blarimie? You should have seen his presentation on Yucca Mountain, they lambasted him with questions on why he helped defeat that site. It was beautiful, he thought he’d give a quick PowerPoint and people would clap and clap all night long at his genius in destroying the industry. Instead it was a Spanish Inquisition. Everyone drilled Blarimie.”

"I didn't mean to—"

"And you should have seen the other panels and discussions, they were about this crazy aircraft carrier guy, why can't we build more reactors instead of decommissioning, what is the industry doing to promote more research? More reactors, business models for the 21st century, less regulations."

Tyler shook his head.

"I peeked into the panel on windmills and less than twenty people attended it. Nobody attended that blowhard Jennings's presentation on wind except a few industry kiss-ups. You should have seen everyone's excitement about nuclear again! Tyler you've done it." Lester threw his fists up in victory.

Rogers knocked again and entered. "Sir, Professor Mallard is calling, shall I put him in the lounge?"

"Professor Mallard's here? Tyler, what's he doing here?"

"I don't know. I didn't invite him. Rogers, can you bring him here."

"Very well, sir."

"Why's he here? Did they find my badge on you?"

"Yeah, they confiscated it."

"Oh God Tyler don't tell anyone I gave it to you, what did you tell them—"

"Relax, I told them I found it in the parking lot."

"Don't tell anyone we're friends. I mean you can but just be careful, I need my job at the plant, if anyone finds out I helped cause this commotion…"

"Don't worry, I got your back."

"Tyler, can I sneak out the back or something. I don't want Mallard to see me."

"Go down the hall and hang out in the billiard room, it's the one we played pool in, you remember right?"

"Okay."

Lester opened the door and looked both ways and tiptoed down the side hall like Inspector Clouseau might do.

Tyler shook his head at Lester's paranoia and closed the door and returned to the couch.

Rogers presented Doctor Mallard and Tyler shook hands with him.

"Doctor Chambers, you created quite a pool of entropy at the symposium."

"So I heard."

"Has Blarimie spoken to you about the signed agreement?"

"He had it couriered over this morning."

"Have you signed it?" Mallard said with a light grin.

"I accept a censure, relinquish my doctorate, and agree never to have anything to do with nuclear again otherwise they'll haul me before a congressional hearing."

"You understand, Blarimie is grandstanding. He doesn't have that kind of influence."

Tyler threw his hands in the air in a *don't know, don't care* fashion.

"I have a different agreement for you." Mallard set the packet of papers he had tucked under his arm on the end table. "Doctor Chambers, you must understand, Blarimie is furious with you. Do you understand why?"

"Because I crashed his party?"

"No. Well, yes, but there's more. Many professionals have dropped out of the SNA. Their membership dropped by half in the past week, all because of your presence at the symposium."

"Me?"

"Blarimie went ballistic."

"Everyone just up and quit?"

"That organization has become a cheerleader for ending nuclear. *Society for Nuclear Advancement*, the name is a cruel joke. It's the opposite of what they do. Tyler, you're young, you're making a spectacle, and you're starting a dialogue in this country that hasn't been spoken since Eisenhower put us on the road toward nuclear."

"That's not true, every president since has had a stance on nuclear—"

"But not a positive one. It's always the looming problem of waste, how fast do we decommission, our reliance on twenty percent of our power coming from it. How do we switch to green energy even though nuclear is far greener than green energy could ever dream of. It's been a negative dialogue. You've turned our trajectory forward."

"All I did was come up with a scheme to get rich quick."

Mallard smiled and adjusted himself in the squeaky leather chair. "If your financial interests and the advancement of nuclear energy cross paths, that's a good thing." Mallard handed the stack of documents to

Tyler. "People see an investor making money, they send billions into the industry. The ghosts of the Shoreham nuclear debacle are exorcised and investors want to invest again."

Tyler examined the stack of papers. "The Society for the Advancement of Nuclear Solutions for the 21st Century?" he read aloud.

"It's a working title, you can change it if you'd like. Those physicists who dropped out of the SNA are reorganizing. We've thrown together a new group that only looks one direction. Forward. They're going to educate the public instead of scare them. They're going to promote it as green energy instead of dirty. They're going to get the industry on board so the technology can move forward to developing countries who are burning coal at an alarming rate."

"I don't get it, what is this?"

"It's an offer to be the head of our group. We need someone who can give this project a path. We need you, Doctor Chambers."

Tyler walked into the billiards and plopped Mallard's paperwork on the corner of the pool table.

Lester scurried over from chair in the corner. "Did he ask about me?"

"No."

"Well what did he want?"

"I guess everyone quit the SNA and is forming a new group."

Lester shook his head and returned to his chair. "I kind of want to quit the SNA too. There's no leadership or vision. Nuclear is a black sheep that America tolerates because we're dependent on it. The second they don't need us, we're all decommed."

"He said about half the members dropped out over the past week and a bunch of people went home early from the symposium including Mallard. Funny but I always thought Mallard as Blarimie's puppet."

"No kidding, I didn't think Mallard had it in him. But yeah, he's always come off as a fall-in-line type of person."

"The whole industry is like that."

"It is. It's sickening."

"He offered me the job to lead the new group."

"It's a bunch of sheep—wait, what did you say?"

"It's kind of silly that he wants me. I told him no of course."

"What do you mean you told him no?"

"Me? Do you know what kind of people are going to be part of that?" Tyler walked over to the pool table.

"What kind of people? What do you mean what kind of people?"

Tyler rolled the solid five across the felt. "You know, scientists, with PhDs."

Lester's mouth hung open as if he waited for a better answer. "So?"

Tyler fell into the couch and tossed his hands over his eyes. "I haven't practiced or done anything since the day I finished my dissertation. I've been designing pool toys."

"What do you mean, you're installing the first American nuclear reactor since Clinton was president. You've done more in the past four weeks than the entire industry has done in the last thirty years."

Tyler imagined the security guard escorting him across the ballroom back in Geneva. Thank goodness they caught him near a side door. Had they paraded him across the entire length of the ballroom to the front door everyone would have noticed the pool noodle king who invaded their party.

"I haven't done anything. This stunt ended my marriage and squandered a fortune. The government is going to shut us down anyways."

"You'll give leadership to this group that desperately needs it. Even if they do shut you down, you're still going to propel the debate forward for the next decade. Thorium will be on the table, people won't be paranoid about misinformation anymore, fusion will be a reality someday and you'll be the guy—"

"He should ask Archer."

"Who's Archer?"

"He's the head engineer of the carrier project."

"But he's the guy carrying out your plan. He's just the tactician. You're the man who stepped up to the plate. You're the one who drew a line in the sand. You're the one they need."

Tyler needed to get away. He would fly to some Caribbean country and spend time with himself. He would charter a plane instead of using his own to make tracking impossible. He needed just a week, maybe two weeks, a nice quiet resort where nobody would recognize him. One of those Panama hats and sunglasses, and he wouldn't shave. He would email Archer to quash the project and work with the government to transition the whole mess back to normal, whatever they determine that to be.

"I need to get away."

"Dammit Tyler you've always been a pushover. You run away, you did this in college, you turned your back on everyone. What the hell is wrong with you?" Lester moved closer and shoved his finger in his face. "You're too stupid to see how smart you are. You have absolute confidence in your ability to fail. That's your problem, it always has been."

Tyler stepped back from Lester. "I don't…run away. I had a company to run."

"You don't have a company anymore and you're still running. You just parachuted the safe way out when it was convenient. You have a chance to correct that."

"No, you're making it sound so easy. Everyone in the world hates me because of what I've done."

"So what. You want to be liked? People who tell the truth and try to change the world are hated. Columbus was hated. Galileo was hated. Darwin was hated and still is. Having enemies means you have convictions. Don't abandon everything now."

"I'm not abandoning—"

"Then what do you call this?"

Rogers entered the billiards room. "Sir, is everything all right?"

"Doctor Wilner was just leaving. Would you show him out—"

"That's how it's going to be? You don't want to face me so you send your butler to remove me? Fine, I'll leave." Lester walked toward the door and past Rogers. He turned back to Tyler. "I'll go back to my moldy plant that's falling apart and wait for them to come and shut it down for good."

CHAPTER FIFTEEN

Tyler sped up Itasca County Road Seven through the darkness as the road winded. He occasionally refocused his eyes from the road to the dark horizon to spot a moving city but he wasn't sure how he'd get on board once he arrived at the base of the logs.

Mechanical problems had stranded the helicopter at Cloquet-Carlton County Airport near Duluth. He wasn't sure where he'd ditch his rental car or how the rental car people would get the vehicle back. He wouldn't even be able to tell them the coordinates of his vehicle. Just that it's parked somewhere in the arrowhead, no complaints, should have taken the fuel option.

Archer assured him that coordination of a new helicopter from Minneapolis-St. Paul International would be complete within 24 hours.

Although they scrapped the main crane back in Vladivostok, they kept the mini crane on Tolkov in case of interrupted air transportation. Tyler would have to rappel up the side in the dead of night like the "Our Gang" treehouse complete with password.

His eyes felt heavy from the oncoming cars that always dimmed their brights at the last possible minute.

He just wanted to get back to his ship and crawl into his tiny quarters. Sleeping was so relaxing when surrounded by tons of steel like you were in the belly of a whale.

He pieced together the conversation he would have with Archer. He would recognize his effort and then tell him he was moving in a new direction. God that sounded awful. Don't say that. How did Ben used to do this, the Harvards were so good explaining bad news and putting a positive spin on it. Maybe he should hire a consultant to end the project—a nice Harvard mouthpiece to give a PowerPoint on how the crew needed to abandon ship and forget this entire fiasco ever happened.

Maybe he should bring a bottle of scotch and break it to Archer over ice in the galley. That was more Archer's style. Surely Archer had quashed an ambitious project every now and then.

A pair of glowing eyes appeared in the road. He slammed on the brakes and punched his palm to the steering wheel blaring the horn.

The car skidded and the deer darted off. Dammit, they were supposed to come out at dawn, not two at night. He released the brake and gained control of the car and sped back up. This time, he'd keep it at fifty, a full five miles below the posted limit. What was the old Jeff Foxworthy-esque saying about Minnesotans? "If you've been involved in not one but two deer collisions, you just might be a Minnesotan"?

Neon lights appeared on the side of the road in the distance. He would violate the male rule of not asking for directions and pull into the parking lot of the local watering hole.

The Walleye Tale had no windows and wood paneling covered the outside. As the neon sign buzzed, a fish, presumably a walleye, blinked different shapes simulating a flopping motion.

There were two men staring each other down with a hulking man, arms crossed standing at their side. He wore a T-shirt with the Walleye Tale logo on the breast.

"You boys got a choice tonight, you can walk way or you can finish this. You see each other's faces. I think it's already finished," the hulking man said.

Both men had blood dripping down their faces. They stared at each other with intensity.

The place was loud and rowdy. There were mostly men with a few bar flies affixed to their arms. The bartender was a standard tough, fortyish tavern wench who probably had broken up a few fights in her time.

"What can I getchya?"

"Would you happen to know where the carrier is?"

"What?" She leaned in closer.

"The aircraft carrier. Is it around here?"

"Oh yeah, the carrier, it's passing through these parts. Just follow Highway Seven, take a right and go west on Twenty-Three, right on Tamarack and go all the way to Colder's field…" She motioned with her arms in tomahawk chopping motions, she pivoted ninety degrees for the turn on Tamarack road.

"Thank you," Tyler said.

"You want a roadie? We're close to last call."

"No, just…" Tyler scanned the bar quickly and realized one beer would be pretty damned good about now. "…just give me a Hienie, or whatever you have that isn't Budweiser."

"Sure, we got Heineken."

He tapped through the updates on his phone that Archer sent him every shift change. He reviewed the diagnostics and scrolled through his Twitter and the comments about the crazy aircraft carrier guy.

"Excuse me, handsome."

Behind him a young girl, maybe twenty, was armed with a broom and dustpan. She smiled and pointed at the floor. A half a bottle of Budweiser was under Tyler's stool—literally half a bottle since it was smashed.

He scooted his stool and the woman swept the remains. "Thanks." She smiled and sauntered to the high-top tables to collect more broken glass.

"Hey, you go see carrier? Tolkov?" The man had a Slavic face and drank a clear liquid on the rocks. He spoke with a thick Eastern European accent.

"That right, seeing the Tolkov."

"Ahh, amazing boat. I serve in Russia Navy, never Tolkov, but Varyag. That's cruise missile and intel."

"Ah, what brought you to Northern Minnesota?"

"Ahh friends, you know, the weather too. Like Siberia only more tropical." He laughed at his own joke.

"I think you're bleeding," Tyler said. The man had blood running down the side of his head, gathering near his ear.

"Ah, miss," he yelled at the bartender. "I need towel."

The bartender came over and handed the man a stack of napkins. He held the stack to the side of his head as he looked over the liquor bottles at the back of the bar gauging his wound in the mirror.

"Mr. Ukraine?" a voice said from behind Tyler and the Slavic man.

A man with long black hair holding a beer tapped him on the shoulder. He had a red puffy cheek and brown skin and appeared to be a Native American.

"Geronimo!"

"My name is John."

"Da, John, John. I buy you drink."

The man slid a stool next to the Ukrainian. "You Russians are tough as nails, you earn the Ojibwa respect."

"You Comanche are nothing like your John Wayne say. You would be famous if you came to Russia bar."

"I'm not Comanche," the Indian man said.

The young barmaid rushed to pick up stools and sweep up glass. Several napkin dispensers and ketchup and mustard bottles were on the floor. A hot pink bra dangled from the Big Game Hunter arcade consul in the corner. The bar's walls and ceiling were covered in stapled braziers.

The woman from behind the bar rushed fresh beers to the patrons and they seemed to fit into two categories. Either they looked Native American or they looked Russian. One held a bottle of beer to his head, another feigned boxing moves on the man across the table from him and tried to teach him how to throw a good left hook. The man across the table held up his hand in a faux block to play along. He too had a puffy chin and a cut on his face.

Tyler scrolled through more Tweets. More jokes from the greenies. More snide remarks about nuclear. A pic of Sergi with two blonde women appeared out of focus since he moved his head as someone snapped the pic. Behind Sergi a piece of pink lingerie hung from the television.

He wished for a moment that he had met Sergi in a different life. The man knew how to enjoy himself. Tyler wondered if he could ever be a Russian playboy. Minnesota boys weren't known for their rowdiness or playboy charm. No matter.

"Hey tall man." The Slavic man tugged on Tyler's arm. "You think Indians can take Russia in hockey?"

The Indian man interrupted. "Indians don't play hockey, we think it's stupid. It's a Nordic sport, and Nordics invaded our land. That doesn't mean Ojibwa do it."

"Hey tall boy, why you come here to see Tolkov? Don't you get internet?" the Slavic man asked.

"Just want to check it out. It's history you know?"

The Slavic man blared a huge belly laugh. "Da, you understand, it big deal, it bigger than Reagan and Star Wars. You know Reagan?"

"Of course he knows Reagan, do you think he doesn't know the presidents?" the Indian said.

"Most Americans know presidents. Do Indians not know Russian premieres?"

"Yes we know leaders. Indians aren't stupid."

"Name last ten premieres in Russia?"

"There's Putin, ahhh, Gorby, ahhh…" The Indian scratched his chin.

"You already messed it up, do you know tall man?"

Tyler dug deep for Contemporary Russian Studies 102. "Let's see, Putin, Medvedev, Putin, first term, Yeltsin, Gorby, Chernenko, Andropov, Leoinid Brezhnev, Nikita Kruschev, Bulganin, Malenkov, and Stalin. I think that's ten," Tyler said with a nervous stutter.

The Indian and the Slavic man both laughed.

"You very smart, tall man, we buy you drink. We introduce you to Sergi."

"Great," Tyler said with a feigned smile.

The two men slapped each other on the back as Tyler returned to his Tweets. He glanced at his image in the mirror covering the back of the bar. The Slavic man and the Indian talked loudly occasionally bumping him. He finished his beer and readied himself to hunt for the carrier. Once again the video games in the mirror caught his attention—a standard Big Buck Hunter, the golf game where you roll the big ball and some sort of bass fisherman console. He again noticed the hot pink bra dangling from the Big Buck Hunter.

He scrolled back up on his Tweets until Sergi's pic popped up again. He had his arms around two women and behind him a blurred pink bra hung off a television screen. But it wasn't a television screen. It was Big Buck Hunter.

Tyler eyed the video game consul and held up his phone to compare the two. It was the same as the pic, the same pink bra hanging from the same game consul.

"Sergi, *Ya kuplyu tebe vypit,*" the Slavic man yelled. "Come! I buy you drink!"

From the corner where the bathrooms were, there was Sergio Stanisavovich. He had his arms around the two women from the pic. A shock of surprise ran up his spine and he jumped off the stool and rushed over to Sergi.

"Sergi?"

"Tyler Chambers. Everyone, this is carrier man, Captain of Tolkov," he yelled.

Tyler became embarrassed but luckily nobody heard Sergi over the noise. "Sergi, you're supposed to be on the boat. On Tolkov."

"Ty, my friend. This is my new friends. Ah what's your name hon?"

"I'm Marissa." She extended her ditzy hand to Tyler.

"I'm Carrie," the other one said as she pushed Sergi's hand from her waist and moved in on Tyler.

He nudged her behind him and spoke in a quiet tone. "Sergi, you can't be off the boat, it's not a diplomatic vessel unless you're on board."

"Oh I get tired, I escape." He leaned into Tyler and whispered, "Tyler, you need rubbers? Marissa and Carrie are how you say, freaky. Wear rubber with them." Sergi reached in his pocket.

"You need to get back to Tolkov now."

Sergi laughed. "Big Tyler, no need for worry, nobody in world knows we here."

"But, you Tweeted a picture of yourself. The whole world knows, literally the whole world. Everyone is watching, including the Feds."

"No, we in Siberia, I mean American Siberia. Nobody come up here."

"Okay, here's what we're going to do. We're going to get out of here. I have a car, we'll drive to Tolkov and we're getting on board."

"No, I not done with ladies."

"You can bring the ladies if you want, but we have to go."

"Ha, listen to you, barking orders like Admiral, you only Captain. Diplomat outrank you." Sergi lunged to the bar, he pulled out a wad of hundred-dollar bills and held one in the air. The bartender rushed over. "We buy drink for everyone. Even Indians. Fuck John Wayne!"

Everyone jeered. The Indians thrusted their glasses in the air and yelled.

The Ukrainian fella came over to Tyler. "Hey you mess with Sergi?"

"No, I was just talking to him."

"Nobody tell Sergi what to do."

Two more Russians approached and surrounded him.

"You want to drag Sergi out of here? You get past us first, eh?"

"I don't want to get past anyone, it's just that Sergi has a prior commitment."

"Commitment, you his mommy?" one of the Russians said.

As Tyler glanced over the Russian's shoulder a man dressed in tactical gear with a submachine gun spoke to the bouncer as he pointed to Sergi.

"You tough guy. You think Russians are animals."

"Not at all, I respect Russians. How do you think I can name all your premieres? Even Andropov."

Tyler purchased a minor reprise with that trivia. Contemporary Russian Studies 102, $4,500 for the two credits, finally paying off.

More law enforcement poured in, dressed in Kevlar with helmets and MP5 submachineguns. Tyler calculated in his head how long Sergi's romp with two women in the restroom while drunk would take, add it to the timestamp of the Tweet and extrapolated how long it took DHS to respond to Sergi's picture. Do people not know about the GPS metadata attached to jpegs? Surely NSA monitored every social media account that had anything remotely to do with Tolkov.

The bar patrons' eyes lifted as the men with machine guns rushed in.

One of the Russians leaned in closer to Tyler and tapped his finger in the middle of Tyler's chest. "Listen tallboy, Sergi big news. He hero in Russia and Ukraine. Nobody tell him what to do."

"I'm sorry," Tyler said. The Indian angrily confronted the FBI agent dressed in tactical gear. Tyler heard some barking of orders and a distinct *stand aside or you will be detained.*

"You big man, you can take me," the Russian goaded to Tyler as he tapped his own chest.

Tyler allowed the notion of battling a buff, drunk Russian with his Columbia PhD fists of fury to linger in his mind.

Three FBI men threw the Indian down to the floor. The Russian broke his stare with Tyler and rushed the submachine gun men. They threw fists at him and he went down, right next to his Indian friend.

The two men with blood running from their chins in the corner attacked two of the FBI men, throwing punches like jackhammers. The FBI men wore tactical gloves that resembled jack-booted brass knuckles. Their jack-fisted punches had no effect on the drunk Indian and Russian.

The Slavic man and other Russian broke their stare on Tyler and ran to help their friend. A man near the door threw his beer bottle by the neck at an FBI man's head. It shattered on his helmet.

Someone hip-checked Tyler and sent him to the ground. They stomped on his shoulder and lunged at another FBI man who just walked into the bar. He went down. Tyler assumed he was Indian from his long black, braided hair. The Indian raised his fists to the air and pummeled the FBI man.

Sergi lay spread eagle on the floor so Tyler ran over and pulled him up. "Sergi, we have to get out of here. They're going to arrest you."

"For what, I do nothing."

"Believe me, they'll think of something."

Tyler dragged Sergi behind the bar and through the kitchen. Carrie and Marissa followed.

They found a door with an exit sign over it. They opened it and another FBI man appeared. The man threw a fist at Sergi who deflected the punch causing it to make contact with Marissa. She went down to the floor. Carrie jumped on the man and screamed as she clawed his face with her purple nails.

"Come on Sergi, let's go!" Tyler yelled.

They ran around to the front of the bar keeping out of sight. Several law enforcement cars and vans lined the street. More FBI agents rushed into the front of the bar.

"There." Tyler pointed to his rental. He popped open the locks and they jumped in and were off. The bar fight created the perfect distraction.

"We have to back for Mary and Larissa," Sergi cried.

"Who's that?" Tyler asked.

"They are my love, I cannot leave them."

"Your love? What about Tasha and Natalya?"

"They are minstrel."

"Who are Mary and Larissa?" Tyler asked as he carefully recalled the barmaid's directions.

"Them," Sergi yelled as he pointed a thumb back to the bar. "I in love with Mary and Larissa."

"You mean Carrie and Marissa?"

"Yes, Carrie and Marissa, they mean world to me."

Tyler had trouble keeping his eyes on County Road Seven from his laughter.

"You bad man Tyler Chambers. You no respect institution of love."

The car skidded along the shoulder as Tyler almost lost control from laughing.

"You terrible man, you terrible man, Tyler. You force me to go back with minstrel Russian women. I better off in Soviet Gulag." Sergi leaned back in the car seat and passed out.

Tyler never thought he'd have to scold a grown man like a parent scolds a child. Sergi wouldn't remember Tyler's words anyways since he was passed out when he dropped him into his bed.

He climbed the ladders in quick repetition. They said never step two at a time as a tall person might do on a flight of stairs or you might go ass over tea kettle. Just take them in quick repetition.

It was quiet on the bridge, Archer must be below deck getting some shuteye. He climbed to the roof of the tower. There was plenty of cold beer up there. He didn't care if it was breakfast time.

The morning sun hung just high enough to cast a tall skinny shadow over the hot tub. The mini fridge hummed his name. He stepped over to retrieve a beer.

"Captain, would you like cup of coffee? There's plenty." Natalya smoked a cigarette in her bikini. She sipped her coffee from a tea set that appeared to be from Russian nobility.

She shifted upright in the deck chair and unscrewed the top of a green thermos and poured coffee into the plastic topper which doubled as a cup.

He adjusted a deckchair back to sitting level and she handed him the thermos topper. "Thank you, Natalya." He smiled, trying his hardest to hide his surprise that she spoke perfect English with a haughty Russian accent that would entice any man.

He balanced the cup in his lap, holding it with both hands, leaned back, and let out a sigh.

"Oh Tyler, you poor thing, Sergio Stanisavovich is driving you to madhouse."

"Yes." He sighed again.

"It's nice to see him drive others crazy for change." She took a drag off her cigarette.

He smiled toward starboard and gulped a slug of coffee. "Sergio Stanisavovich. What do you see in him?"

"He's playboy but he's charming. He's caring when he wants to be. And I get to go places I wouldn't normally."

"Where are you from?"

"Moscow. But I've been all over Baltics. That's East Europe."

"You mean with Sergi?"

"No, school mostly, I was raised in Moscow, but did undergrad at Rezekne in Latvia and masters at Novosidirsk. My thesis put me at Sarov, that's Russian Federation nuclear research facility."

"Yes, I know what Sarov is." Tyler's eyes widened when he realized he was sitting next to another doctor.

He coddled the topper enjoying the warmth. Although it was clear and the sun's fingers touched the back of his neck and head, a Minnesota morning chill lingered in the air. Maybe 60 degrees, but probably only 50. Minnesota mornings were so refreshing. Nail-biting cold at 5 AM, 80 degrees by late morning.

His eyes wandered to Natalya's legs. They were firm from the cold. She could wear the hell out of a bikini, even in arctic weather.

"Why are you doing this, Tyler Chambers?"

"Doing what?" Goodness, surely she didn't notice his wandering eyes.

"This." She motioned port with her cigarette.

"I have no idea," Tyler said with a groan.

"Doctor Chambers, I admire what you do here."

"Thank you but I have no idea what that is."

"You're a sincere man. Most men of power never admit they accidentally succeeded. You are different."

"Maybe someone stomped on my pride once and I want to do some stomping myself. Why are you here? Is Sergi husband material?"

Natalya laughed. "Oh goodness, no. He takes me places but I

mean…he is supporter of women. The feminism."

"You think Sergi is a feminist?" Tyler grinned as clandestinely as possible.

"The way it works in Russia is only the most talented women rise to the top. They break the glass, you know?"

"Yes, the glass ceiling."

"Glass ceiling. But it is still man's world, if women break the glass they need to take certain men along the way, it's a fair trade."

"A tradeoff? So you and Tasha are…well."

"You think I'm bimbo?"

Tyler gave her a surprised look.

"You know bimbo?" she said.

"Yes, I know bimbo, you are not bimbo, a bimbo. You're not a bimbo."

"But Sergi is small price for getting out of Moscow and breaking glass."

"You don't care that he's exploiting you?"

Natalya laughed again showcasing her Russian charm. "Please, I am exploiting him. When news of the Tolkov being sold to American firm spread, I did everything to get ticket."

"What was your thesis on?"

"Fusion. Sarov researched weapons but the knowledge could be put to energy use."

As Tyler's grip on the empty thermos topper tightened, it popped out of his hand and jumped about six feet in the air performing several turns and bounced around on the deck. "Can I have a warmup?"

Natalya set her cigarette and cup down and retrieved the topper.

Tyler averted his eyes aft as she kneeled down to retrieve the cup hoping this Russian beauty wouldn't notice his glance. Yes, it was a good decision including shots of her in the Discovery doc. She poured him a fresh dribble and placed in on the table.

"Thank you," Tyler said trying not to let his voice crack like a pubescent eighth grader.

She plopped back in the deck chair and took a sharp drag off her cigarette.

"Why did you fight so hard to get on this boat in the middle of nowhere instead of staying at Sarov?"

"Russian people are looked down on for their scientific accomplishments. We have Sputnik, we have the ISS, many Russians and Slavs at Hadron Collider. Nobody remembers anything except Chernobyl. I think that is despicable."

"Russians have done amazing things with reactors."

"Yes, nobody knows though. When I'm done with my time with Sergi and Tolkov, I will go to Ignition Facility in California. You know of NIF."

"The National Ignition Facility in San Francisco? You're going there?"

"That's the future. That's where I want to get to. Here on Tolkov we are moving a few inches at a time. If it takes that long to get there, I will wait. You will put good word in for me?"

"I don't know how good my word will be after this is over."

"Tyler, you will be talked about for centuries to come in any conversation about energy. You are Rockefeller of twenty-first century."

He smiled at Natalya and admired the sunrise. For a brief moment he let go and allowed Natalya's words to linger in his mind and trusted them to be true.

They enjoyed the bright sunrise as well as the briskness of the Arrowhead cold summer morning. Tyler finished his coffee and stood from the deck chair.

"Thank you for the coffee. I'm heading to bed."

"Good night, Captain," Natalya said. It was the first time Tyler saw her smile.

He descended the ladder, cut past the bridge and slid down several more ladders. When he entered the lower decks he ran into Archer. His hair was still wet from a shower and he was clean shaven.

"Captain." He extended his hand. "Long time no see."

"Good to be back."

"How was Geneva, did you find a plant manager?"

"Still looking."

"What did you want to see me about? Do you have time to meet?"

Tyler's rehearsed speech about abandoning ship could wait just a little longer. "Just wanted to go over some numbers. I think the diagnostics on my phone answered my questions. I'm going to get some sleep."

"Excellent."

"And keep an eye on Sergi. He escaped last night."

A look of surprise fell over Archer's face. "Oh. I wasn't aware."

"It's been a long night."

"I suppose it has."

He hiked down the corridor to his captain's quarters as Archer ascended the ladder.

He pulled his shirt and pants off and crashed into his bunk. As his eyes drifted he thought of Jonah and the whale. Somehow the belly of a whale gave comfort to its occupant. Steel surrounded him in every direction and the creeks as the whale rolled over the logs soothed him. He opened his eyes and the pipes along the ceiling appeared to move ever so slightly. It was as if the metal beast was alive and life pulsated through its veins, even in the lower decks. It made him yearn for the comfort of his bedroom, of his library, of his exotic cars…

In a quiet, woodsy area just off Itasca State Highway Seven, a brook tricked through the bottom of a ravine and meandered through the forest. A doe tip-toed to the edge and scoured for predators. After satisfying herself that it was safe, she lowered her head to the brook and sipped from the clear water.

A burst of a dozen shots echoed through the air. The doe lifted her head but it was too late. She caught eight holes in her torso, each trickled with blood. Her knees gave out and the weight of her body crashed down to the rocks.

An Indian and a Ukrainian leaped from behind a fallen tree. The Indian looked at his hunting weapon, an MP5 which had the selector on full auto.

The Ukrainian handed the Indian the bottle of vodka. "Let me see. How many shots you have left?" He pulled the magazine out and pushed his thumb on the top cartridge to gauge how much resistance the spring gave. "Lots left," he mumbled.

They hiked to the bank of the creek.

"One, two, three, four…nine hits," the Indian counted.

"No, eight, that not bullet hole."

"Hmmm," the Indian conceded.

The Ukrainian pointed the weapon at a tree and peered through the red dot sights. “Very space-age. In Kiev, police have AK-47, same as army use. These tiny rifles are very nice hunting guns.”

“Hmm, much lighter than Mossberg too,” the Indian said as he tipped the bottle of vodka toward the morning sun.

“You say….eh prayer to Indian God for taken hunt, yes?”

“No, old stereotype. We just cut the tenderloin and leave the rest for wolves.”

CHAPTER SIXTEEN

Tyler and Richard watched the metrosexual lumberjack focus his concentration on the cocktail shaker. He raised it to his right shoulder and shook in short bursts. He looked like a person who might shake fruit at the grocery store to test for the perfect Honeycrisp apple.

He set the shaker down and sampled the contents with a bar spoon. He smacked his lips as he evaluated the taste and tossed the spoon into the sink. He carefully squeezed the eye dropper from the bitters bottle to add one more drop of cherry vanilla concentrate into the shaker.

After another cha-cha beated shake, he placed the shaker next to the hookah. He put a tablet of tobacco into the device and pressed the button and the machine scorched the tablet and sent flavored smoke through the pipe which the lumberjack submerged into the cocktail shaker.

He set two cocktail glasses next to Tyler and Richard and filled them with purple smoky liquid.

"Enjoy, gentlemen."

"An interesting establishment," Richard said.

"Do you think the guys would like it or is it too trendy for them?"

"Hard to say, we've gone to the four corners of the globe to find the perfect everything. Perfect burgers, perfect wings, perfect cioppino."

"Cioppino? You mean the seafood stew?"

"Yeah, it's a thing. There are connoisseurs in New England who eat it like it's a wine tasting. We tried Sicily, but it's not a thing there even though it's a Sicilian dish. Maine is where the real cioppino snobs reside."

"I'll have to try next time we're in Cape Cod."

"Tyler, tell me how everything is going?"

"Well..." Tyler sipped the chilled surface of his cocktail. "...seven miles a day, lawyers keeping the government in line, Indians excited, Putin called me. Seems like everything is going smoothly."

"I'm going to ask you this, because I know you know the answer and I'll bet you want to brag just a little but…how much a day do you incur in legal fees?"

"Around ninety thousand a day."

"Jeez." Richard sipped his cocktail, smiling. "That's a rite of passage. When you ruffle enough feathers to break fifty Sterling a day, er, what is that, thirty grand US dollar in legal fees, you know you've arrived." He raised his cocktail glass. "Cheers, mate."

They touched glasses.

Richard cocked his head. "This is really interesting. It tastes like a fag. I mean a cigarette, did I just say that? It tastes like one of those flavored cigars. I mean in a good way. How did you find out about this place?"

"Grew up around here."

"Are we still in Minneapolis proper?"

"Just outside the city, Robbinsdale."

"Charming suburb."

"Mean Gene Okerlund is from here."

"Oh goodness, I haven't watched wrestling since the '80s."

"Can I ask you something Richard?"

"Sure."

Tyler had practiced his question several times in the mirror. He closed the divider between him and Rogers in the limo and recited it several times on the way over. It was a good question, a logical question. Rational, flattering, a question protégés asked of their mentors.

Richard lent him his full attention. It wasn't very Minnesotan to give one such direct attention. Tyler found it difficult to make eye contact and retreated to another drink from his cocktail.

"I wanted to know, if you don't mind me asking. When someone goes on a business venture, how do you…when you…"

Richard tried to understand.

"I'm having troubles, so…if you…" He glanced at Richard who still lent him his full attention and patience.

"Yeah, you can ask me anything, mate."

"Well…" Tyler shifted in his chair and started again. "How do you…" He sighed and tried again. "How do you do it? How do you do it, Richard? I'm not cut out for this. I can't sleep, I can't focus, I can't do anything, I sweat all the time, I'm just not cut out but I bought this thing, I bought into it and I'm not going to make it. I'm dying here."

"Okay, okay, okay. I've gone through the same thing."

"What do I do? I take sleeping pills and they don't help, alcohol doesn't help, I've tried just—"

"Okay, don't do any drugs, okay, just, here's what you want to do…I mean I don't know what to do, but, you know you're doing something. You're trying to change the world, people despise that."

"Everyone hates me."

"That's not true."

"Yeah, everyone. The power companies, my employees at Fusion, board of directors, they think I betrayed them, my wife. She hates me."

"I'm sure she doesn't hate you."

"She's divorcing me."

"Oh my!" Richards's eyes grew bigger. He quickly regained his composure. "I'm sure she's just bitter."

"What do I do?"

"Okay, take it easy."

"I'm backing out."

Richard pushed his drink aside and raised his hands to try to get Tyler to shut up and listen. "Okay mate, listen carefully. I know what you're going through. I've been there. I'm still there. It's a struggle every day. Elon does it, Dave does it."

"I want to go back to the way things were. I was so fat and happy and content. I just rolled around in my easy chair in my library and read books."

"I know, mate, comfort. Something warm and familiar."

"Do you miss the days where you didn't have this weight on your shoulders?"

"Yeah I remember those days."

"When?"

"Well, my first record shop. Shop downstairs, office and recording space upstairs. I lounged in my beanbag chair and listened to music and smoked herb. I switched between doing that and manning the shop and talking with customers and the newest upcoming band. Yeah, I miss those days."

"I wanted to work in a lab. I wanted to work in academia and do nothing but research on fusion. I never thought I'd be rich. I got caught up in a business venture and next thing I know nuclear fusion is a distant memory. I got lucky. I suppose you could have a beanbag chair and all the pot you want now."

"And you could go back to work in a lab if you really wanted to. You know I miss the old days but I don't yearn for it. I look back and those were some good years but if I still ran a record store and smoked reef every day I think I'd feel pretty pathetic. I love what I've built and I believe my best days are ahead of me."

"What do you do when everyone is against you? Everyone hates you."

Richard rubbed his hands together searching for the right words. "When I went up against British Airways, I was the devil. I was worse than Hitler, I was the most hated man in Britain. People thought I was attacking the royal crown since BA was the official airliner of the UK. Most people hated me for changing the status quo. Everyone thought Britain should have one airline and anything else was an insult to the crown. And I can't tell you how many decisions I made in the recording business that angered fans. But I did it to stay ahead of the industry and to move forward."

"What do I do?"

"Sometimes you follow the trail but sometimes you blaze a new path. The synergy comes flowing. Remember who said that?"

Tyler allowed just the faintest of grins to linger. He recalled this advice that he dished out while eating wings and slamming Trappist Ale. "Sounds familiar," he mumbled.

"You know mate when you said that, the three of us already knew it. I think you said it for you."

Richard twirled his glass with his fingers. "Tyler. There are people in this world who move it forward. We come up with the ideas of the future but that's easy. It's trudging forward with them that's the hard part. Invention is easy, innovation is difficult."

"I miss my lab coat."

"I miss my beanbag…my hi-fi headphones. Headphones are so perfect these days, I miss the metal ones that looked like tin cans. Those old headphones, you really knew they were there."

Richard's words relaxed him or maybe it was the alcohol doing its job. When he left the trendy bar, he'd go right back into the world that hated him.

"You know Ty, when a man gets what he wants he starts thinking about life. Certain people are ambitious and when they have the means they find a way. It wasn't an accident that I ran into you at that mud race."

Tyler's attention jumped. Richard smiled at him with the same glimmer in his blue eyes from behind the mud at the warrior dash all those months ago.

"You looked me up?"

"You think we just let anyone into our little club?"

"Why me?"

"Your background in science, your lack of fulfilling something in science, your wealth. The perfect combination for a white knight to strike down the boogie man."

Tyler thought back to the last time he strolled the research lab at Columbia. He wore business casual while they had lab coats on. He remembered the iciness as he shook hands with his soon-to-be-former colleagues. Where the hell was he going again? A foam tube? "Best of luck," they all said. *Best of luck*, the professional way of saying F-off. Would he turn in the courtyard to see if anyone watched him leave from the lab windows? Nobody was there. They had already gone back to their stations. Off to start a business with Rachel. Academia was a distant memory.

"I have to go back to my ship, don't I?"

Richard nodded. "Yes, but not for anyone else. For you."

Tyler nodded and smiled at his friend.

"Ty, you're in an exclusive club. Nobody's involved except the most creative and inspiring characters of the world. Go forth. Make great leaps. Try big, fail big, even if you fail, you'll have a good tax write-off for years to come."

Tyler laughed.

"And don't be afraid to anger people. If you have enemies then it means you stand for something."

CHAPTER SEVENTEEN

Tyler peeked through the kitchen blinds, carefully lifting one blind as to not let anyone outside know he was watching. They were out there waiting for him just beyond the property line. This would be bad for Rachel and therefore bad for him since it would call the unwanted attention she was quite specific about.

The Scarsdale Police obviously didn't care about the protest in front of their estate since they assigned the heaviest officer possible to their cause. The officer wore a gun belt but nobody would know it from the front since his stomach hung past his belt buckle and groin area. He leaned against his squad car with big cop sunglasses and arms crossed. A student of the *you better not cause me to get out of my comfortable position* school of thought.

The Chambers Manor had majestic walls surrounding the backyard and sides but the front was exposed to the street. The garage was out back and the awning on the west side offered shade when Rogers pulled the cars around to pick him and Rachel up. A grand spectacle, yes, but now it would work to their disadvantage.

"Sir, they are quite savage if you'd excuse my commentary," Rogers announced.

"Yeah, angry too." Tyler continued to survey the crowd.

No Chernobyl in Minnesota, No Chernobyl in Minnesota.

They thrusted their signs into the air with perfect unison. *Build more windmills. Solar is our future. Sink the Tolkov. No nukes on the Iron Range.*

Tyler felt particularly sour about the no nukes sign. There was no way a fission plant could explode. Meltdown maybe, but there was no possibility of chain reaction. It was like considering a Ford pickup a bomb since it had a gas tank full of combustible liquid. Tyler stared harder at the protesters since he could see his wife seething from the corner of his eye.

"Mommy, what are they saying?" Thora bounced up and down in her Belle dress. She loved how the frilly bottom part bounced in rhythm with her.

"Go put your shoes on," Rachel snapped.

Thora darted to the side parlor like a little fairy running through an enchanted garden.

Tyler plucked the blinds shut as he turned to Rogers. "They are animals, they have no respect for our political process." The blinds offered him some privacy from Rachel's anger.

He tried desperately to ignore her as he attempted to keep Rogers engaged on the subject. Surely this would prevent her from broaching the subject of their agreement where these shenanigans were to stay in the Arrowhead region.

"Sir, I recommend that I pull the SUV around and you and Mrs. Chambers and Ms. Thora cut through the backyard and through the south gate to Sheridan Drive."

"A good plan, Rogers. Rachel is that okay?"

"Fine."

Rogers stepped away.

"Rogers," Tyler said.

He came back through the door and pivoted, giving Tyler his full attention.

"You'll have everything under control?"

"I'll do my best, sir."

At times Tyler despised Rogers's succinct style. The weight of his wife's scowl beat the back of his neck like a noon sun.

"Will there be anything else?"

"No, please proceed." Tyler retreated to the blinds, to gather intelligence of course. "Boy, they really are loud. I'm surprised the Wenburgs haven't called the mayor's office."

"Do we allow a profiteer of energy to exploit Native American's land?"

"No!"

"Are we going to allow technology designed by the same people who made Chernobyl to sit in the heartland?"

"No!"

The woman known as Lotus paced back and forth like a leopard stalking its pray while shouting old sound bites from the Cold War anti-nuclear movement into a megaphone. Tyler wondered if she would remember his face from Robert Yellowfeather's office. How on earth did they find out where he lived?

"Those people are nuts." Tyler refused to understand that Rachel was burning a hole in him. "They would have us go back to the Stone Age."

Rachel stomped out of the kitchen. Tyler had won that battle, although he certainly didn't feel like a winner.

Tyler held hands with Thora as they passed through the back gate. The SUV waited across the south lawn next to the curb. Rogers motioned them toward the vehicle.

"Hey there they are. They're leaving!" someone yelled from just beyond the hedge.

A storm of protesters charged from around the hedge. They ran to the sidewalk along Sheridan, careful not to step on the property and give the police reason to move in.

"You're going to radiate everyone. Traitor. War profiteer!"

Rogers walked swiftly and held Rachel's arm as he motioned her to the vehicle.

No nukes on Indian Territory, no nukes on Indian Territory.

There they go again, confusing fusion and fission. He tried to ignore them.

As he pulled Thora along, she still bounced, showing off her little yellow dress to her audience making Tyler wonder if she thought they were there for her.

Out of the corner of his eye, he caught a man throwing an object, his arm making a quick jerking movement. By reaction, Tyler ducked out of the way and raised his hand to his face.

The object missed him by inches and struck Thora in the cheek. It was an egg. She had a surprised look on her face. The white and yolk drizzled down to the lacy part of her princess dress.

The protesters went quiet for a moment. Rogers beamed at the crowd with a sour look that Tyler had never seen before. He looked as though he exercised incredible restraint. Rachel snatched Thora in her arms and rushed into the SUV as Rogers put himself in front of the two.

Tyler scanned the crowd. He locked eyes with a man in the front. The young man had a guilty-as-sin look on his face. The other protesters started to chant again but they inched away from this man as if to distance themselves from the culprit. Tyler stepped toward him with unflinching eyes.

The young man kept thrusting his sign up and down and tried to keep with the chant, but the more Tyler closed in, the more uncomfortable the man became. Adrenaline shot through Tyler's veins. He clenched his fists by his side and gnashed his teeth.

The man backed into the crowd, trying to disappear and not notice an angry father marching toward him. He tried to break eye contact and feign ignorance on who threw the egg as Tyler stormed closer to him. It was no use. Tyler knew it was him.

The SUV pulled away and Rachel, Rogers, and Thora were gone. The chanting died down as Tyler confronted the man who hit his daughter with the egg.

His face was inches from the man. He towered over him. The man's eyes bulged behind his thick glasses. His mouth hung open, sweat ran down the side of his face.

Tyler unclenched his fists and locked eyes with him. "You will come with me. Is that clear?"

The man closed his mouth and swallowed not daring to disagree.

He spotted Lotus who held the megaphone to her side. "You will come too." He panned the group of protesters who stared at him with angry eyes. "The rest of you will come with me."

Two luxury bus-style limousines thundered along Highway 9 with the cooling towers approaching in the distance. The ride was quiet with the occasional light chatter. Tyler stared at the highway from the front seat as Lotus clung to the megaphone in her lap.

Lester led the group through the innards of his Reactor Number Two. The archaic computer displays with dizzying green diodes from a science fiction film caused the environmentalists' heads to dart back and forth. They provided diagnostics for the giant pressurized water reactor which powered a million homes in New York State.

"The uranium atoms are split, that's called fission, and it produces heat. The heat makes the water hot and it goes through the pipes to the steam generator and that steam spins the turbines—the big monsters that make all the noise." Lester motioned with his hands as he spoke into the bull horn over the hum of the turbines.

The environmentalists' eyes fell into the back of their heads from the mind-numbing array of input from Lester and Indian Point Two. They also glanced suspiciously at the rad tags clipped to their shirts.

Tyler wondered if his little excursion would work. People still wanted to believe in aliens despite no evidence. More people died each year from slipping in bath tubs than shark attacks, yet sharks are feared. Cell phones caused brain cancer despite no evidence. Every bad thing ever said about GMOs yet no evidence. Astrology, cryptids, ghosts, karma, intuition. Ironically, the people who believe these superstitions are always critical of faith-based religions. God is just a fairytale but watch for brain cancer from your iPhone.

The heads bobbed back and forth and Tyler empathized as best he could with the tour group. He remembered how he wasn't always a star swimmer. That first time his father made him jump off the diving board, he wore a kids' life vest, and his mother waded in the pool. He inched his toes to the edge of the board but his little feet just wouldn't leap forward. After swimming the equivalent of the circumference of the earth by his senior year, he wondered how there could have been a time when the water frightened him.

The environmentalist group removed their noise-cancelling headphones as they exited Indian Point Two. Some of them rubbed their ears, others rechecked their rad tags, just to make sure they didn't indicate exposure.

"Any questions?" Lester announced.

"Where's the radioactive waste put?" one of them asked.

"Don't they just dump the radioactive water into the river?" another interrupted with.

"Oh heavens no," Lester said. "The pressurized water in the reactor is recycled over and over and the steam vapor is a totally different system. It has to be cooled with regular water and that's what we get from the river. That's why nuclear plants are generally near a body of water."

"But those rod things. Those are radioactive?"

"Yes, they are put in what's called dry storage casks."

Lester waited as if a follow-up question should be asked by the tour group.

He smiled awkwardly then continued as though someone asked a question. "Dry storage casks. It's a container made of steel and concrete that protects from radioactive—"

"How big are they?"

"Well, I suppose we could go look at them."

"Wait, they're here?"

"Yes, we store them on site."

The faces in the tour group were petrified with fear as every eyeball fixated on Lester Wilner.

"Do we wear radioactive outfits?" one of them finally asked.

"No, just what you have on is fine."

"Are they in some underground vault or something?"

"No, you might have seen them from the parking lot."

"They're just sitting out there?"

Tyler broke in to help his friend. "Lester, tell you what. Have someone bring us a Giger counter and a banana."

Tyler handed the Giger counter to Lotus. "Go ahead, that's the radioactive waste. See if it beeps."

The environmentalists looked with paralyzed stares.

Lotus approached the towering cask with a skeptical swagger. The cylindrical cast was about twenty feet in diameter and sat upright like a mini grain silo.

She waved the Giger counter over it and when the light clicking noises convinced her of her thoroughness she walked back to the group.

"Now I want you to test this." Tyler pulled a banana out of his pocket.

She waved the device over it and a feint peep tricked from it. “Is this banana radioactive?”

“Yes it is. It has potassium so it gives off about one microsievert of radiation. That’s more than the dry storage cask.”

“But it’s radioactive because you retrieved it from the break room of this place.”

“No, all bananas are radioactive. So is your television, so is your granite countertop, everything displays trace amounts. But the dry storage casks give off less than the banana.”

“But how can you sleep knowing that these things are in your back yard?”

“Because I believe in science. It’s well established that radiation is easily containable.”

Lotus’s eyes dodged left and right. Tyler remembered his little feet inching closer and closer to the edge of the diving board with his heart racing. He wanted to shove Lotus off the diving board.

“It’s okay if you want to ignore environmental science for urban legend—”

“I’m not ignoring science. Mister Chambers, I don’t know why you brought us out here.”

“See the three cooling towers? Those are three of the one hundred reactors we have in the US.”

“A hundred of these?”

“Correct, one hundred on the nose. They provide twenty percent of the power to America.”

“Where do they put this waste?”

“Most of them store it on site, like what you see here.”

“That’s insane.”

“I agree.”

An environmentalist raised his hand. “Why don’t they have a storage place to put all this?”

Tyler turned his head sharply and locked eyes with a young man who had his hand up. He had a curious look on his face that was filled with idealistic sincerity. There was hope. Tyler imagined his toes inching forward so they were just barely over the edge of the diving board. Maybe this young man would be the first to jump.

“There is a place,” Tyler said.

"Where?" the young man asked.

Tyler looked at Lester and then glanced back at the tour group of environmentalists. "Everyone get back on the bus. Everyone back on the bus and I'll show you."

Tyler hung up his smartphone after speaking for five minutes with NetJets. From behind the bus driver, he watched the cooling towers disappear into the horizon in the rearview mirror.

The two buses parked at the edge of the runway of West Chester County Airport. A fueled Airbus 320 waited at the edge of the tarmac. The group departed the two buses and the gate crew quickly ushered them to the plane. Before everyone was seated, the flight attendant sealed the door and the plane's twin engines vibrated to life.

"Could everyone find a seat please? Fasten your safety belts," she said.

She quickly went through the FAA safety regulations with the mock seatbelt and air mask. The plane turned sharply onto the runway and lunged into the sky.

As they made a rough landing the environmentalists jumped and the cabin filled with comments about the bouncing. The plane turned from the end of the primitive runway and a sign next to the modest tarmac read: *Welcome to Jackass Aeropark, Amargosa Valley, Nevada.*

Buses were waiting for them at the front of the terminal. As everyone disembarked, the dry desert heat knocked everyone back since it contrasted the humid heat of the East Coast. The buses kicked up a smoke screen of dust as they trudged toward their destination.

Tyler was the first to get off the bus after the two-hour ride. He shook hands with a man in a hardhat. The environmentalists' eyes ballooned as they stared at the entrance which resembled an opening for what could have been Godzilla's lair. Men with desert fatigues and rifles pulled the doors open. They bore the heat with a certain patience and relaxation in their manner.

As the group walked off the bus, a man with a white hardhat handed out yellow hardhats. "Everyone must have a hardhat on when inside the facility."

Tyler led the group to an uncovered train that resembled an oversized roller coaster. "Everyone fasten your safety belts and hang onto the bar in front of you. If you need help with your belt, raise your hand." The man in the white hardhat boarded the tram last.

The engine rumbled causing the seats to vibrate and they disappeared into the tunnel. As the tram turned to a downward angle, Tyler and Lotus grasped the hand bar in front of them to stable themselves. Lotus's eyes bulged as her mouth hung open. She said something to Tyler but the industrial rumbling of the tracks overwhelmed her words.

They emerged from the darkness into a lighted area. The man in the white hardhat stepped off the front of the tram. "We're here. Everyone unfasten your belt and watch your step as you enter the repository."

There were other men with hardhats and flashlights waiting for them in the dark. Lotus clung to Tyler's forearm as the men led the group.

They were ushered toward a vault door two feet thick. One environmentalist approached Tyler. "Mister Chambers, are we allowed to be in here?"

"Yes. I made arrangements."

"But you just told them you were coming with a bunch of us?"

"Yes."

"How do you do that?"

"I know a few people who worked on this mountain."

They were ushered through the vault doors and they walked briskly. The environmentalists had their arms out as if they were waiting to run into an object or a wall, but they never did.

Lotus's arm shook and Tyler put his hand over hers to calm her.

"Everyone ready your eyes for the light," the man in the white hardhat yelled.

Giant stadium lights appeared in the distance and they glowed from a dark amber to a yellowish glare and eventually a bright white.

Everyone glanced around in amazement at the vast emptiness that was lit as bright as any room in a home.

"You could fit a football stadium in here," one environmentalist observed.

The group spread around the area. Lotus was no longer shaking and let go of Tyler's arm. She wandered to where the 50 yard line would be and marveled at the ceiling, the lights, the walls, and the vastness of the empty space.

"Take a look," Tyler yelled. "Go ahead, spread out. Don't be afraid."

The environmentalists no longer used their hands to guide themselves and they walked about without fear of tripping over or running into anything. After they satisfied their curiosity, they came back to the 50 yard line and gathered around Tyler and Lotus.

Tyler started speaking. "This is the depository you were asking about. The government carved a space out of the bottom of this mountain to store all the radioactive waste in the country. There's a thousand feet of rock in every direction. The waste would still be stored in the dry storage casks, it's just that they'd be put here."

"So, when are they putting them here?"

"Never. Right now they stay next to the parking lot, like you saw back there at Indian Point."

"Why wouldn't they just put them here?" one environmentalist asked.

"Because people are scared."

"Can you blame them, it's radioactive waste," another yelled.

"Would you prefer it be her or next to the parking lot outside of Peekskill."

"I'd prefer if it didn't exist," a voice from the group said.

"But it does and it has to be put somewhere. Every plant has those dry storage casks sitting next to the parking lot. You can Google Earth any of them when we get back to the surface and see for yourself."

"But, solar and wind—"

"Even if we turned off all one hundred reactors, we'd still have spent fuel rods that need to be put somewhere for a long time."

"Why didn't they just put it here?"

The lone dissenter caused a hush within the group. Did he get through to one person?

Tyler walked toward a man in an LSU hoodie with a goatee. "It was closed by the Obama administration because of political concerns."

"They probably thought it was unsafe," a female voice yelled from the back of the group.

Tyler turned to her direction. "No. The US Office of Accounting cited politics as the reason, not science. Remember the casks stored next to the parking lot? That's a few feet of steel and concrete with no more radiation than a banana. This place has a thousand feet of rock in every direction."

"Why did they shut it down?" the man in the LSU hoodie asked.

"Because people are paranoid. They don't want to listen to science—"

"That's not science. What about Fukushima and Chernobyl?" a woman from the back yelled.

The LSU hoodie yelled back at her. "Fine, nuclear is horrible but why not just store what we have here. We can shut down the plants but where do we store the waste that already exists?"

The woman stood silent. Tyler had created dissent in the ranks. The first road to turning people. Even if they weren't sold on nuclear at least someone bought the logic of Yucca Mountain.

"He's trying to divide us. Don't you see what he's doing," a voice yelled from the back.

"Hey I'm allowed an opinion. Should I shut up and never talk again and just fall in line?"

"That would be good." The group laughed.

Lotus stepped through the group. "Nobody is allowed to tell someone else to shut up. Open communication is one of our core principles and dissent is part of what we do. Mister Chambers is giving us information and I'm confident our principles will shine through with truth as their partner."

A skinny Asian woman spoke up. "Lotus is right, the man should be allowed to speak. Don't you have any faith that our views can stand up to his ridiculous scrutiny?"

Tyler winced his eyes. *Thanks...I think.*

The airbus cruised over the Midwest thundering back to the east coast. Tyler logged into the display of the carrier on his phone. He read through the daily status reports from Archer. He swiped through several diagnostics and camera angles. The ship crept forward at its usual point three an hour. Archer had everything well at hand.

He checked the social media avenues. His PR people found the social media accounts of the sixty environmentalists and followed them with Tyler's Twitter account.

I'm being kidnapped by the aircraft carrier guy. It's not so bad.

This guy is fucking nuts.

I'm going to grow a second dick.

Lots of radioactive waste.

Go to a nuclear power plant, post a pic of nuc waste. It's usually next to parking lot. #picofnucwaste

Lotus joined Tyler in first class. "Mister Chambers. Why are you doing this? It's a nice tour, but I want to go home."

Tyler put his phone away. "I guess I want the chance to convince you."

"Me?"

"People like you. People who think as you do."

"You mean, idiots like me who don't believe in science?"

"Not at all. Science isn't just one experiment. It requires many to build consensus even among scientific minds. And there's nothing wrong with holding onto long-held beliefs since they were forged by observation and inference which are parts of the scientific method." Tyler thought about standing on that diving board again. When he jumped in on that fateful afternoon, he never again wanted to wade in from the steps at the shallow end. He became a diver that afternoon. He made it a goal to jump 100 times into his mother's hands, and maybe a few times without her help. "Lotus, I want to find common ground with you and others who think as you do. Maybe we're on the same side and we don't know it."

"I doubt that."

"Are you one of those people who is set in their ways and would never consider something counter to their long-held beliefs? If so that's fine by me."

Lotus looked at him skeptically.

"I know, reverse psychology, dirty tactic."

"Mister Chambers, my mind is as open as the horizon. If anyone shows me something new, I'm always grateful."

Tyler smiled as he stood from his seat and headed to the cockpit. He knocked on the door.

"Yes, Doctor Chambers?"

"How long to Jersey?"

"Two hours, forty minutes," the co-pilot said.

"I'd like to make a slight change to our destination."

The pair of bus-style limousines bumped along the gravel road. It was about an hour from Yeager Airport outside of Charleston. They were approaching the mining site and the industrial smell of the coal made everyone's nose twitch. A bulldozer drove from the pits and dumped coal into the parking lot.

Everyone stepped out of the limo buses into the sweltering heat. The stretch buses each held 30 passengers and they were filled to capacity with hot, annoyed environmentalists.

Tyler led the group to the mountain of coal. "Come on, climb to the top with me." He wondered if he should smash tablet-sized chunks of coal to the ground for effect.

He endured the clumsiness of his dress shoes moonlighting as hiking boots and wasn't shy about getting them grungy. The others followed to the summit of the coal pile.

He allowed the group to get closer to the apex before he spoke. "Look at this mountain," he yelled. "You are standing on 350 tons of coal. This is the amount of coal you will use in your 76.4 years on Earth. It will generate 700 megawatt hours of electricity for you and you alone. If you only used coal for your power, this mountain is your mountain.

"The CO2 you make from this is roughly one thousand tons. How does that sit with you?"

The environmentalists looked around confused, trying not to trip on the sharp shale. "How can 350 tons make 1000 tons of pollution?" one of them asked.

"The carbon combines with two oxygen molecules in the air. That's the *oh two* part in CO2."

"One person will use this whole mountain?"

"That is correct, one person."

Lotus climbed to where Tyler stood with her megaphone in hand. "You're going to convince members of Green Earth First that coal is dirty?" she said sarcastically.

"My plant will replace this mountain." Tyler held a piece of coal in the air. "Do you see this? This is about five pounds. This is how much uranium you'd use in your lifetime. This five pounds could replace this entire 350 tons of coal." He dropped it back in the pile.

"Mr. Chambers. There's nobody here that needs to know that coal is dirty. That's why we're trying to replace it with wind and solar."

"Wind and solar?"

"Yes, wind and solar."

"Wind and solar can only reduce this pile by so much. And they are expensive. I can produce nuclear for less than coal."

"It's not always about price. Some people will be willing to pay more for green energy."

He wondered if he had lost them. Price indifference threw a wrench in basic microeconomics. "This mountain is the American Dream. Americans will not settle for less."

"The American Dream is why we're the world's biggest polluters. You don't have to convince me this mountain is atrocious. I know. We already know this."

"You will not replace this mountain with wind or solar. I can replace every ounce of it with my plant."

"Wind and solar can replace this too."

"The wind doesn't always blow and the sun doesn't always shine. Uranium fuel rods don't care about the weather."

He was losing them. These people did not have their feet properly on Earth, they were somewhere in a utopian haven where only renewables existed. Don't say that, don't insult them, don't push them away. He would sell them dammit. He would find a way!

"Everyone back on the bus," he yelled.

On the bus ride back to the airport, everyone buried their noses into their smartphones, tweeting pictures and posting on Facebook the mountain of coal they ascended.

Tyler scrolled through the pictures and comments the group posted.

Standing with the crazy aircraft carrier guy somewhere in West Virginia.

A lifetime of coal, this is why we need wind.

Americans should learn to live with less. Atrocious that this much energy is what we use.

The buses pulled onto the tarmac where the plane waited for them. They shuffled back into the luxury Airbus A320-200. The plane held 180 passengers in traditional economy rows but Tyler had the crew assemble the World Executive configuration within minutes of booking the charter.

Instead of a long skinny movie theater, the plane cabin resembled the VIP section of a hip nightclub. The environmentalists sprawled across the couches and comfy seats. Tyler took the private room at the front of the cabin as it taxied to the runway. Everyone left their dirty, coal-stained shoes near the door at the urging of the flight attendant.

She quickly handed out hot towels so nobody would get coal dust on the tan and white surfaces.

The plane sped down the runway and launched into the air. Tyler put away his phone, momentarily ignoring the snarky remarks across social media.

After the plane achieved cruising altitude the seatbelt light blinked off and the flight attendant brought out a choice of sushi or vegetarian lasagna. Hot sake was also an option and the environmentalists had no complaints.

Tyler leaned back in his seat allowing the sake to do its job.

A man carrying his carafe and cup planted himself next to him. He opened the tray table and set them on top and filled his glass with hot sake. “Mister Chambers? When are we going to be in Dubai?”

“Moring, six AM local time.”

“Don’t we have to do any customs and immigration paperwork?”

“No, not for refueling, we’ll be on the ground for about 45 minutes and then back in the air.”

“And we don’t need passports in China?”

“No, we have special permission from the government. Everyone just has to stay with the guide. We won’t be there long. It’s taken care of.”

The man downed the tiny cup of sake. “Why did you do this?”

Tyler glanced at the LSU logo on the young man’s sweatshirt. “I guess I wanted to convince a tough audience since I had nothing better—”

“No, I mean, the whole thing. The aircraft carrier. What was your moment?”

Tyler pondered this question as he lifted his sake carafe and realized it was empty. The LSU man poured him a shot from his. “I think it was pent up for a while. And I just decided it needed to be done.”

The LSU man let out a sigh. “I know what you mean. Does your wife have a say in any of this?”

Tyler wanted the man to share another pour with him. “My wife…”

The LSU man let out a diminutive laugh. “Say no more, I get it. You know my girlfriend, girlfriend at the time, we were into microbrews. We hit these breweries in Brooklyn that were popping up everywhere. Loved it. We had such a great time. Then I bought this brew kit and she flipped out. I mean it was like 800 dollars and we could afford it. I mean we could kind of afford it, but I didn’t ask her, just surprised her. I thought she would love it but we started on the outs after that stupid brew kit. No idea what I did wrong but it started with that damn brew kit.”

“Maybe it meant to her that you’d never go to another brewery again.”

The LSU man nodded gently and glanced back at his sake carafe.

“Gentlemen, may I take that and offer you a blanket or pillow? We’re about to go lights out. Quiet time.”

“Sure,” LSU said.

Tyler and the LSU man handed the flight attended their sake cups. He turned off the light and they drifted off.

The three buses arrived just outside Zhengxing, a suburb of Chengdu in the Sichuan Province in Central China. They weren’t as nice as the charters in Charleston but the trip was only twenty miles from the airport.

The fresh-looking road reeked of recently laid asphalt. Tyler noticed that the traffic lane stripes were freshly painted. As the bus glided to the outskirts of Zhengxing several flatbed trucks with bulldozers and other heavy construction equipment flew by them.

The buses turned on to a gravel road and the smoothness gave way to bumpiness. Everyone looked around to see where they were but the first bus kicked up too much dust to make an observation.

When they stopped, the guide and the translator stood to make an announcement.

“Get off bus everybody, please.” She wore a tan pantsuit and smiled gently when finished interpreting.

Construction equipment growled everywhere and scaffolding climbed a five-hundred-foot smokestack in the distance next to two buildings with only girders constructed.

They disembarked the buses and Tyler gathered everyone around with the construction project to his back. “This is the Zhengxing coal plant. It’s slated to go into energy production at the end of the month. Look at it. Does it look finished?”

The environmental group peered into the distance. The scaffolding covered the buildings and smokestack like ivy and orange earth-moving vehicles crowded around the base.

“Look over there, see those flatbed trucks?” Tyler pointed. There was a fleet of flatbed trailers and several semis parked in front of them.

“Do you know what those are for? When the heavy equipment is done here they load it on a flatbed immediately for the next site. There is a wagon train of coal plant producing heavy vehicles that is on the tightest schedule you can imagine. If this were an American project that plant would still be a year to completion. These plants are pumped out in assembly line fashion.”

“Mr. Chambers, this is awful.”

“The future of energy is coal,” Tyler announced as he raised his hands.

“But coal is dead.”

“Maybe in America but in China it’s just getting started. You see China is coal and coal is China. They are building a nation that will be dependent on it.”

“Mr. Chambers, the UN convention on climate change—”

“Doesn’t matter. The treaties don’t apply to this and even if they did, China would ignore them.”

“Hey you don’t know that,” a random voice yelled.

“Look over there.” Tyler pointed to the skyline. “That’s Chengdu, the fastest-growing metropolis in China. They are not going to stop growing, every Chinese person there wants to be like the West. See those slums?”

The environmentalists squinted.

“See that grey housing and the high rises behind them? Every month they tear down the old housing which doesn’t have electricity and they build modern housing, office buildings, government centers. This is a city that doesn’t want to stop growing and won’t let anyone get in their way.”

“There’s no reason solar and wind can’t come to China.”

“Oh yes there is. It’s expensive. Ten cents a kilowatt hour over two and half cents for coal. They're building coal because that's the future here, not solar, not wind."

"Mister Chambers, it's not true. It just isn't."

"Oh no, look at that plant." Tyler grabbed Lotus by the arm and turned her to the coal plant. Tyler didn't care how much she didn't want to look, he made her look. "There's no men sitting around on break, there's no downtime for these vehicles. Look at the floodlights they have."

The towering lights looked as though they belonged in a baseball stadium.

"They run their equipment twenty-four seven and when the sun goes down they turn on the lights so they can work into the night."

His words penetrated her. She looked away and desperately didn't want to look but Tyler made her.

"This country is building seventy-two coal plants a year. That's one every six days. They have a hundred and fifty-five slated to be built. This is not a country that is going to consider wind or solar except for posterity. They will build solar panels near the capital and a windfarm that's just big enough to be photogenic. Other than that, developing countries see renewables as an impediment to growth. They only do it when it's convenient and someone else pays."

"No, it's not true. What would you have them do, build nuclear plants instead? A hundred and fifty-five nuclear plants?"

"Remember that mountain you were standing on? Remember that?" Tyler closed in to her as he shouted down at her. The other environmentalists huddled around him ready to step in if he got too close. She refused to see but Tyler refused to relent. "Look at those high rises and developments. Count the number of tower cranes you can see. There's one point three billion people in this country and they want what you have, the American Dream. They are not going to let wind and solar stop them."

Tears welled in her eyes as Tyler held her. He was getting through and he didn't care how much it hurt.

"I can stop them, Lotus. I'm telling you I can stop them from building these."

"How?"

"By making nuclear so damned irresistible they can't say no. When they see how cheap I've made it, when they see how easy it is to do, when they see the figures and the numbers, they will stop their plans immediately. The Chinese government has that power. They won't listen to the UN, they won't listen to Western countries, they won't listen to environmental groups, but they will listen to the numbers."

"Hey, the UN can stop the pollution. They signed the Kyoto Protocol."

"The Kyoto Protocol doesn't require them to do anything. Read it on Wikipedia, go ahead and look it up." A few of the environmentalists pulled their phones out.

"Don't you understand, there's over a billion people here and it's getting bigger. Those billion people are going to each have their own mountain of coal. Economic growth is going to be their master, not solar, not wind. They're seething for the cheapest energy they can get. Trust me that won't be windmills."

"He's right. Says they don't have to do anything for the Kyoto Protocol. India neither," one of the environmentalists said.

Tyler stopped, stunned by the voice of reason. This person had jumped into the pool on his own.

"That can't be," another said.

"It's on Wikipedia. I can check the citing."

"And do you know who's in line after China? Indonesia. Another three hundred million who see the American Dream and won't let some environmentalists get in their way. If China can get away with it, so will they."

Tears streamed down Lotus's face. "No, Indonesia is years away—"

"And after Indonesia, India is next in line. They have vast reserves of coal. Another billion people who see green energy as cutting off their supply of life, their future, what you and me as Americans enjoy every day."

The light for seatbelts binged. Tyler stepped out of the master suite and planted himself in an empty seat and buckled his seatbelt as the plane descended.

The wheels gently hit the runway with just a hint of orange peeking over the horizon.

There were lots of arms in the air in seventh-inning-stretch fashion.

Lots of yawns and throat clearings. Everyone was safely back in New Jersey.

The plane taxied to the terminal and a stair truck drove to the plane door. The stewardess fixed her makeup to ready herself for the bobble-headed buh-byes.

Tyler unsnapped his belt and headed toward the front as the flight attendant opened the door.

She smiled at everyone and gave them a faux-sincere ‘goodbye’ as they exited.

Lotus still clung to her bullhorn as she made her way to the front of the plane. “Mister Chambers, thank you for your hospitality.” She extended her hand and her eyes showed her to be a slumber zombie like the others. “You really opened my mind and I want to present some of these ideals to my people at Green Earth First.”

He regarded her as she left the plane. The water surrounded him and it wasn’t that bad. His mom barely held on to him and he didn’t need her after all. The next dive, he would get to the edge of the board and bark at her to get out of the way. Lotus had jumped in and it wasn’t that bad.

He joined the flight attendant in her goodbyes and shook hands with the environmentalists. Their sincerity shined through, after all they had flown around the world in the lap of luxury.

A shy gentleman reached out and shook Tyler’s hand. “Thank you.”

“Thank you for coming,” Tyler said.

“Sorry about the egg.”

“It’s fine.”

“Is your girl okay?”

“She’s fine. I appreciate that.”

The man looked faint. “Good, sorry.”

“It’s fine. Thank you.”

The man who hit Thora with an egg was the last of the environmentalists to descend the stairs.

CHAPTER EIGHTEEN

Tyler walked to the front desk and a woman in a maroon blazer directed him to the Oak Room on the 52nd floor. When he arrived his legal team waited patiently. Thomas shook his hand and the group of seven walked into the conference room.

A meeting room with white linen tables and convention chairs, and refreshments greeted them as they entered. The seven ignored the peace offering and took seats at the U-shaped table array.

On the other side sat Norring and a few of his underlings. Rutledge occupied the corner with a cup of coffee and a cookie on a napkin resting on his thigh.

"Doctor Chambers, we appreciate you taking this meeting," Norring said. "I want to get straight to the point. We seem to be clashing on the project you've undertaken…"

Norring went on occasionally glancing over his shoulder at Rutledge. Rutledge was an ominous presence. He had subtle cues for Norring—the secretive nod or subtle shaking of his head as Norring spoke.

"Why are we here?" Thomas interrupted.

"I'm sure you know the US government does not look favorably on this venture your client is undertaking and we will do all we can to stop it."

"You have…and you've been defeated."

"There are still options and we intend to exercise those options."

"What options?"

Norring turned to Rutledge to gauge his response and then back to Thomas. "We aren't willing to divulge those at this point. But let it be known that we intend to oppose your client's actions vigorously."

"Noted," Thomas grunted.

"With that said, we are also understanding of your client's motivations in his selection of this particular venture and we know the expense and risk can be high. For that reason we are prepared to make Mr. Chambers an offer to purchase the project in question."

"Not interested."

"You haven't heard the offer."

Norring slid documents across the table to Thomas. "The highlights are fifty million in cash. That's about ten times what it would normally fetch in scrap, and decommissioning of the power plant which the government would pick up. Doctor Chambers walks away with a boatload of cash and he wouldn't be burdened with the decom which can run in the hundreds of millions."

Tyler glanced at the massive contract sitting in front of Thomas. Norring's offer had a certain enticement to it. He would lose a ton of money and his net worth would go from a billion down to fifty million but he could walk away from this mess he created.

He appreciated his dream team but for a moment a relaxation entered his body. His silk pajamas cradled him, the soft light of his library warmed his shoulders. The books smelled so comforting. Oh how he yearned for the simple life his books afforded him. The last few weeks had wreaked havoc on his family and life. Norring's offer hummed a song from the sirens.

"We know your venture is making progress albeit slow progress. You have end of day to accept. If you reject we move forward with our plans to confiscate the boat."

The meeting broke up and Rutledge, Norring, and their legal team left abruptly. Tyler's lawyers stayed seated.

"Everyone," Thomas announced. "I think it would be best if I spoke to Tyler. I look forward to hearing everyone's feedback on the offer from the perspective of your areas of expertise. Have your opinion drafted to me by end of business."

The dream team pushed in their chairs and packed their notepads and briefcases.

Thomas moved to the chair next to Tyler. He knew what was coming. Lawyers could be incredibly convincing even if you paid them not to be.

"Tyler, this is a good offer. They'll even foot the bill for the decom and he's right, that's expensive as hell."

"What do you think they have up their sleeve? What were they referring to?"

"I don't know but that's not the point."

"What else is there?"

"Tyler. This is an amazing publicity stunt. You've achieved what you came to do if getting the country to talk about nuclear was your goal, but—"

"No. My goal was to start an energy company."

"You're never going to make it. They will find a way to stop you. They might even just ignore the law and claim national security. That's the card up their sleeve."

"I covered that, that's why we have diplomatic status, so we can leverage American assets in Russia."

"They're offering a carrot but make no mistake, the stick is coming and it's going to be big. Take the deal."

"I don't want their crummy deal or a better deal or any deal. I'm moving forward."

"I'm happy to have your business but I must tell you that you have to end this stunt. It's already cost you most of your fortune."

"I'll make it back once we reach the reservation."

"You've reduced a billion dollars to nothing. At least you walk out with something. You can do whatever you want with fifty million behind you. It's a good offer. Take it and put an end to this thing."

Thomas didn't shake his hand when they left the conference room. He disappeared into the stairwell.

Tyler pushed the button for the elevator. He stepped in and hit the lobby button. As the doors closed a hand sliced between them and they opened back up. A portly man lunged inside. Tyler froze. Rutledge pressed the button for the lobby again. He glanced at Tyler.

"Well, Doctor Chambers. Quite a talker aren't you?"

"My attorneys are much more apprised of the laws governing our venture."

"Yeah, it's quite a group of Johnnie Cochrans." He closed in to Tyler and glared up at him. Although he couldn't have been more than five three and Tyler boasted a foot and a half on him, he had the uncanny effect of making Tyler not know what to do with his legs.

"You should apprise yourself of the law," Tyler said, trying not to let his voice crack.

Rutledge raised his finger to Tyler's face. "You listen to me you trust-fund baby, I've been in this racket a long time. You flaunt the law but I know how to slam the curtains of government on charlatans. I can put any utility out of business. I can stop anything remotely related to energy policy. That stunt with The Onion article was cute, but you're in my arena now and I don't lose with home court advantage."

"Mister Norring seems confident in the scrap offer."

"Mister Norring is mine. He's under my direction. His involvement is a formality of my doing. He wouldn't know the first thing about dealing with grand-standers. When this is over, I'll be reassigned back to agency head."

Rutledge put his finger down and turned to the elevator doors, giving Tyler his personal space back. He let his hands hang at his side and glanced at the floor numbers above the button panel as strangers in an elevator usually did.

Such a tall building. There were still quite a few floors left where Tyler had to bask in the awkward silence. He knew that later seventeen perfectly witty comebacks would jump in his mind but none would come now. It didn't help that the elevator walls and doors were paneled in mirrors.

From underneath the painting of Crazy Horse in Robert Yellowfeather's reception area, Tyler checked his phone and he curiously did not have any texts from Rachel since she climbed in the back of an SUV to escape a raging band of environmentalists. Gina shot him a text though:

Tyler, we received an invoice from NetJets for $1.4 million. Do you know what this is for?

Tyler sighed. He recalled a time when he and Lester ate at Peter

Luger's in college and how the table was a vast wasteland of bread crumbs, dishes, porterhouse bones, grease stains, and empty scotch snifters. The bill arrived and felt like a bucket of cold water to the face. Surely there was some sort of mistake. They read over the itemized check and yup, everything seemed to be in order.

Sixty or so environmentalists into 1.4 million dollars. Six went into fourteen around 2.2, 2.3 times, drop a zero, around 23,000 dollars per head. Tyler could put off answering this text for a few hours.

Thomas didn't point his finger in Tyler's face like Rutledge did. He was calm and professional in his demeanor but he came to the same result as Rutledge. Funny how the message is more convincing depending on the package it's wrapped in. Even though they both arrived to the same conclusion, Rutledge was wrong and Thomas was right. It would be so easy to accept the money and end this. Rachel might even come back to him. No she wouldn't.

"Doctor Chambers? Chief will see you now."

When he walked in, Robert gave him a great big bear of a handshake and motioned him to a chair. Tyler would do his best to convince Robert that his heart was still in the project.

"So basically the royalty would be eleven percent on revenues less present value of decommission costs upon the power plant's end life." Robert tapped his fingers on the new agreement sitting on his desk.

Tyler gave Robert a confused look. "Wait it was nine percent on gross revenues. Now it's eleven percent on net revenues? That's less money. They're asking for less money?"

"I was able to negotiate less because the eleven percent is more than the ten percent royalty the Ojibs get from the casino. That's a particularly strong sticking point for our tribe."

"So they're willing to accept less money if the percentage just sounds bigger?"

"Bragging rights, they can say they get a higher royalty from their power plant than the Ojibs do from their casino."

"Amazing. Sure. I'll send it off to my attorney." Tyler shook his head and threw his hand in the air in a dismissive manner.

"Great." Robert handed the thick agreement to Tyler. "Is everything still rolling along, Tyler?"

Tyler ran his hand over the new royalty contract. "I'm not sure this is going to happen."

Robert's mouth hung open for a moment as he stared a hole in him. "Tyler, it has to happen. What are you talking about?"

"Nothing. Just...."

"If there is something, you need to say it."

"Just the government causing problems for me. I met with their attorneys from the Energy Department."

Robert raised his hands. "You know what, I've had to deal with the Feds most of my life. They've made hell for us on the rez, but we win a few victories here and there. Stay strong my friend, you're a hero on the reservation. Even the Ojibwe think you're a god. Matt Osceola called me and wanted to know about you. He wanted to meet you but I told him to fuck himself. He can count his poker chips and I'll count my megawatt hours."

Tyler smiled. "Megawatt hours, very good."

"Been reading up on energy. I'm ready to take this reservation to the future."

"We'll see."

"You're not thinking of throwing in the towel to these politicians? That would be horrible for Indians everywhere. You're uniting tribes better than Crazy Horse did. You're the talk of Reservations from here to Oklahoma."

"Why is everyone talking about me?"

"Anyone who gives as big a *fuck you* to the US Federal Government is a hero to Indians everywhere."

Robert's intercom buzzed. "Chief, Lotus here to see you."

"Ah, send her in."

Lotus walked in and Robert grasped her hands. "It is good to see you my waabigwan."

"What's that mean?" she asked.

"Flower."

"That's sweet. Mister Chambers!" Lotus rushed over to embrace Tyler as he stood.

"You two know each other?" Robert asked.

"Mister Chambers is going to rid the world of coal plants by getting everyone to switch to nuclear power."

"Well, trying..."

"Mister Chambers I have to tell you something. They kicked me out of the Green Earth First group."

"Kicked out? Why?"

"I tried to convince them about nuclear power. They fired me as program director."

"I'm so sorry…"

Tears streamed down Lotus's cheeks and she lunged into Tyler's shoulder. He put his arm around her and held the royalty contract in his other hand.

"I'm sorry Lotus. That's terrible."

Robert shot Tyler a snide grin. He grabbed a Kleenex box and offered it to Lotus. "My dear, you've obviously suffered greatly and you cared deeply about your cause. Tonight is about healing. We'll fly my private jet to Duluth and we'll watch the sun go down over Lake Gitche Gumee. Have you ever been on a G5?"

"I've been on Tyler's private jet."

Robert shot him another sour look.

"Chief, I came here to tell you I have to cancel our dinner."

"Non-sense. You need a shoulder to cry on and the Minnetrista people are experts at healing the heart and soul."

The NetJets invoice flashed through Tyler's frontal lobe as he wondered when his 1.4 million would show a return.

Lotus grabbed a Kleenex from Robert and dabbed her eyes. "All the people I know and worked with for years won't talk to me. The Sierra Club, the NRDC, none of them want anything to do with me. I can't be a liaison to the reservation anymore?"

Robert tried to hold her hands but she pulled free from him. "I have to meditate and figure how I can fix this."

"Meditate? A journey quest is what you need." He reached for her hands again.

"You said those weren't real." She pulled away. "I have to go." She took Tyler's hands. "It was really good seeing you again Mister Chambers but I have to fix this. I'm sorry I was wrong about you." She fought back more tears.

Robert closed the door behind her. "Dammit Chambers, you jocks are still stealing women from schleps like me."

"Jock? I don't think swimmers have ever been called jocks."

"You have a way with women. How did you get that fluff head to be a cheerleader for nuclear?"

"What do you mean *for*?"

"You didn't hear her? She said she's for nuclear."

"I guess she did say that."

"Tyler that's huge. I've worked with these environmental wackos for a decade. They're the biggest idiots on the face of the earth. If you can win them over you can win anyone over. There's a presence to you, man. These hippie chicks swarm guys like you. You did at Columbia too. They go for the jocks."

"I guess so."

"Tyler, you are going to be more famous than Geronimo."

CHAPTER NINETEEN

Tyler's phone went off in his quarters and he answered.

Captain, you're needed on the bridge.

"Aye." He hung up the phone and put his clothes on. He washed his face quickly and hand-combed his hair.

He wandered through bulkhead after bulkhead and ascended the ladders in lock-and-barrel fashion. Up eight flights he went, happy that there was no elevator on board except the one for lifting planes from the hangar to the deck.

He stepped onto the bridge and it was quieter than usual. The diagnostic panels appeared calm, the helmsman leaned back in her chair, shuffling through the different cameras making sure everything operated within normal parameters.

Tyler walked up to Archer. "Status?"

"Captain Chambers, Mrs. Chambers has paid us a visit." He motioned to navigation.

Rachel's red suit stuck out from the ship's grays. She leaned over the navigator as he explained the controls and terrain mapping.

Archer leaned over to Tyler and in a soft voice, "We had to admit her, sir. She owns half the boat."

"I'm sure it'll be fine. As you were." Tyler walked to the nav station. "Well, you found the way."

"Yes, only way is by helicopter, very exclusive."

"Rachel, what are you doing here?"

She glanced around the layout of the bridge. "I guess I own half this operation, so I decided to drop by to get the tour."

Tyler gauged Archer's reaction. He was stitched to the main monitor and too much of a gentleman to roll his eyes or make a subtle facial expression to show his annoyance from Rachel boarding them. "I'm happy to show you around."

They walked through the bulkhead to the hall.

"Are you trying to get me out of their hair?"

"No. Well, maybe a little. They're under a lot of stress. Did they show you how everything worked?"

"Yes. The giant spike, the tractors, the cameras. It's quite an operation."

"It's pretty impressive below deck too."

"All right, message received. Let's see the downstairs."

He grabbed the railings of the ladder and slid down with his heels hitting the floor with a thud. He turned around and glanced at Rachel with his hands out ready to catch her.

"I'm not going down that way. Do you know how long it took me to get up here?"

Tyler looked at her red heels and climbed back up the ladder. She put her hand on his shoulder and clung to the railing with the other. She stepped sideways one stair at a time as he led her down.

"I didn't think of wearing comfortable shoes," she said when they reached the next level.

"There's a few women on board who wear heels. They usually take them off when they climb the ladders and put them back on when they get to the top."

"You mean Natalya and Tasha?"

Tyler stopped in the middle of the ladder. "How do you know them?"

"I watched the documentary on Discovery."

"Oh yeah, of course."

They walked into the hangar and Rachel's eyes glazed over the vast space. She chuckled. "This is where they store the planes?" She grinned when she noticed the strobe lights and disco ball. They were attached to motorized frames and looked as though they swiveled to the beat of the deejay.

"Not anymore, now it's Sergi's nightclub."

"His nightclub?"

"Restaurant too, they have quite a gourmet selection flown in—cavier, octopus, elk steaks."

"And he just lives here?"

"Until the boat arrives, he's stuck here so he gets whatever he needs."

Rachel ran her hand along the felt of the blackjack table. She picked up the bedpost queen, turned it over and admired the aircraft carrier logo.

"We have a dealer flown in from Black Bear Casino, along with cocktail bunnies and a cigarette girl."

"Even a cigarette girl?"

"We're technically under Russian law and smoking bans haven't come to Russia yet."

They made their way to the living area. He opened the door to his captain's quarters. She stepped through the bulkhead. "This is smaller than our first apartment. Isn't there a bigger room available?"

"Sergi has the Admiral's quarters. He's on the boat twenty-four seven so he gets the grand room."

She rested on the edge of the cot and dropped her Prada heels on the floor. "Wow, my feet are killing me. You climb all those ladders every day? No elevator?"

"Everyone does. It's a good day-breaker routine. Gets the blood moving."

Rachel rubbed her feet. "And you guys eat in the galley, just like the Russian sailors did?"

"Sergi had his favorite chef flown in from Yalta. If he wants quail and caviar at three in the morning, he gets it. The rest of us eat regular cafeteria food, but sometimes we sneak a lobster from his stash."

"What are they going to do with that space in the hangar when it's at the reservation?"

"Offices. They'll build it out to a couple of floors, cut some slots in the side of the ship for windows."

She had a look on her face that hadn't been there for months. Her strict exterior had faded and she had a humble quality in the way she regarded him.

She sighed and shook her head. "Tyler, what are you going to do when this ends? You'll get to your Indian reservation or they'll stop you in a week and then what? We won't have anything."

"We'll have our own power company."

"You think this giant hunk of metal will make money?"

"I can show you the projections."

"I don't need to see the projections."

He inched around the personal compartment on the wall, as to not bump it when he joined his wife on the cot. "Do you remember what it was like to build Fusion from nothing? It was just a silly outdoor equipment supplier but I loved building it with you. I never thought I'd build anything working as a professor or acting like a cog in a giant government research project."

She rested her head on his shoulder. "I miss those days too."

He desperately wanted to put his arm around her. Would she jump and slap him if he did? He certainly deserved it.

She picked up her shoes. "I'd better go."

Her eyes told him she didn't want to leave. He should have put his arm around her. "Come see the nest."

"The nest?"

"The roof of the tower. You can see the tractors and the wires, it's quite a view. We could have dinner up there."

"I'm not climbing any more stairs."

He opened his locker. "You can borrow my Crocs."

She laughed as she shook her head. "They won't fit."

"One size fits all."

The sun dipped below the stern of the boat. Tyler and Rachel had cleaned their plates of the duck breast and cranberry sauce. The Caspian beluga caviar was gone as well. Rachel wiped her lips with the cloth napkin and placed it on the plate. She ran her finger over the etched crest of the Rudnisky family. She set her silverware on top of it so it wouldn't blow away.

"That was amazing," she said.

"Sergi has caused me some headaches, but he's also brought a certain dignity to our cause."

She went to the front of the nest and gazed out to the bow.

The cool breeze caused strands of her hair to come loose. She crossed her arms to stay warm. Tyler grabbed his suit jacket from the deck chair and laid it over her shoulders. She pulled the lapels tight.

As he inhaled the fresh breeze he stepped closer and he caught her scent, right between her ear and her shoulder. The smell was so distant and yet so familiar. His eyes locked onto the back of her neck. How he wanted to kiss her there.

Her scent caused memories to flash through his conscience—only the good ones. He nudged closer and breathed in every molecule he could. He would never have a chance to be this close to her again.

The temptation to touch her swelled in his hands. He would rest them on her shoulders. It would last for a moment. She would jump, turn around, maybe slap him, but the fleeting moment would be worth it.

He couldn't resist. When he touched her, she didn't jump. She reached to her shoulder and touched his fingers. He placed his lips on the nape of her neck. She gasped. He kissed her on the side of her neck and turned her around and she locked eyes with him. Her lips were flush and open and ready for his.

He kissed her and ran his hands down her body.

The sun's rays were blotched out by the haze of the diesel fuel giving their world an orange glow.

He unbuttoned her blouse. His jacket and her blouse fell to the floor, she unbuttoned his shirt and kissed his chest.

They pulled off the rest of their clothes. He found himself between her thighs, it was the first time in so many months. He kissed her all over.

"Wait, stop," she said. She caught her breath. He waited for her. She turned around and put her hands on the base of the railing and pointed her waist in the air for Tyler to embrace. He grabbed her hips and they found a rhythm and pressed with their embrace as if it were their first time with each other.

He opened his eyes just before he climaxed. They gazed forward over the flight deck, the wires disappeared into the horizon. They were so thin, like spider webs reaching into nothingness with tiny orange dots dragging them.

The ship creaked and cracked from the shifting weight of the logs.

The wires twanged and chirped while Tyler and Rachel pushed forward with their love.

The hot tub bubbled and steam poured off it from the cold, but that made it all the more cozy. The Minnesota passive-aggressive weather, which reached 75 during the day and dropped 45 at night, had given the Chambers a full display.

Tyler had his arm around Rachel as the tip of the sun disappeared into the horizon.

How could he have been in a life where she wasn't part of him? He lived that life for the last two years. She gave him coldness, absentness, and apathy and he was guilty of returning those to the person he cradled in his arms. How could he have lived that life?

She nudged out of his embrace and climbed out of the hot tub. She unabashedly walked naked over to the wine fridge and retrieved a chilled bottle of aquavit. She poured two flutes and set them on the edge of the hot tub and climbed back into Tyler's embrace.

They sipped their chilled vodka and watched as twilight turned to dark. Tyler desperately wanted to ask his wife about their marriage and talk about everything that needed to be talked about but a little devil on his shoulder kept telling him not to. Or maybe it was an angel.

There'd be no more sleeping in the east wing, there'd be no more awkward morning breakfasts, he was ready to be with Rachel. She was back.

He briefly thought back to the mud girl at the warrior dash all those months back. She piqued his interests and she was so desirable. But those memories faded. He remembered back to that warehouse in Jersey City that was strewn with garbage and grime everywhere. It was their weekend job to clean it up for when their first employees would arrive on Monday. They rolled up their sleeves and dove into it heaving everything into the dumpster. They beautified it, making it look like an empty canvas ready to be filled.

By Sunday evening they were in a bar for pizza and beer before day one of building their company. Tyler wiped a streak of grime from Rachel's cheek. They were tired, dirty, and stinky. The grease from the pepperoni and the chill of the cheap beer made excellent rewards for a Columbia MBA grad and a physics professor who dug through junk and trash all weekend. A calm before the storm when they would bring the pool noodle to every pool owner in America. The mud girl faded from his memory. Rachel's elegance behind that mask of grime appeared in her place.

They finished their aquavit and set the two flutes on the edge of the hot tub. She nudged even closer to him since the cold settled in.

"Remember when I rang the opening bell?" she asked.

He broke his stare of the horizon. "You mean on the exchange?"

"On the balcony overlooking the trading floor. Remember that?"

"I remember."

"We worked so hard at building that company and going public meant a new chapter, but it wasn't. It was us stepping away from the company we built. We were turning it over to a bunch of strangers. I didn't know it at the time, but it set in after a few months when I realized we weren't welcome at our own company anymore."

"You figured that out years before I did."

"I thought it would be a new life for our baby. I rang the bell, trading started. Our underwriter clapped, you clapped, the president of the exchange shook our hands, and just like that, our company was gone."

She nudged away from him so she could face him. "Tyler, I want to be a part of this. That's why I was so angry at you. Not because you did this but because you did this without me. You left me behind."

"I promise, I'll never start another business without my business partner."

"When I watched the documentary on Discovery about this ship, I saw you in it."

"But I wasn't interviewed."

"I mean..." She squeezed his fingers. "...I could see your work. Archer was the star but I saw your creativity in everything. Your vision of the future inspired me. I remember that when we started Fusion. You had so many ideas and I was your tactician who made them come to life. You always talked about changing the world with nuclear power at Columbia and I saw that when I watched the show."

"When we get this thing hooked to the power grid, we'll celebrate with a nice vacation, we'll have a nice dinner, we'll drink too much wine, and a week later...we'll go right into our next venture. It will be just like the first time."

She sunk back into his arms. “Let’s make this happen. I don’t want to do philanthropy again until we’re in our eighties.”

Tyler stumbled into the mess hall. He poured himself a cup of coffee from the communal drip and made his way to the pastry counter. A platter of perhaps fifty Egg McMuffins wrapped tightly in paper with the McDonald’s logo stared him down. He briefly imagined the spectacle of the helicopter landing in the parking lot of the nearest McDonald’s to make the breakfast run.

He joined the other crewmembers at the aluminum table who were coming to for first shift when he heard his name over the loudspeaker.

“Captain Chambers, dial helm.”

He set his McMuffin down and rang the bridge from the wall phone. “This is Chambers.”

“Sir, we had an incident last night. Some of the protesters made it through the state trooper lines and vandalized one of the tractors.”

“I see, is it still functional?”

“The damage appears to just be graffiti.”

“Can we just quickly paint over it?”

“They’ve arrested about a dozen people.”

“You know what? Have the helicopter on deck in five. I’m going down there myself.”

He finished his McMuffin and drank his coffee in the helicopter. He crumpled the wrapper and shoved it into his pocket.

Tyler had had enough of the environmentalists. They didn’t deserve an uneventful arrest for petty misdemeanors. They’d get 100 hours of community service for trespassing and vandalism. The courts were always lenient on protestors.

He would file a civil suit against each of them, their group, and the groups affiliated with them. He’d make an example out of them and follow them with attorneys for years if necessary. The line had to be drawn.

The pilot put them a hundred meters in front of the lead tractor where the state troopers had the protestors in cuffs. Tyler climbed out as the engine of the copter died down.

He walked through the morning haze to the troopers and protesters as he glanced down at a pair of five-gallon paint buckets and several paint rollers on the ends of broom handles.

"Mister Chambers," Lotus yelled.

The supervisor of Tractor Crew One approached Tyler. "Captain, it appears that these folks painted one of the tractors during shift change when they were replanting the spike last night. No damage to the vehicle other than the paint job."

Tyler clenched his fists when he spotted Lotus. He would never punch a woman, let alone one in handcuffs, but the temptation overwhelmed him. His eyes grew beady as he demanded an answer. "What the hell is going on?"

"Mister Chambers I hope you're not angry at what we did but nobody listens unless you take action."

His mouth hung open and his eyes grew wide and he froze when he spotted the vandalized tractor.

Tractor One was partially painted bright green and a black peace symbol was drawn on the side.

He turned back to Lotus and realized what she had done. He recognized the others from the plane trip including the man who threw the egg.

"Sir would you like us to take them in and press charges?" the trooper asked.

"Officer, thank you for your quick response to this, but I don't wish to press charges. Would you mind removing everyone's handcuffs?"

Maybe the monster NetJets invoice had been worth it.

The trooper and his men removed the cuffs starting with Lotus's.

"I hope you're not angry. We just decided that it needed to be done. We formed a new group called Environmentalists for Nuclear Energy. We only have a few members, but we wanted to align ourselves with your project—"

Tyler embraced Lotus. She put her arms around him.

"I love it. I love it, Lotus," Tyler whispered in her ear.

He let go of her and tears welled in her eyes. "I'm glad you're not angry."

"It's not finished."

"They caught us before we were able to finish. We were going to paint a peace symbol on the roof so the news copters could see it."

He admired the tractor again and turned to the Tractor Group One supervisor. "How long until the spike is in place?"

"One hour, sir."

Tyler put his hands on Lotus's shoulders. "Okay Lotus, you guys have one hour to finish the job so you'd better get moving."

CHAPTER TWENTY

Rachel had insisted on a more private location after she studied Tyler's spreadsheets, so they met in the forward airplane repair bay.

She wore the same outfit as yesterday only she discarded the red jacket. Her black hair was pulled back in a ponytail.

"Sit down," she said.

Tyler pulled a metal folding chair which scraped against the metal floor and she slid a tablet across the table.

"Tyler, these people are robbing you blind."

"What are you talking—"

"The wages are over the top. What you're paying for land use hovers around Manhattan rates. These tractor drivers earn obscene amounts."

"I set the prices high to get what I needed. If one landowner says no the neighboring leases become useless since we'd have to go around."

"But look at these forecasts. We're going to run out of money. Why did you pay them so much?"

"I kept the project a secret and told them it was transporting heavy equipment."

"Okay, that part was smart."

"I offered them a ton so they'd sign without asking too many questions."

"What is this increase in your projection of cash?"

Tyler looked at what she pointed out on the tablet. “That’s a contingency for the landowners we’re rolling across.”

“Contingency for what?”

“Since word’s spread, most of them want to renegotiate.”

“Tell them to get lost,” Rachel snapped.

“I can’t, they won’t let us cross their land. Any one of them could put everything to a halt and we’d have to go around. We can’t afford that.”

“But you have a contract.”

“If they complain to the local police, or if they let protesters on their land, then that’s it.”

“Tyler, they’re blackmailing you, plus if you give into one, the rest will want a raise too and you’ll have a domino effect. We need to put a stop to this immediately. Let’s call a meeting with this one.” She pointed to the survey map. “Who’s this?”

He crooked his neck and inspected the map. “Farmer Olson lot.”

Mister Olson walked into the Itasca Inn with his attorney. He pulled a chair out for his client across from Rachel and Tyler. He wore a straw hat and overalls fitting into every stereotype one would expect from a soy bean farmer.

“Mister and Misses Chambers. Who is representing you?” Olson’s attorney asked.

“We don’t need representation at this point,” Rachel said.

“I see ma’am. May I present Christopher Olson? His property is around ten miles west of your ship. He has signed a lease with you in good faith to pass through his farm on or about three days from now. My client has requested a reevaluation of the terms based on new information and circumstances.”

“He wants to renegotiate?” Rachel said.

“Good faith is implied in both parties in every contract. Mr. Chambers never told Mr. Olson of the scope of this project, so adjusting the consideration is in order.”

“He had ample time to review the agreement and make inquiries. He signed the document,” Rachel said.

“Be that as it may, my client feels additional compensation is warranted.”

"Listen to me, Mister Olson—"

"I kindly request you direct your remarks to myself, Mrs. Chambers."

"Very well. Tell your client that we have this agreement. Tell him that if he doesn't observe the terms he will be the subject of infinite litigation. We expect him to fulfill—"

"Our understanding of the situation is that it would cost a great amount for the ship to go around the Olson farm. By allowing you to pass across his land he's saving you a seven-figure expense."

"So he's doing us the grand favor of saving us money by gouging us and holding our operation hostage."

"There's no blackmail here. Situations have changed."

Rachel held the lease in the air. "Do you see this Mr. Olson—"

"Address your remarks to me Mrs. Chambers."

She ignored to the attorney and leaned across the table into Mr. Olson's space. "Tell your client that he is doing us a big favor by breaching this agreement. We have meetings with every property owner from here to the reservation. All of them want more money and want to hold our operation hostage. I'm grateful Mr. Olson has volunteered to serve as an example about what happens when you breach with us. He could actually save us a lot of headaches by breaching."

"Wait a minute now."

Rachel slammed the lease on the table. "Tell your client that we will go around his property at great expense and he will foot the bill because of this breach. The out of pocket for this operation is roughly one million dollars a day so Mr. Olson would be on the hook for eight million dollars."

Mr. Olson pulled at his attorney's arm. "Wait Henry, can they do that?"

"Inform your client that this agreement is with him personally, not some shell corporation, and that everything he owns including his land, house, everything in it, the shirt on his back, even that straw hat would be ours. And believe me I will happily pay attorneys' fees for years if it means stripping Mr. Olson of everything down to his overalls."

Tyler watched as Mr. Olson and his attorney walked out of the motel with long faces. They peered at Rachel from the lobby one last time before leaving. She buried her nose in her tablet and read over the collective labor agreement. She was too busy scrolling through the pdf to notice and she most likely had already forgotten their faces. But Tyler peered back for her. He shot just the slightest of grins to Farmer Olson and his hired gun.

Leeroy Skerritt lifted his stalky figure from the lobby couch as Olson and his attorney passed by him. He walked into the glassed meeting room and planted himself across from Rachel and Tyler. He set his notepad in front of him and reached inside his cheaply fitted suit jacket for a Bic pen.

Rachel set her tablet down on the table. "We've reviewed the revised agreement and it's out of the question."

"Understand, they expect to be well compensated for a venture that requires a unique skill set."

"Unique? It's driving tractors across land, it's no different than any other job. And fifty dollars an hour is well compensated. That's a hundred Gs a year to drive a tractor."

"These boys were shipped up from the cities, they have to be away from family."

"And that is why it's fifty and not the standard thirty. They are already paid a premium."

Mr. Skerritt let out a sigh and shook his head. Look miss, we know time is of the essence on this project. That means the price goes up. And you can afford it."

"We're paying the originally agreed-on amount."

"That's a problem. If this revised agreement isn't executed by midnight, then my boys are *finito*. Now I don't want it to come to that…"

"If they walk off the job, I will hire replacements."

"You can't find that many replacements. Every operator is a Teamster and our interstate chapters stick together."

"We don't need the Teamsters; we can fly workers in from Russia."

Skerritt smirked and rolled his eyes. "You'll get visas, just like that, you can find safety-certified workers that OSHA will approve? I have friends in the Department of Labor and ICE, they're happy to cause problems for you at a moment's notice." He smiled as he leaned back in the chair.

"We're not under their jurisdiction."

Skerritt chuckled. "The hell you aren't, lady."

"It's a diplomatic vessel and so are the tractors. OSHA, ICE, Department of Labor—they can't touch us. Our operation takes place on Russian soil until it gets to the destination."

"Well, still, if we walk—"

"Mr. Skerritt, if you walk you might actually save us a lot of money. Instead of paying workers $50 an hour, we can fly in Russian drivers who will accept $10 an hour. We'd lose a day of work, but your union would compensate us for that since you signed an agreement and then reneged. It won't cost the drivers who go on strike that much since you can just dip into your interstate strike fund since your chapters stick together."

"You can't just replace workers that quickly."

Rachel threw her hands in the air. "Yes we can. The family of the diplomat aboard the ship has direct ties to Putin. He could halt dozens of state projects so drivers could be shipped here at a moment's notice for ten bucks an hour. So what will it be?"

A bead of sweat appeared on Skerritt's head. His eyes dodged back and forth and his confident swagger faded.

"Mister Skerritt…"

"Listen here you…" Skerritt thrust his finger at Rachel as he searched for a word.

"Are you going to call me the B-word?"

Skerritt shifted in his chair and pouted his lips.

"Hey." Rachel tapped her red polished index nail on the table. "Your mom's a woman, your sister is, and your daughter. You're really going to call me that?"

Skerritt breathed heavily and spoke in a subdued tone. "Ma'am…I was not going to call you the B-word."

"Good. I tell you what. You go back to your Teamsters, you tell them that we were going to bring in Russian ringers for ten an hour but you talked us out of it."

Skerritt let out a frustrated sign and nodded in agreement.

A tingle flowed through Tyler's stomach. He recalled Rachel smacking around Fortune 500 companies like Target and Wal-Mart back when they negotiated their pool equipment in their stores. She was good. His business partner was back.

"Eyes, cam one," Archer ordered.

The monitor displayed what laid ahead just a mile from the reservation border.

"Zoom in."

The monitor enlarged the image and a grainy, hazy display of military might formed a wall in their path.

Tyler watched the monitor which had CNN playing. The CNN cameras showed the tractors from above. The anchor spoke of how the footage was filmed hours ago as the military banned news helicopters within a five-mile radius of their operation.

CNN switched back to the footage of the tractors. It zoomed in on the 99 orange dots and the single green lead dot. The black peace sign on the roof of the cab was unmistakable. Tyler thought of Lotus and how he first met her in Yellowfeather's office and how he thought her a bimbo and how now he grinned widely at her passion and fervor.

"We're at a thousand meters," the lead tractor voice announced over the comm. *"Request further instruction."*

"All tractors, stop," Archer said. The com relayed the order.

Rachel stepped onto the bridge and stood next to Tyler.

The yellowish green line sensor changed to a solid green indicating little tension. The feet per minute and mph dropped to zero. The wire ropes made a faint scraping noise from dangling and bumping into one another. The rumble of the diesel engines in the distance fell silent.

"Sir, we're at full stop," the helmsman said.

"Pan camera one along the horizon," Archer ordered.

The monitor showed several armored vehicles. Humvees, mounted with machine guns. One had rockets attached to its bed, another vehicle resembled a woolly mammoth, perhaps one of those IED-resistant behemoths used in Iraq. The outline of soldiers with their black weapons pointing to the sky highlighted the government's resolve. Several black dots hovered in the air which could only be gunships.

Archer stepped back to Tyler. "They block our path. An entire line of armor. I think they're serious this time."

"Captain, a helicopter is approaching. It's not a military bird," the helmsman said.

They watched from the observation deck as the helicopter landed and a man with a package under his arm ran toward the tower. After a few seconds he ran back to the helicopter as it lifted off.

"Captain Chambers," a crewman said out of breath from climbing the ladders. "A FedEx for you." He handed the envelope to Tyler who promptly pulled the red strip and emptied the contents on to the strategy table. It was a one-page letter and a folded US Geological Survey map.

Archer spread the map over the table as Tyler read the letter.

"It says the Department of the Interior has designated land ahead as a wildlife sanctuary," Tyler said.

"But where?" Rachel said as she walked over to the map Archer inspected.

"It's just a red line," Archer said. The three leaned over the map trying to decipher the government's intentions.

"There's coordinates in this letter for the new area," Tyler said.

"This line is right in our path." Archer tapped his finger on the monitor. "If I'm not mistaken the line is just in front of the armored units." He glanced back at the map.

"These coordinates are odd," Tyler said.

"Yeah latitude and longitude," Archer said.

"But they're nearly the same. They're one one-hundredth of a second off."

Archer examined the memo coordinates. He activated the calculator app on his smartphone and tapped in the numbers. "If I'm not mistaken the red line on this map isn't a line at all. It's long skinny plot of land. About thirty miles long, only fifty feet or so deep."

"A long skinny wildlife sanctuary. We try to go through that and they arrest our bulldozer drivers," Tyler said.

"They can't stop a diplomatic ship with environmental regulation," Rachel said.

"They can," Tyler said in a quiet tone to his wife. "My attorneys warned me about this. The immunity laws don't apply to immediate threats to natural habitat."

"Then we challenge them."

"They're not going to move, they have an army there," Archer said.

"It's not over, Tyler. If they want to make a spectacle, we call in the media. Who did you say your publicist was?" Rachel asked.

"We can't afford to sit here idle for months before a court decides in our favor."

"We put the pressure on them just like you did the first time they tried to arrest everyone on board."

"The lawyers have done everything. Besides, we can't get them here in time. We need a solution now."

"I'll go down there. Let me at Rutledge. I know his type," Rachel said.

Tyler walked to the helmsman and looked over her shoulder. He stared into the distance at the tip of the lake on the reservation where they were to dock. It was close enough to reach out and touch.

"Tyler. Tell me what kind of guy he is," Rachel said.

"No. I'll go."

She leaned in close to him and whispered, "Are you sure that's a good idea?"

"I'm going to talk to this guy. I'm going there by myself."

He scrolled through his phone contacts and instructed the com to dial a number. The other end rang over the speakers.

"NRC, Robert Rutledge's office."

"This is Tyler Chambers. Is Mr. Rutledge in?"

"What is this regarding?"

"I wish to meet with him to discuss terms."

"He's no longer with this agency."

"I know he's there. Can you just put me through?"

"Please hold," the cold female voice said. After a short pause, "He's busy."

Tyler walked back to the map and laid his fingers on the red line. "Can you put me through to Mark Norring?"

"One moment," the voice said.

As he stared at the speaker, the numbers ran through his head of how much it would cost to go 25 miles south and 25 more north to get around the line. It was too much. A battle of financial attrition with Uncle Sam left no survivors.

"Mr. Norring is in a meeting."

"I want to meet with Mr. Norring to discuss terms. If I can be at the Northern Lights Resort in one hour, will Norring take the meeting?"

"He's can't just—"

"I know he's in Northern Minnesota. Would you please ask him? No attorneys, just him and me, one hour from now."

Tyler ran his finger along the red line of the survey map. They wouldn't raid the boat this time. They would simply arrest the tractor drivers as they crossed the sanctuary line. The boat would be a giant rock.

"He'll take the meeting, one hour," the voice said.

CHAPTER TWENTY-ONE

Tyler stepped off the helicopter at the far end of the parking lot near the RV camp. He walked briskly as the chopper lifted into the sky. The casino parking lot expanded as far as ten soccer fields. As he closed into the hotel, he zigged and zagged through parked cars.

He stepped inside the casino and his senses were overwhelmed with cold air and an infinite number of beeps and dings and alarms from slot payouts.

He scurried past the gaming floor and the front desk to the elevator bank.

The quiet of the fourteenth floor made the hotel feel secluded from the bustle of the casino. He found 1425 and knocked.

Norring opened the door. “Doctor Chambers, please come in.”

The room was clean with two queen beds and the standard allotment of four-star hotel amenities.

“You didn’t bring any representation?” Norring asked.

“No, like I said, just you and me.”

“Very well.” Norring crossed his legs.

“Thank you for meeting with me Mr. Norring.”

“The government’s stance on this issue you’ve pushed on us has been one of openness. I’m going to be very open with you. You have two choices, either abandon this ship and the government will confiscate it and disassemble it, or you can press on and the government will arrest you for attempting to damage a wildlife sanctuary. We'll still confiscate your ship and disassemble it. I'm sure you realize our cash offer has been long dead."

"Because now you have the military behind you?"

"They are merely helping us enforce the law that you've fragrantly tossed around like chattel."

"We'll call the media in. There will be twenty-four-hour coverage and all the heat—"

"What? You're some sort of charity cause? You're like baby Jessica falling down a well? You think you're going to garner the sympathy vote?"

"You're head of the Atomic Energy Commission? And you're against what we're doing?"

Tyler glanced over Norring's shoulder out the window. He barely made out the gray dot known as Tolkov. Norring came back into focus.

"We'll arrest everyone on that ship. Your famous engineer, that fake ambassador. Trust me, nobody is going to care if we lock him up. He's a silly playboy. Putin won't fight to get him back."

Norring continued with the litany of laws Tyler had ignored. He delivered his words in much different fashion than Rutledge. Blowhards like Rutledge issued threats like a schoolyard bully. Norring's threats contained little passion. It was as if he recited a script that Rutledge had shoved in his lap. He wondered if Rutledge eavesdropped on their meeting from the john in the neighboring room.

As he gazed into the horizon at the gray dot he lost focus of Norring's words.

Norring was that no-man that Richard had warned him about—the lawyer/accountant who discouraged people from taking risks. He wondered if Norring was really such a man or if he had him pegged wrong. Rutledge valued this man but only as his puppet. His threats and accusations sounded like dictation from Rutledge but they lacked his passion for cajoling and bullying.

"…you're violating every safety protocol. It's Chernobyl, Three Mile Island, Fukushima all over again. My job is to put you away. Away for a long time and make sure any of your followers know what happens when someone uses the law as a throw rug. The game is over. You may have fooled—"

"Come work for me."

"What?"

Tyler took a break from the gray dot and gave Norring his full attention. "Come work for me."

"Are you insane?"

"You obviously care about safety. Do you believe that what you're doing with the Atomic Energy Commission is the best way to encourage safe nuclear energy? Someone working inside the industry could be many times more effective, especially someone with your strong regulatory background."

As Norring stood he upended his chair which fell to the carpet with a soft thud. "You are crazy. You're certifiable…I can't just up and leave…I mean…what capacity are you talking about?"

Tyler picked up the chair and they sat back down at the table.

"When we have these two reactors plugged in and running we're going to commission several more. When people see that they work and they're safe, we put more of them in. Since the government will be on board, we don't have to sneak around with a big old navy ship. Hell in Russia they already do this, they have nuclear plants on barges that they just sail into a city and connect to the power grid—"

"But my role?"

"You'd be my lead of safety, you'd report directly to me and your role would be the most important in the company. I would value your experience and input. By doing your job you'd instill confidence in nuclear over time. That's our biggest challenge and you'd face it head on. You'd no longer be an impediment to progress but an engineer to the future."

Norring walked to the window looking out at the gray dot. "You really think there's a future for nuclear in America?"

"With you I can do it."

Norring's eyes darted as his wheels turned. He loved the idea but wasn't ready to admit to it. Tyler could tell a certain pain that lingered in Norring was leaving his body. This man wanted to walk out on Rutledge and join the real nuclear movement. Tyler knew because he had been the same man a few weeks earlier.

CHAPTER TWENTY-TWO

Tyler gazed out the main bridge window onto the twilight of the flight deck. The string of lights going from the nest to the bow started coming on to light the party below. Everyone was dressed in black and whites and evening gowns. The pre-party band died down—a five-piece orchestra that brought a certain class to the lumbering beast which docked in her new home and displayed her new name, Wawasayg.

He threw his sailing blazer on, affixed his captain's hat to his head, and admired himself in the reflection of the windows.

"Captain Chambers. You're wanted on deck."

Archer's strong baritone voice caused him to jump. "After the party is over you'll have to call me Doctor. Wilner is going to be the new Captain."

Archer joined him at the helm.

Tyler put his hands on the ship's wheel. "I guess we have to gut most of the tower to make it more compliant with safety standards. The ladders are going to be replaced with stairs and they're working in an elevator to make it handicap accessible."

"Welcome to the private sector."

Tyler laughed. "They're keeping the bridge though."

"That's good."

They watched as the emcee came on the stage and motioned the guests to move from the cocktail tables and bar to the dancefloor. His voice over the giant speakers sounded muffled through the windows.

"You're almost up. Do you know what you're going to say?" Archer asked.

"No. I've got this one though."

Archer admired the view of the flight deck and the guests dressed in tuxedos and evening gowns. "You know Tyler I visit the Petronas Towers about every five years. And every other project I've been involved in. I'll come back here in a few. But I always move one way and that's forward. I take everything I learn with me and see what this crazy world throws at me next. We were put on this earth to move mountains and that's what we've done these past few weeks."

The speakers popped and the emcee's announcer voice filled the air.

"I couldn't have done this without you." Tyler extended his hand to Archer and the two shook.

"Sad it's over, Captain. But God what a rush."

Tyler pulled out his smartphone. "Want to show you something." He showed him pictures of a cylindrical container on a double flatbed truck. "It's gen three."

Archer admired the pictures as Tyler flipped through them. There were several more modular containers on flatbed trucks.

"I don't think I can help with this."

"No, we don't need to sneak around with these. Those are my next reactors. Korea's engineering them and shipping them to Macon, Georgia, right by the sea, so no portage this time."

"Impressive." Archer handed the phone back to Tyler.

"The government is on our side this time. Norring is overseeing it personally. He's not at the party. I wish he was but he wanted to oversee every aspect of the next reactor."

"Quite a trooper."

"Time for my speech," Tyler said as he took a deep breath.

They glanced one last time at the bridge of Wawasayg and stepped off.

They slid down the railings in their good clothes. Their freshly shined shoes smacked against the metal floor with each level. Archer and Tyler rushed down the six flights as though they were a couple of teenage boys late for Sunday school.

Tyler stepped out of the bulkhead to the flight deck.

"...and there's your Captain now," the emcee exclaimed.

The crowd of about five hundred erupted into cheers. Tyler had a big smile on his face and held his hand high as he headed toward the stage.

Everyone clapped and yelled as he walked through the crowd. Sergi stuck his hand out to Tyler and yelled congratulations into his ear. Tasha and Natalya clapped and nodded at him giving him alluring smiles. Tasha wore a blue evening gown and Natalya's was green. The gowns didn't cover much more than their bikinis.

A man with thick glasses lunged out with a big smile. Drew Carey shook his hand vigorously. Tyler barely recognized Mara, the helmsman since the back of her head usually faced him. But she had let her hair down and wore a darling blue gown. She greeted him with a small bow and a big smile.

Gina offered him a firm handshake, maintaining her professional demeanor though she trembled a little with excitement. He touched her arm and smiled warmly at her.

David O. Sacks grabbed Tyler and gave him a big bear hug and didn't seem to want to let go. Elon reached over and pulled him away. "Congratulations, Doctor Chambers." They shook hands and Elon went back to clapping.

Richard grabbed Tyler and kissed him on the cheek and gave him a huge hug. "I knew you had it in you, mate. I knew you'd do it." Dammit, Tyler knew Richard would be the one to kiss him.

Chief Yellowfeather gave him a firm handshake. He wore a suit with his giant Stetson. On his arm Lotus clapped vigorously as she cried, God bless her. Her green evening gown had a combination of radiation trefoil symbols and peace symbols patterned all over. He smiled and hugged her. The man who hit his daughter with the egg stood next to her and shook his hand. He had an awkward look on his face but his sincerity still made it through.

Wilner clapped and so did his new staff. Tyler recognized a few older faces from his Columbia days. There were a bunch of young engineers clapping too. They were the next generation that would learn from Wilner and his team and make a home for themselves around the Minnetrista reservation.

And there she was. Tyler's business partner, Rachel. She looked stunning. She held Thora's hand as she bounced in her little pink dress. He grabbed Rachel by the waist and locked his lips to hers sending the crowd into an even bigger frenzy.

Thora latched onto Tyler's leg. He crouched and grasped her little body in his arms. He stood and she latched back onto his leg.

Rachel pulled her away. "Sweetie, we have to watch Daddy's speech. He's going to be up there talking." Thora's eyes widened as she gazed at the towering podium as her father ascended the stage.

Tyler approached the microphone with a new-found confidence. There was no nervousness, he didn't feel stressed, everything was illuminated and he knew the words would come out with little effort.

He looked out at the crowd of people. His people. Just a few months ago his life had been over for years. He promised himself that he would never retire again. Maybe a vacation after this but never retirement again. His life wasn't over, just a chapter coming to an end which meant a new one would open soon enough. And this chapter would include his business partner.

ABOUT THE AUTHOR

Scott Seeger calls Saint Paul, Minnesota home. He doesn't like dogs or people and lives alone.

ABOUT THE READER

In 1984 a staffer handed President Reagan a book which he later called 'unputdownable'. The book was *The Hunt for Red October* and the one word review launched the career of Tom Clancy.

While you might not be the president, you do have a strong voice through the miracle of the internet. Amazon reviews are the lifeblood of the independent author and are vital for up and coming writers seeking exposure. Please support us by leaving an honest, well thought review on Amazon, Goodreads, or both.